Service
Dress Blues

Books by Michael Bowen

Screenscam
Unforced Error
Putting Lipstick on a Pig
Shoot the Lawyer Twice
Service Dress Blues

Service Dress Blues

Michael Bowen

Poisoned Pen Press

Copyright © 2009 by Michael Bowen

First Edition 2009

10 9 8 7 6 5 4 3 2 1

Library of Congress Catalog Card Number: 2009924174

ISBN: 978-1-59058-667-9 Hardcover

Poisoned Pen Press
6962 E. First Ave., Ste. 103
Scottsdale, AZ 85251
www.poisonedpenpress.com
info@poisonedpenpress.com

Printed in the United States of America

This story is dedicated to MEB, RN.

Disclaimer

Service Dress Blues is a work of fiction. The characters depicted do not exist, and the events described did not take place. They are products of the author's imagination. Conversely, any perception of a resemblance between characters or events in this story and characters and events in the real world will be the product of an overactive imagination on the part of the person doing the perceiving.

Chapter One

Hell is knowing what you're missing. Gunnery Sergeant (Ret.) Champ Mayer had heard that from a chaplain somewhere, and he figured the padre was onto something. The constable loitering at the Cloverleaf Motel's registration desk, for example, was missing plenty about the naked guy on the floor. Soon Mayer would clue him in and make his life hell in the process.

Right now, though, Mayer was concentrating on the naked guy himself—kid, really, nineteen if he was that.

Pinching the kid's nose shut and pinning his tongue roughly against the back of his front teeth, Mayer locked lips with him for the eighth time. A gale-force lungful of breath redolent of Jim Beam and Skoal rushed down the kid's windpipe. Mayer rocked back on his heels and released the nose. He kept the tongue pinned, though. He hadn't liked fishing it back from down the kid's throat, and he didn't want to do it again.

That one did it. With a hint of a shudder, the kid started breathing again. The breaths were shallow and the kid was still out like a boot after a twenty-mile night-hike, but he was breathing. Mayer released the tongue.

Now he looked up at the constable, who was intently studying the monitor for the lobby's security camera. The video loop showed the kid striding up to the desk about forty minutes before, if the timer was right, with a bulging duffel bag in his left hand. In grainy black-and-white he set the bag down and with a looping, southpaw flourish signed a card the desk clerk pushed at him. Then he disappeared screen right and the loop started again. Mayer couldn't have said why, exactly, but he could tell the kid on that tape was a soldier.

The constable finally felt Mayer's gaze. Even in a faded checkerboard plaid flannel shirt and aging denim jeans and with every one of his fifty-two years showing in the salt-and-pepper stubble on his seamed face, Mayer came across as someone it would be imprudent to ignore. The constable turned his head and tried unsuccessfully to meet Mayer's eyes.

"An ambulance is on the way."

"Well that's real good." Mayer's tone asked whether the constable was expecting a medal or something. "When it gets here they're gonna want a name to plug into a computer for some medical history before they try anything too ambitious with this youngster. You got one for 'em?"

"No idea. Signed in as John Smith and paid cash. SOP at a flophouse like this. Whoever dosed him took his bag and everything else except his lighter. Even his cigarettes."

Mayer glanced over at the young woman in shiny vinyl pants who was nervously smoking a few feet away. She washed her hands a lot, Mayer knew, but even so he could see a faint orange tinge on the tip of her left index finger. Nothing like that on the kid, and no tell-tale discoloration of his teeth.

"How do you know he had cigarettes?"

"The lighter."

The woman took three baby steps and crouched next to Mayer to whisper at him.

"This is great, what you're doing, honey, but I'm on the clock."

Mayer jovially smacked the damsel's rump and grinned at her.

"The commodore and I have things to talk about darlin', so why don't you just go warm up the sheets?"

With only a *pro forma* pout at the swat—after all, the customer is always right, at least if he doesn't go too far—she jumped to comply. She deftly caught a room key the clerk tossed to her. She and Mayer hadn't gotten around to registering yet, but the clerk didn't stand on formality with regulars.

"Do me a favor, constable," Mayer said then. "Call the United States Naval Academy at Annapolis and see if they're missing a mid—'cause if they are, that's where this kid oughta go."

"It's almost midnight. No one's gonna answer the phone."

"There's a midshipman on watch at every duty station twenty-four hours a day. They'll answer the phone all right."

"But there must be two-thousand kids at that place. You think they're gonna know whether one of them missed bed-check?"

"There are more than four-thousand midshipmen in the brigade, divided into two regiments. Each regiment is divided into three battalions. Each battalion is divided into twenty companies. Each company has a company officer and two stripers in charge. And one of them for damn sure knows if he has a mid unaccounted for."

"Why do you even think he's from the Academy? Just because he has a crewcut?"

That did it. A Camp Lejeune beam lit Mayer's eye. His left eyebrow twitched. When he spoke his words came in a deliberate, unhurried cadence and his voice was low, so that the constable unconsciously leaned forward as he strained to hear.

"Two reasons. First, this pillow shop is nineteen-point-four miles from the Academy, so it's within the twenty-two mile radius where a plebe with town liberty can legally go—and why would anyone his age come to a pissant dump like Fritchieburg if he could get laid in Baltimore or Washington? And second, that shoulder-board of yours wouldn't pass inspection at the Academy. You need one of these."

He stopped talking long enough to dig his own lighter from his pocket. It was a brushed steel Zippo—the lighter that won World War II—embossed with a USMC globe-and-anchor seal. As he opened it and thumbed the friction wheel, a fragrant blue and orange flame popped up. The constable retreated, as if he thought Mayer were actually going to attack his epaulet with the lighter.

"Most midshipmen don't smoke these days, but they almost all use lighters to burn the fuzz off their shoulder-boards and melt shoe paste when they polish their shoes."

"Look, we got priorities. Fritchieburg is part of a county-wide metro squad. This probably isn't the only kid got cold-cocked by a hooker in Anne Arundel County tonight."

Mayer sighed.

"Constable, do you know the most important thing that's going to happen tomorrow?"

"Your day off, I hope."

"The Army-Navy football game. Which will be attended by the Corps of Cadets from West Point and the Brigade of Midshipmen from Annapolis. And by the President of the United States. Who will start the game sitting on the Army side and at halftime cross the field and sit on the Navy side. All in front of something like eight-thousand cadets and midshipmen who've marched in without a security check. It's a hundred to one that whoever slipped this kid a mickey walked out of here with a United States military identification card and a duffel bag holding a service dress blue uniform. Someone in service dress blues will fit right in at that game."

Mayer paused. The deputy blinked and swallowed. When Mayer spoke again, his voice was very, very quiet.

"Now you be makin' that call, son."

Chapter Two

December 6-9, 2008

Ole Lindstrom never hit his wife except with his open hand, which in Loki, Wisconsin, made him a liberal. Lena liked to give as good as she got, and since Ole had six inches and sixty pounds on her she'd been known to use blunt objects to even the odds a bit. When deputy sheriff Moose Svenson saw Ole lying on his living room rug with his scraggly, gray-blond hair stuck in a pool of his own blood, Lena would have been his prime suspect even if she hadn't been standing there with a cast iron skillet dripping something red onto the orange shag carpet.

"You have the right to remain silent. Anything you say—"

"Skip it, I didn't do it. You got a cigarette?"

Svenson sighed and an exasperated *it's-just-not-fair* expression spoiled his broad face. Lena had told him—more than once—about how a Chicago cop had billy-clubbed her across the backs of her thighs at the 1968 Democratic National Convention for just *standing there*. Everyone in Sylvanus County had heard the story at one time or another. But he didn't see why she had to take her negative attitude about law enforcement officers out on him, disrespecting him this way when he was just trying to clean up Loki's first major crime in three winters. He looked at her—snow white hair tied back in a neat bun, rosy red cheeks courtesy of the Northwest Ordinance Tavern around the corner and six country blocks up County Highway M, nowhere close to drunk even if her robin's egg blue eyes were a little glassy—and sighed again.

"Lena, I got to read this to you. You have the right to remain silent. Anything you say can and will be taken down—"

The doorbell rang. Without waiting for an answer an EMT swung the storm door open so that his partner could wheel a gurney into the room and over to Ole's body. Moose managed to finish reading Lena her rights while the two med techs examined Ole.

"Why aren't you going after the guy who broke in here and conked Ole?"

"Didn't you hear what I just read? Don't say anything. Anything you say I got to write down and tell in court."

"Well you write down that I found the back door wide open when I got back from Northwest Ordinance."

"Lena, you're *holding* the frying pan he got hit with."

"Well of course I am. It's evidence."

Svenson face reflexively morphed into a *why-me-Lord?* expression.

"Lena Lindstrom, you are under arrest for the murder of Ole Lindstrom. Now put down that frying pan and—"

"Attempted murder," the first med tech said. "Looks like Ole needed more killing than Lena had in her. I think he's gonna make it."

Moose wasn't buying that. The first thing he'd done when he came in was check for a pulse and if Ole still had one Moose had missed it. He might not be dead *yet*, but no way he was gonna make it.

Moose would linger in stubborn disbelief on this point until the following Tuesday morning, when Ole showed up at the Sylvanus County Justice Center in Appleburg to bail Lena out. Ole was heavily bandaged and looked even more short-tempered than usual, which was saying something. It took considerable gumption for Moose to approach him.

"Lena says there was an intruder," Moose said while Ole was fussing with the paperwork.

"You caught him yet?"

"Did you see an intruder?"

"I got hit in the back of the head. I didn't see nothing but stars and I didn't see them for long. Don't suppose you found any footprints, did you?"

"Only three-hundred or so. You guys might wanna think about shoveling that driveway once in awhile."

"Yeah, that's on my list." Ole pushed the bail papers across the counter to a uniformed clerk.

"Ole, I haven't heard you say she didn't do it yet."

"You haven't heard me say you're a goddamn Republican, either, but that doesn't mean it ain't so."

"We've got to talk about this sometime soon."

"Listen," Ole said. "I ought to be lying in a hospital bed right this minute. But this blessed country doesn't have a rational health care system, so some desk jockey at an insurance company told the doctors to kick me out with a handful of ibuprofen and a pat on the back. For the next couple of days I'm not gonna be talking to anyone except Lena Lindstrom, and I won't be saying much to her."

A heavy metal door with a diamond pattern of steel wire covering its opaque glass panel swung open. Lena and a matron stepped through.

"You'll be sorry you stuck me in that jail cell, Moose Svenson," she said as the door began to swing shut. "I told all the ladies you're holding what their rights are, and I gave them the number for Legal Action of Wisconsin. When the sheriff is up to his neck in writs, you just tell him you're to blame."

Moose met this pronouncement with a prudent stoicism. Lena swiveled her gaze to Ole.

"How are we getting home?"

"Gary fetched the Ford. It's waiting outside."

"He's good for something, anyway. Let's go."

They left the imposing granite and cream city brick building that housed Appleburg's police department along with the Sylvanus County Jail, its sheriff's offices, and the precincts of a few county officials without enough pull to get offices in the courthouse two blocks away. The steps and sidewalk had been shoveled and ice-scraped down to bare pavement, for it's hard to survive an upper Midwestern winter psychologically if you don't fight for small and temporary victories against the snow and ice. They found the Ford hybrid SUV right where Ole had told Gary Carlsen to park it and climbed into the thing—Ole at the wheel, bandaged head and all—without exchanging a word.

Their silence continued for the first ten minutes of their drive. When Lena saw Appleburg in the rear view mirror and spotted the sign saying Loki was ten miles away, she spoke.

"You figure I need a lawyer?"

"If you don't then no one ever will, I guess."

"How about whoozit, Thorstrom or whatever, back in Appleburg?"

"He's a goddamn Republican."

"Everyone in Sylvanus County is a Republican except you and me and a couple of English professors at Joliet University—and I'm not even sure about them."

"Plus Thad Thorstrom couldn't win a case against a drunk Indian if he had his mother on the jury."

Lena waited for Ole to say something more. When a full mile had clicked past on the odometer without another syllable from her husband, she spoke up again.

"You don't think I'm the one who whaled on your brain-pan, do you? 'Cause if I'd done it you would've been halfway to Valhalla before you hit the floor, I guess."

"No, I don't figure it was you. What I do figure is I'm going to be paying a lawyer instead of going to the inauguration in Washington, D.C. next month—that's what *I* figure."

Ole slapped the steering wheel with the heel of his right hand. Lena could tell he was struggling to keep the Viking *berserkers* in his DNA from making him do something that would generate more paperwork for Deputy Svenson. They finished the rest of the ride in silence.

As soon as they got in the back door, Ole went straight to a large room on the other end of the house, tacked on to the back almost as an afterthought. A wood-carved sign over the door read "Gaylord Nelson Democratic Club of Sylvanus County." If there had been an intruder, it figured he was after something and Ole wanted to see if anything was missing. Lena went to the living room to check the voice mail that had piled up while she and Ole were guests of the county.

Against the background of the droning, indistinct, mechanical recorded voice from the answering machine in the living room, Ole checked the computer and the drum of CD ROMs next to it. Then he checked the rack of hand-labeled DVDs. They were really the only things of more than sentimental value in the room unless you were heavily into American flags which, furled and unfurled and in a variety of sizes, stood ready along one entire wall for the next rally or public announcement Ole organized.

He found nothing amiss. Then a sudden, panicky thought fluttered across his semisedated brain. Hands trembling a bit, he pulled open the thigh-level drawer above the white oak storage cabinet that defined the door end of a secretary/credenza stretching across most of the room's front wall.

He saw the key and sighed with relief. He picked the thing up, as if to assure himself of its reality, and then laid it back in the drawer's curved tray with some paperclips and rubber bands. With a rare and silent prayer of thanksgiving, he gently closed the drawer.

Lena's voice, shrill and imperative with a tinge of angry panic, shattered his momentarily mellow mood.

"Ole Lindstrom, get in here."

Sighing heavily, he left the club room and lumbered down the hallway into the living room. He winced a bit as he noticed the stain his own blood and tissue had left in the carpet.

"For planning purposes, woman, is this just a hissy-fit or am I in for the full-blown psycho-bitch from hell routine?"

"Shut up." Her voice was now strangely subdued. She stood slouched at the end table where the phone sat. Her head was bowed in what someone other than Ole might have mistaken for submission.

"What is it, then?"

"Harry's in trouble. Pretty big trouble, maybe."

"At the Academy?"

"Where else, you think? Ole, we got to get a lawyer damn quick I guess."

Ole blinked at this new information. His head throbbed, and his body screamed simultaneously for caffeine, nicotine, and alcohol, but data were somehow getting through. One was pertinent.

"What day is it?"

"Tuesday."

"I'm seeing a lawyer tomorrow afternoon. From Milwaukee. Gary is supposed to pick the feller up in Appleburg and run him out here so he doesn't kill himself on the way. I'll talk to him."

"Better call Gary and remind him. Otherwise he'll be resting on his Laurels tomorrow instead of running that errand." She straightened from the subdued stoop and looked straight at him, a spark in her eye and a half-smile playing at her lips. "That's what I said, Ole Lindstrom. 'Laurels,' with a capital L."

Chapter Three

Rep Pennyworth met Gary Carlsen in front of the memorial to Senator McCarthy at the Sylvanus County Courthouse. Yeah, *that* Senator McCarthy. Not Gene; Tailgunner Joe, eponym of an era and an ism.

"Ole always has people wait for me in front of the shrine," Carlsen said, flashing an *aw-shucks*, heartbreaker smile. "It's his way of saying, '*This* is what it's like to be a Democrat in Sylvanus County.'"

"I'm duly admonished."

"The truck is out front."

Carlsen swept a mop of very light brown hair from in front of eyes with a blue cast that was soft but not pale, a hint of gray adding nuance to a robust tidewater hue. At just under six feet he was almost three inches taller than Rep, and only a hint of paunch sneaking over his belt marred a sleekly muscled, gym-rat build. Rep thought he had to be pushing thirty, only six or seven years younger than Rep himself, but he affected the anxious-to-please earnestness of a college senior angling for a strong grad-school recommendation from a senior professor.

Exiting the courthouse, they walked through brisk cold and brilliant, sting-your-eyes winter sunshine to a metallic green Ford hybrid SUV sporting an "Impeach Bush/Cheney" bumper sticker and a parking ticket. Before climbing behind the wheel,

Carlsen shed a bright yellow North Face ski jacket with the stub-end of a lift ticket still tied to the zipper and stowed it in the back seat. This exposed a long-sleeved white dress shirt that he wore open-collared, and an oversized biker's wallet stuck in a rear pocket of his blue jeans and linked by a chain to a belt-loop. Rep clambered into the front passenger seat.

"The chauffeur service wasn't my idea, by the way," Rep said. "Mr. Lindstrom insisted on having you meet me in Appleburg because he said if I tried to drive my Taurus into Loki I'd end up stranded there with a broken axle."

"What do you know about Ole?" Carlsen asked as he started the mammoth vehicle and pulled out onto Christiana Avenue.

"He wants a copyright lawyer, he's willing to pay travel time for house calls a hundred miles from Milwaukee, and the check he sent me for the retainer cleared on the first try. The check was drawn on the account of something called the Paper Valley Political Education and Values Fund, so I figure he's involved in politics. What else should I know?"

"'Involved in politics' is a world-class understatement. He called the presidential vote right in every county in Wisconsin to within one percentage point in last month's election. Look closely at the pictures on the walls when he takes you into the club room. You'll recognize a lot of the faces. But at the moment the main thing you need to know is this."

Reaching across to Rep's side, Carlsen punched a button on a DVD player mounted next to the glove compartment on the ample dashboard. The tiny screen filled with an array of freshly-scrubbed, bright-eyed teenagers on risers, their faces beaming with earnest, up-with-people expressions. Mostly white but with a handful of black, Hispanic, and Asian faces sprinkled in. A simple, catchy tune began playing on a piano off-screen. Rep recognized a folk melody, Shaker perhaps, that he knew under the title *'Tis a Gift to be Simple*. After eight bars and a brisk arpeggio, the piano stopped briefly. When it resumed, the adolescents started singing in unison, their clear, innocent voices and the upbeat tune clashing with stridently muscular lyrics:

Come now you people who are bold and are free!
We can make our lives the way we know they ought to be!
We can decide for ourselves without some plutocrat's decree!
We can live in a world that is peaceful and free!

Speak now, and let your voice be heard!
Children yet unborn will be grateful for our words!
We are the future and we will not be deterred!
We will speak now, and make our voices heard!

We dream for tomorrow while we work for today!
We are not afraid to fight and we are not ashamed to say
That we know where we're going and rejoice along the way!
'Cause the whole world is listening to what we have to say.

Let's speak now, and make our voices heard!
Children yet unborn will be grateful for our words!
We are the future and we will not be deterred!
We will speak now and make our voices heard!

"Okay," Rep said as the screen went blank.

"Ole wants to talk to you about copyrighting those lyrics. More important, he wants you ready to sail into court on a moment's notice the second someone infringes."

"Fair enough. I'm not sure the lyrics say 'platinum' to me, but I'm just the lawyer. You don't need a hit to register a copyright."

"Selling CDs is the last thing Ole is worried about."

"What's the first thing?" Rep asked.

"The Attorney General of Wisconsin. He's a Republican."

"Nobody's perfect."

"It gets better. He's the *only* Republican in the United States to win a statewide election for a Democrat-held office in 2006. In-the-United-States. Take a second and think about that."

"Impressive."

"Impressive cubed," Carlsen said. "Republicans are hungry for winners these days, so the odds are he'll be running for something else soon. Maybe as early as 2010."

"Making Attorney General an open office."

"Right. Now skip to the next track on that DVD."

Rep obeyed. The screen this time showed a woman at a podium. She looked like she was in her mid- to late thirties. By squinting Rep could make out something about Conference of Non-Governmental Organizations on a banner stretched across the wall behind her. The woman seemed to be finishing up a presentation. After thanking the audience and the organizers on behalf of the Institute for Cultural and Artistic Liberty, she stopped, glanced to her right, and looked back at the audience as an unseen voice invited questions.

'That was a symposium at NYU four years ago," Carlsen said. "Before the lady there came to Milwaukee to head up a goo-goo outfit called The Wisconsin Policy Project."

"'Goo-goo'?"

"Good Government. It's independently financed and administratively autonomous, but loosely affiliated with the University of Wisconsin-Milwaukee."

"That's where my wife, Melissa, teaches," Rep said.

"I know. That UWM connection is one of the reasons you made the short list for this gig. Now listen carefully. The fun part is just about to start."

An off-camera male had been asking a question—or, more accurately, making a speech punctuated by occasional upward inflections suggestive of interrogation. He spoke in an urgent tone somehow made even more indignantly earnest by a heavy New York accent. In court the "question" would have been called argumentative and compound. Something about the United States government subsidizing and otherwise coopting Euro-American cultural organizations to use as fronts for undermining progressive parties and unions and otherwise interfering with internal affairs in European democracies and did she deny that the ICAL had taken secret government money and didn't she think this was outrageous and didn't it make her ashamed to be an American? Unfazed, the woman waited three beats before answering. "Those things happened during the Cold War. The Cold War is over. The good guys won. The bad guys lost. You're welcome. Next question."

That's where the DVD stopped.

"That's Veronica Gephardt," Carlsen said. "She was general counsel for the US branch of ICAL when that tape was made. She moved to The Wisconsin Policy Project three years ago. WPP's theme this year is the End of Domestic Violence."

"She'll fit right in at UWM."

"UWM provides office space and infrastructure as long as WPP raises its own money. What UWM gets out of the deal is some national visibility and attractive intern slots for a few graduate students every year. Now: Guess how Ole got his hands on that tape."

"No idea."

"He started discreetly floating the idea of Gephardt as a dark horse Democratic candidate for attorney general. Nothing public. Low-key hints to political insiders and a whisper here and there to political reporters in Madison and Milwaukee. Within a month one of our party's standard-issue suicide bombers started circulating the tape to discredit Gephardt."

"*Discredit* her?" Rep asked in genuine surprise. "Maybe it's just me, but I'm kind of glad we won the Cold War."

"That's because you live here on planet Earth and function in the real world—like most voters. Ole wants Democratic candidates who appeal to people like you instead of to hard-left ideologues who'd rather sit on the sidelines polishing their halos than win elections."

"That doesn't sound like it should really be a controversial position."

"You're not a Democrat, are you?"

"As I said, noboby's perfect."

"The true believers think they have a vested right to run the Wisconsin Democratic Party. Ole begs to differ. He thinks Gephardt is perfect for an end-run around the party's institutional apparatus."

"Even though she's never held public office?"

"*Because* she's never held public office. She has the closest thing to a feel-good career that any lawyer can claim. She's a progressive who goes to church now and then. As you saw on that tape she gives good sound bite. And she's an outsider."

"An outsider who's not afraid to wave the flag a little," Rep said.

"Gold star for Rep! Ole is very big on the flag. He remembers when Democrats used to own the flag, and he thinks we should take it back. He seriously believes that he can make Veronica Gephardt the first woman attorney general in Wisconsin history."

"Which is where the song comes in?" Rep guessed.

"Bingo. The idea is to make her not just a candidate but a movement. A breath of fresh air. A generational change. A paradigm shift. The rising star in a transformative election. That's the theme. The song is the hook. An attention-getting device, an instant brand."

"You make her sound like a new line of soap that you've market-tested with a brace of focus groups."

"Ole Lindstrom doesn't do focus groups. Hillary Clinton had focus groups. Ole has a golden gut—and no candidate who listened to him ever lost a twenty-five point lead in the polls in six months."

"Does Gephardt know about Lindstrom's plans for her?"

"She has nibbled at the bait, but I can't say we've reeled her in." A phone resting in one of the console cup-holders next to Carlsen erupted in eight digitized bars of *Solidarity Forever* and he picked it up to glance at its screen. "Sorry, I'd better take this. Gotta pay the rent."

Rep turned to look out his window at deeply banked snow and naked birch trees lining the east side of the highway as

Carlsen shifted to a suggestive, piano-bar purr. Even so, Carlsen's half of the conversation came through loud and clear.

"Hey, Laurel, what's up, doll?…Look, girl, tell you why I called. Listened to the tape on my way up and *no one* lays down tracks like you do, babe. No one.…Uh huh.…But there's one thing. Toward the end there you were doing that 'shawn' thing again. You know what I mean? Like, usually when you say 'action' or 'satisfaction' you say the 'tion' part the way most people do: 'shun.' But when you cop that sultry temptress attitude you start going all '*ack-SHAWN*' and 'satis-*fac-SHAWN*. Like you're auditioning for some saloon-singer job on North Thirteenth Street.…I know, baby. You're right. I'm a bad, bad boy…Yeah, I wouldn't blame you if you did…No sweat, though. I'll stop by tonight and we can overdub right from your place, right over the phone.…Okay, babe. Peace out."

Shaking his head, Carlsen clicked the phone off and put it back in the cupholder.

"That girl can be a royal pain in the butt, but she is *worth* it."

"Friend?" Rep asked.

"Colleague. *Professional* colleague. Like I said, she can lay down tracks. Despite what Lena insists on thinking, I've never slept with her. It's my one claim to distinction."

"More information than I really need."

"Oh, I'm not saying she's a hooker or anything like that. Hookers get paid. Laurel just likes it. I mean *really* likes it. If Laurel ever goes to Austria her first weekend will be called 'the Congress of Vienna.' She's a power-tripper. She is absolutely convinced that someday I will get her in the sack with a President of the United States. And I'll tell you what: I might just bring it off before I'm through."

"Okay," Rep said.

"By the way—do you know any lawyers who do criminal work?"

"I sublease my office from Walt Kuchinski, who I think is the best criminal lawyer in the state. Why?"

"Well, there was a little complication with Ole and Lena, over the weekend. Long story short, someone conked Ole with a skillet hard enough to put him in the hospital for three days. The cops think Lena did it. They've charged her with attempted murder."

"What does Ole think?"

"He got hit from behind and he didn't see who did it, but he says it wasn't Lena."

"What does Lena say?" Rep asked.

"She blames an intruder, identity unknown. She and Ole had some harsh words during their weekly Saturday night at the Northwest Ordinance Bar. He got up to walk out, she grabbed him, and he either slapped her or pushed her back into her seat, depending on whether you believe Ole and Lena or the other twelve people in the bar. Anyway, he hoofed it home and she sat and drank for awhile. When she finally made it back to chez Lindstrom herself, she says she came through the back door into the kitchen, heard a strange noise from the club room at the other end of the house, and hurried off to see what was going on. As soon as she reached the living room she found Ole on the carpet. I drove up just in time to hear Lena screaming like Brünhilde having her first orgasm. Lena says the scream came when she stumbled over Ole's body."

"Lena needs a lawyer."

"Yep."

"I'll give them Walt's number and tell Walt they might be giving him a call."

"How does a trademark lawyer end up being partners with a criminal lawyer?" Carlsen asked.

"Walt and I aren't partners. My partners are all back in Indianapolis. They said if I wanted to open an office in Milwaukee they'd want me to find some cheap space, and Walt had some."

"If you had it goin' on in Indianapolis, why did you want to do an urban pioneer number in Milwaukee?" Carlsen asked. "No, wait, dumb question. Your bride got the gig at UWM and you wanted to back her up, right?"

"Got it in one."

"You might share that little story with Lena if you get the chance. She'll like it—and if you want Ole's business it's not a bad idea to have Lena on your side. She goes upside his head every now and then, but anyone else who tries it better be ready to deal with Lena—and when that lady decides to bring it, you'd better have your A-game on."

"Noted."

"I know what you're thinking. You're thinking you've already got Ole's business. But Ole and Lena are political animals. Nothing is permanent. There are no guarantees. Everything is on the line every minute, and every question is a test."

Rep unconsciously tapped the end of his red silk bow-tie and then smoothed the front of his royal blue shirt. He didn't do business casual, didn't really approve of it even though it had become endemic among lawyers under forty. He kept his charcoal hair cut barely long enough to part and comb across his head. He sometimes wore contacts but usually couldn't be bothered with them and often, like today, wore small, gold-rimmed glasses instead. He sensed that Carlsen had been trying to prod him into a little verbal joust, just for the exercise, but he hadn't risen to the bait. By now, avoiding conflict and confrontation was a habit as ingrained as the tie-touch he'd just done.

"I'm the one who checked you out, you know," Carlsen said.

"I hope you liked what you found."

"You know what I really loved? That trial-lawyer trading card thing you did. That was beautiful, dude."

"I didn't come up with the idea. I just did the trademark and copyright work."

"The idea goes nowhere without the intellectual property. Even I know that much. You got the licenses. How did you manage that? And how in the *world* did your client get people to pay ten bucks apiece for packs of fifty trading cards with trial lawyers instead of baseball players on them?"

"Same answer to both questions. Trial lawyers have very healthy egos. Tell one of them you're putting together a pack of America's greatest trial lawyers: Clarence Darrow, Max Steuer,

Racehorse Haynes, Melvin Belli—and him. Does he want in? If
so, just sign this piece of paper. And by the way, the cards are only
ten bucks a pack if you place a minimum order of twelve—just
in case you want to pass some out to your clients."

"You kidding?" Carlsen squealed, smacking the steering wheel
in elation. "They bit?"

"Eighty-thousand sets sold at last count."

"I love that! I so love it! You got people to pay you for the
privilege of giving you a license to use their name and likeness.
That is prime stuff, man."

"It's all in the small print."

"You know what? You could be on the coast. I mean it. LA.
You could be billing twenty-two-hundred hours a year at seven-
hundred an hour. That's gotta be four times what you're making
in Milwaukee."

"Maybe." *Certainly. Obviously.*

"Reason *I'm* still in Milwaukee," Carlsen said, "is that you
don't go to the coast to break in. D.C., same thing. You go there
after you've already got the goods. You've got 'em, dude. And
LA is a lot more exciting than Milwaukee."

Rep felt the armor plating start to encase him, and he fought
to keep from seeming chilly or unfriendly. He didn't remember it,
but he knew that when he was fifteen months old three cops had
come to the tract house where he lived and arrested his mother
for felony murder. She was guilty. She hadn't pulled the trigger,
but she'd driven the car the killer rode away in and for the law
that was plenty. She'd gone to prison—the death penalty was on
hiatus in the early 'seventies—and the official record said that
she'd escaped. She had. He hadn't learned any of this until he was
in college, he hadn't seen her again until his early thirties—and
if the FBI happened to ask, he'd never seen her again, period,
and had no idea she was out in LA, making a living off people
who paid her to hit them and act out fantasies about childish
punishments. Rep had decided sometime around his second year
in law school, before he'd even confirmed that his mother was
still alive and before he knew anything about the hairbrush-and-

paddle stuff, that his mother's story was one-hundred percent of the excitement he needed for the rest of his life.

None of this, however, could he say to Carlsen. So he said something else.

"Let me ask you something. Suppose someone offered to sell you six-hundred extra waking hours every year. No catches, no deal with the devil, no drugs, no side-effects. Just fifty hours of discretionary time every month that you wouldn't otherwise have. How much would you pay for that?"

Carlsen looked at Rep, then turned his gaze back to the windshield and scanned the highway for fifteen thoughtful seconds.

"Heavy question, dude. I guess I'd pay a lot."

"So would I," Rep said. "I don't know how much. But I know it's more than I could net every year in LA."

Chapter Four

Wednesday, December 10, 2008

"How about a Bud?" Ole Lindstrom called roughly five seconds after Carlsen brought Rep through the Lindstrom's back door and into their kitchen.

Rep almost said, "You bet, thanks." His lips were actually forming the first syllable and he was a nanosecond away from reaching for the water-beaded can of Budweiser that Lindstrom pulled from a harvest gold refrigerator and held out to him. Then a glimpse of black and gold cans of Miller Genuine Draft in the refrigerator reminded him of Carlsen's every-question-is-a-test admonition. He nimbly switched verbal gears.

"Uh, sure, if that's what you're drinking. But personally, I'd rather have a beer."

"Looks like you found one of the smart ones," Lindstrom said to Carlsen, grinning with unalloyed delight at Rep's rejection of the non-Wisconsin brew. "Dig out some MGDs to bring back to the club room with us."

While Carlsen foraged for the beer, Rep followed Lindstrom out of the kitchen through a cozy dining room and a slightly more capacious living room to an L-shaped hallway. The hall led to what had probably been called a rec room when the house was last listed for sale about forty years before. Rep didn't need the GAYLORD NELSON DEMOCRATIC CLUB OF SYLVANUS

COUNTY sign over the door to tell him that Lindstrom's use for the room had nothing to do with recreation.

Carlsen was right about the pictures. Black-and-white eight-by-tens in cheap, black drugstore frames dotted all four walls, sharing the space with laminated newspaper headlines, handwritten letters on White House stationery, and a couple of autographed *Time* and *Newsweek* covers. The suits and haircuts on most of the men in the photos—they were almost all men—evoked the late 'fifties to the mid-'seventies. Some of the faces were mysteries to Rep, and he had to squint to make out signatures like "Bill Proxmire" and "Pat Lucey" beneath the friendly inscriptions. Just as Carlsen had predicted, though, Rep had no trouble recognizing many of them: Robert F. Kennedy, smiling and determined as he shook Lindstrom's hand over the scrawled words, "Thanks for the help with Wisconsin, Ole (Alaska too)!" John Kennedy's trademark charismatic grin highlighting the inscription, "Ole—we owe Wisconsin to you!" Hubert Humphrey, Gene McCarthy, Lyndon Johnson, George McGovern, Jimmy Carter, Walter Mondale, all featuring messages that started with Lindstrom's first name.

Three televisions flickered along the near wall to Rep's left as they walked in, stashed on shelves above the wooden drawers and storage cabinets. One tuned to CNN, one to Fox News, and one to MS/NBC, they flashed their images and crawls in muted silence. In front of the intersecting wall, running down from a computer work station wedged into the far corner, sat two long folding tables placed end to end and crowded with computer printouts and bulging manila file folders. Lindstrom circled behind the tables and sank into a non-descript, brown tweed desk chair that might have been picked up cheap when a retiring small town lawyer sold off his office furniture.

A six-by-eight foot American flag spread across the wall behind Lindstrom. With its top almost brushing the quarter-round molding at the ceiling, it hung more than halfway to the floor. Raised calligraphy on a card beside the flag attested that it had flown over the United States Capitol on January 3,

1959. "Thanks Ole! Bill Egan" looped in triumphant letters across the card.

Hustling into the room behind them, Carlsen put a Miller Genuine Draft in front of Lindstrom and tossed another to Rep. He kept one for himself and plunked a spare next to a bulky Excel spreadsheet printed out on oversized paper. While he expertly popped the top on his can with one hand, Lindstrom gingerly fingered the substantial bandage still dominating the crown of his head with the other, brushing spiky bristles around it where hair cut by the surgeon last Saturday night had just begun to grow back. With a flick of the beer hand he invited Rep to sit in a Naughahyde armchair on the other side of the tables.

"What do you know about politics?" he asked then. "I don't mean policy-wonk stuff. I mean street-level, curbstone, retail politics?"

"Nothing."

"Good. I won't have to flush a lot of nonsense out of your head before we get down to business."

As a token of getting down to business, Rep pulled out a legal pad and balanced it on the triangle formed when he rested his left ankle on his right knee. After a sip from his beer he focused on Lindstrom.

"Did you compose the lyrics for that song that you want to copyright?" he asked.

"No, Lena did. Except for 'plutocrat's decree.' That was my contribution. Everything else came from her. The copyright should be in her name."

"Getting a formal copyright registered shouldn't be a problem in itself," Rep said. "Unless someone else has already copyrighted something very similar. I can run that down in a hurry."

"How?" Carlsen asked.

"By doing lawyer stuff," Lindstrom said impatiently. "That's what we're paying him for. Here's what I want to know. Let's say we get the copyright and then someone in, say, Kansas City starts running our little ditty to support some reactionary troglodyte's campaign. What do you do about that?"

"Gary said you'd want to move fast, so we'd have templates of all the pleadings ready to go ahead of time. Five minutes after you get the information to me, I call a law school classmate in Kansas City and PDF the basic pleadings to him. He plugs in the details about the infringing conduct and heads off to the Clerk of Federal Court's office with a briefcase full of paper and a check for the filing fee. Best case, we're in court asking for a temporary restraining order before the next news cycle."

"'News cycle.' You *have* been talking to Gary, haven't you?"

"Guilty as charged. Fair warning, though. This kind of rapid-deployment stuff means spending a lot of money to get ready for something that might never happen. Is the risk of infringement really that great?"

"Only if the song works. If it doesn't catch on, no one will bother to rip it off. But if our tune is all over Youtube getting a thousand hits an hour within two days after we roll it out, every two-bit political hack from coast to coast will know it. Think about those lyrics for a minute. Change 'plutocrat's' to 'bureaucrat's' and 'say' to 'pray' and you convert Lena's stirring paean to progressive values into a reactionary anthem. If it generates the kind of buzz I'm hoping for in Wisconsin, the bad guys will have it on the air in three days in Ohio, Missouri, or Colorado. Voters don't like whining, but they don't like stealing more. You get a temporary restraining order against them the first time they try it and there won't be a second time."

Rep settled back in his chair and took a deep breath. He pushed his wire-rims a couple of millimeters back up his nose. He glanced at the only words he'd scrawled so far on his legal pad: "Copyright/ Lena." Then he looked back up at Lindstrom.

"This is about more than the song, isn't it?"

"You betcha, counselor." Lindstrom took a long pull from his MGD and smacked the can back on the table with a tinny thump. "You said you know nothing about politics. Well, there's only one thing you really have to know to be an expert."

"I'm listening," Rep said, smiling gamely and spreading his arms to invite instruction.

"Most elections aren't won, they're lost. The other side screws up and you're standing there as the only alternative. You take office by default. Nixon in 'sixty-eight, Carter in 'seventy-six, Clinton in 'ninety-two, Bush-one in 'eighty-eight and Bush-two in 'oh-four. But every once in awhile, if the stars line up just right and everything works perfectly, you actually *win* an election. FDR in 'thirty-two, Reagan in 'eighty. When that happens, you don't just take *office*, you take *power.*"

"On the way up Gary called that a transformative election or a paradigm shift," Rep said.

"I call it kicking Republican butt." Lindstrom abruptly rocked forward, planted his right elbow on the table, and put the ball of his thumb against the first two fingertips on his right hand in what Rep called a 'this *will* be on the test' gesture when Melissa did it. "I want to take an absolute political neophyte and steal a statewide office away from the Republicans in a purple state. I want to put a package together that will do that. Because if I pull that little trick off, I won't be a political fossil anymore. All I'll have to do is sit right here and wait for that phone to start ringing. I'll have a chance to play in the major leagues again. I'll be headed back to the show. That's what this is about."

"Got it," Rep said.

"I already have the package put together. Candidate, message, theme, hook. I've run the numbers, county by county. I've got the sound-bites. Gary has the web-site ready to go live. I've got the story-boards for the first round of TV commercials."

"TV is key," Carlsen interjected. "That's where political consultants make their real money. The campaign manager gets a cut of the media buy."

"When lawyers do something like that they call it a conflict of interest," Rep said.

"That's where three extra years in school gets you," Carlsen said, grinning.

"The catch is the candidate," Lindstrom said. "Veronica Gephardt is my girl, but I haven't closed the deal with her yet."

"And even though you have the material for an irresistible pitch," Rep said, "there's a risk that she won't have the stomach to make a run for elective office."

"There's a risk that bothers me a lot more than that. Most Wisconsin politicians think I'm a relic from the age when men wore fedoras to work. The worry gnawing at my gut is that somewhere along the line someone will whisper to the candidate, 'What do you need Ole for? Why not just take these dandy ideas and let some glossy, digital-savvy kid run your campaign?'"

"So you need to have the whole package protected: hook, theme, concept, storyboards, soundbites and so forth."

"Right."

Rep kept his expression carefully neutral. In his mind's eye, though, he saw a federal judge glaring down at him from the bench. *You ever heard of the First Amendment, counsel? Or did you cut class the day they covered that in law school?*

"It's tricky but it might be doable," he said after a thoughtful pause. "An idea for a novel or a movie is one thing. A political idea is, well, a political idea. That's what the First Amendment is all about. The trick will be to find a way to frame your concept not just as the ideas themselves but as particular, unique, and creative expressions of those ideas. How much of the package can you give me to take back to Milwaukee with me and review?"

"Enough."

Reaching toward the floor, Lindstrom leaned so far over to this right that Rep feared the chair was going to tip over sideways. He picked up a thick, black vinyl binder bristling with multi-colored plastic tabs, laboriously righted himself, and tossed it on the table. Rep leaned forward to retrieve the tome. He flicked through it briefly.

"I can't promise to get back to you by the next news cycle on this," he said, "but I think I can have some ideas for you by the middle of next week or so. Will that work?"

"It'll have to work," Lindstrom said, shrugging. "Now, we also have a little criminal case going for us up here. Did Gary tell you about that?"

"Yes. The police seem to think that Lena conked you on the head."

"Right. That kind of thing in your line at all?"

"No. I went into copyright and trademark law because I wasn't sure I could handle the excitement of trusts and estates. Criminal law isn't my cup of tea. But the best criminal lawyer I've ever seen in action is Walt Kuchinski, and his office is about forty feet from mine."

Rep took out one of his cards and wrote Kuchinski's name and number on the back. He leaned forward to hand the card to Lindstrom.

"Maybe I'll give him a call," Lindstrom said.

"Maybe *I'll* give him a call, since the idea is for him to be *my* lawyer," a female voice said sharply from near the doorway.

Rep twisted around in his chair to see Lena Lindstrom striding in, carrying a platter laden with oatmeal-raisin cookies. She was wearing a mustard yellow chamois shirt and faded blue jeans, softened a bit by a candy-apple red apron with something embroidered on its breast in elaborate white script. Carlsen reached for the platter as she approached the gray folding chair where he'd perched, but with a curt, "Guests first," she jerked it away from him and offered it to Rep.

Murmuring his thanks he took two cookies that were still warm. He noticed hand-painted rosemaling designs in vivid red, blue, and gold decorating the platter's edge. He found this reassuring. Like the apron, it was the kind of homey touch you wouldn't stumble over if you were advising, say, Karl Rove.

She set the platter on the front edge of the farther work table, where Ole and Carlsen could both reach it. Then she picked up the fourth beer, opened it, and parked herself on the corner of the same table. This allowed Rep to read the script embroidered on her apron:

WHEN IN DOUBT
GO NEGATIVE

Great, Rep thought. *I'm not counseling Karl Rove, I'm advising Lucretia Borgia.*

"You're right, of course, that you should call the lawyer," Ole said. "When I said I'd call him I was referring to myself as your surrogate."

"Right," Lena said. "You and Bill Clinton ought to be competing for surrogate of the year." She accompanied this with an almost but not quite winsome giggle that sent Miller Genuine Draft dribbling from the corner of her lips down her chin.

"I'll get in touch with Walt on my way back to Milwaukee and tell him to expect your call."

"Lemme ask you something," Lena said. "Do a little polling. Do you think the government should discriminate on the basis of race in conferring economic privileges? I don't mean affirmative action. I mean should the government say, 'Here's a way we'll let you make money, but only if you're the right color.'"

"Is this a trick question? I'd say the answer is no. Is the government doing that?"

"Next time you're in Madison," Ole said, leaning back in his chair, "ask for a license to open a casino. See what happens."

"Casino gambling?" Rep asked. "You think you can make that a wedge issue?"

"It's all in how you spin it. You can't be in favor of expanding casino gambling, because then you get some of the Protestants mad at you. And you can't be in favor of restricting casino gambling, because then you get the rest of the Protestants and all of the Catholics mad at you."

"Along with most of the atheists," Lena said.

"But what you can do," Ole went on, "is say that whatever the rules are, they ought to be the same for everybody. You shouldn't have one particular racial group—"

"Native Americans, for example," Lena interjected.

"—allowed to make wampum hand over fist fleecing patsies while everybody else is shut out of the teepee."

"Especially if they do it by pouring money into the Madison shakedown machine, otherwise known as the Wisconsin Legislature."

"That's the hook you were talking about, I take it," Rep said.

"It is." Ole nodded his head in emphatic confirmation. "The key is getting out front on the issue and being pitch-perfect in the way you frame it. Then whichever position the other guy takes, he either makes somebody mad at him or everybody mad at him."

The doorbell rang.

"I'll get it," Ole said jovially to Lena as he levered himself up from his chair. "If it's your lawyer I'll call you."

Lena laughed around a swig of beer and favored Ole's rump with an affectionate backhand as he walked past her.

"Is this Walt I'm gonna call any good?" Lena asked.

"He knows his way around a jury."

"How long has he been at it?"

"He's been a trial lawyer for over thirty years, but he's technically been representing defendants for even longer than that. When he was in the Marines his buddies recognized his latent talents and they'd have him represent them in the informal disciplinary proceedings that they call 'Captain's Masts' on board ship."

"Did he now? Well, then, he might just do, I guess."

A vigorous throat clearing announced Ole Lindstrom's reappearance in the doorway.

"Mr. Carlsen," he announced with playful solemnity, "you have a caller. She's offering to give you a ride back to Milwaukee, if you can tear yourself away. Laurel something-or-other."

"Laurel Wolf or Laurel Fox?"

"I'm not sure," Ole teased. "I'll go ask her."

"No!" Carlsen said as a look of sit-com panic flashed across his face. He leaped to his feet and sprinted for the door.

"Which one is it, really?" Lena asked after Carlsen had disappeared.

"The Native American, not the slut."

"That would be Wolf."

"Well we'd better get out to the living room and tell Gary that I'll take our lawyer back to wherever he parked his car in Appleburg so that Gary can accept the generous offer he's receiving."

Without waiting for the others he set off on this mission. Rep and Lena followed him and reached the living room just as Carlsen, to his evident elation and vast relief, was getting the good news. Carlsen lifted a black-haired, sepia-skinned lass in wraparound sunglasses almost off her feet for a passionate kiss and then, with a quick wave to the Lindstroms and Rep, hurried off with her toward a Ford F150 pick-up truck parked at the curb.

"Lucky boy," Ole said.

"Unlucky girl," Lena said wistfully. "Old story, I guess."

"I'll pull the truck down the driveway so you don't have to skate over too much ice to get to it," Ole said.

He exited toward the dining room. Rep was about to step toward the front door when Lena brushed his arm. Puzzled, he looked over at her. She walked a few steps to a harpsichord—*not* a piano, he realized with some surprise, but a harpsichord with yellowed keys in distressed maple that looked like it was two-hundred years old—and idly fingered a photo album.

"You said your Walt friend used to be a Marine," she said. "We have a sort of a military problem that may be a lot more important than that silly charge they're throwing at me."

Rep looked at the album. On the cover, slipped in between the blue binding and the plastic sheathing over it, was a four-by-six print. It showed the breast of a dress white uniform tunic with a nametag embossed white on black over the left pocket. The name-tag read LINDSTROM 12.

"That's our nephew, Harald," she said quietly. "Closest thing we have to a son. He's a midshipman at the Naval Academy. Class of 2012."

"Congratulations."

"Ole and I called in every chit we had to help him, but he really made it on his own. He's real smart, and he's tough enough, I guess. He wants to be a Marine officer."

"Has he gotten himself in some kind of scrape?"

"Looks like it."

Most of the flint-hard, go-ahead-just-try-to-hurt-me tone had vanished from her voice, replaced by an aching hint of vulnerability. Rep, who had been wondering a few minutes ago whether he should write a condolence card to the Wisconsin Republican Party on the imminent loss of its testicles, now felt a surge of sympathy for her.

"What kind of trouble?"

"Not sure. Something last weekend. I don't know the whole story, but it wasn't just the usual drunken whoring or anything like that. Whatever it was, it caused a big stink. It could get him thrown out, I guess. Do you think your Walt could be any help with that?"

"I don't know. He'll tell you one way or the other, though, and he'll give it to you straight. And maybe there's something I can do."

"I thought you said this kind of thing wasn't your line."

"It isn't. But my wife's brother, Frank, is a lieutenant-commander in the Navy. He just finished a tour teaching at Annapolis. He's been rotated to another assignment now, but he may be able to pick up some useful information and give you at least some general advice about what to do next."

"Well I'll tell you what," Lena said, so fiercely that Rep had to resist an urge to back up. "If you and your friends can get our nephew out of this mess with a whole skin, I'll gladly do four or five years for conking Ole. I'm seventy-two years old and I've been to jail. More than once. I could do five years without changing my socks."

Rep believed her.

Chapter Five

Melissa Seton Pennyworth's fingers hesitated over the keyboard of her desktop computer in the modest Curtin Hall office provided to her by the University of Wisconsin-Milwaukee. She sternly instructed her ego to repress the mischief that sparked her green-flecked brown eyes. She knew that her penchant for flippancy in bureaucratic communications, which was chancy enough for a junior faculty member when directed at assistant deans, could be downright reckless in emails to people with real authority—like UWM's general counsel, Robert Yi Li.

She took a deep breath. Then she began sketching a tentative response to Li's most recent email which (like every email he sent) was flagged IMPORTANT and had arrived with an irritating *beep!* when it reached her computer. Editing mentally as she typed, she made a determined effort to root out any hint of freshness or spontaneity in her writing and replace it with the plodding stodginess that would be called for by the Stylebook for Interdepartmental Memoranda if such a thing existed:

Dear Mr. Li,

I fully appreciate the honor of representing UWM at the "Ask the Professor" promotion planned by the Milwaukee Brewers baseball club for this spring. I assure you that, notwithstanding the qualms suggested by your note, I have neither aesthetic nor ideological objections to standing in cap and gown on top of the Brewers dugout in

front of an anticipated crowd of forty-thousand people or
so, to answer baseball trivia questions in competition with
professors from Marquette University, Alverno College,
and the Milwaukee School of Engineering. I recognize
the institutional interest in demonstrating a commit-
ment to and interest in all facets of community life—and
in particular in showing that we're not "just a bunch of
ivory-tower stiffs," as you elegantly phrased it, but on the
contrary (to borrow your eloquence again) "can kick back
and chill with the best of the eighteen- to twenty-six year
old male demographic."

With deep regret, however, I must decline the honor.
I am sure you do our colleagues an unintended injustice
when you suggest that I am the only junior faculty member
at UWM "who can tell a drag bunt from a cut-off man."
While we all have heavy workloads, moreover, I fear that
my schedule of second-semester classes and administrative
committee responsibilities, in combination with an article
that I have committed to complete before June, leave me
without sufficient time to give the Brewers project the
attention that it undoubtedly deserves.

MSP

She read the piece through. She frowned. Parts of it seemed
to lack the stultifying dullness that the occasion demanded. Each
time she toyed with changing a phrase, though, a bit of sparkle
seemed perversely to insinuate itself into the message somewhere
else. She adjusted the collar of the yellow blouse she was wearing
over a black turtleneck sweater and under a black v-neck sweater.
(She had grown up in Kansas City, and not even four undergraduate years at the University of Michigan had prepared for
Milwaukee winters.) No further inspiration reached her. The Muse
of Serviceable Prose was apparently taking the afternoon off.

It would have to do. Shrugging, she hit SEND. She consoled
herself with the thought that at least she had completed the most
annoying task she would have to confront for the rest of the day.

Then her husband called.

"Where are you?" she asked, hearing the whine of tires over pavement as she answered the phone.

"Headed south on Highway Forty-one. Driving past the naughty book store this side of Fond du Lac. Maintaining speed and ignoring the exit."

"How did things go in Loki? Did you get the copyright case?"

"Not only that, I might have gotten an attempted murder case for Walt."

"Attempted murder? Who tried to kill whom?"

"Wife allegedly brained husband with skillet and he ended up in the hospital for a three-day nap. He allegedly clocked her one first but that was a good deal earlier, so the skillet-conking wasn't exactly in the heat of battle."

"That would have been a pretty standard premise for a TV sit-com episode in the 'fifties," Melissa said.

"It's a felony in Wisconsin."

"I'm guessing alcohol was involved."

"Safe bet. Do you know Veronica Gephardt, by the way?"

"Afraid not. Should I?"

"She's head of a study center affiliated with UWM. My new client would like to turn her into a politician—and I have a sneaking suspicion that he's going to ask you to help him do it."

"Let me just check my job description," Melissa said thoughtfully. "Let's see, that would be under 'H.' 'Hackwork comma Academic.' Yes, that's there. 'Hackwork comma Bureaucratic.' Yep, that too. Hmm. Nope. 'Hackwork comma Political' isn't here. So unless he wants her to run for Provost or Chancellor it doesn't look like I can help."

"I'll take that as a maybe. By the way, am I going to get Melissatude for the rest of the day, or was that a one-shot deal?"

"Sorry, honey. Sarcasm is a fault that I should try harder to overcome. I just finished a note to a big shot in non-academic administration and I guess I hadn't quite gotten all the bitchiness out of my system."

"The Lindstroms also have an issue that your brother Frank might help us with," Rep said then. He described what he called the "drunken-plebe mess."

"I have more sympathy with that one."

"I thought you might. Wasn't Frank your favorite sibling growing up?"

"He was my most useful sibling, which may be the same thing. He's the one who told me that boys don't really think smoking is sexy, no matter what they say. More important, he taught me how to take a punch—and then he taught me how to throw one."

"Both useful skills, with an important place in any self-respecting liberal arts curriculum. I've already called Walt about both issues, and unless I miss my guess the Lindstroms will be in touch with him before the day is out."

"I'll send Frank an email this afternoon."

"Thanks. I should be back by the usual time."

Melissa hung up and turned back to her keyboard. She had just turned fifteen on the I-Day not quite twenty years ago when she and her parents came with Frank for his induction into the United States Naval Academy. From the time she was two or three she remembered looking up to him in near adoration, even when she was furious with him, thinking of him as almost superhuman. On that I-Day, though, he'd had a deer-in-the-headlights look in his eyes and a nervous quiver in his limbs that left her shaken. He had stepped onto the Naval Academy grounds looking at eleven months of being a plebe—one of eleven-hundred-plus first-year midshipman whom three-thousand upper-classmen would treat as the lowest form of human life. Eleven months of screaming stripers, of rounding every indoor corner on a run, never sitting down outside, calisthenics at five a.m., white-glove inspections, hazing, push-ups on any pretext or no pretext, dress parades, midnight watches, sleep deprivation, all on top of a grueling class schedule. And she remembered the gleam in his eye and the strut in his step in May of the following year, when he officially stopped being a plebe and became a Midshipman Third Class.

She had a soft spot for plebes.

She took considerably more time composing her email to Lieutenant Commander Francis X. Seton than she had on the missive to Robert Yi Li.

"The attempted murder rap is a trial lawyer's dream," Walt Kuchinski told Rep not quite three hours later as they were walking through the chilly evening to a parking ramp where the Germania Building reserved spaces for its tenants. "The cops caught Lena with the blood literally dripping from her hands. Well, not literally. But holding the murder weapon and standing over the body, which is close enough. And I think I might get her off. She could actually walk."

"By pointing to an unknown intruder who didn't take anything or leave any fingerprints?"

"Don't sound so skeptical. Lena tells me their driveway is lousy with partial bootmarks. Who knows whose they are or how long they've been there?"

"If Lena heard a sound in the club room while she was coming in the back door, though, the intruder would have had to go out a rear window into the back yard or side yard. Otherwise Lena would have run smack into him."

"Or smack into her. Let's not eliminate half the human race from the universe of potential suspects. We'll want as many as we can get to accompany us on our search for reasonable doubt."

"Good point."

"You're onto something, though. I'll have to take a careful look around the property when I pop up to Loki for a little face-to-face with my client."

Kuchinski towered over Rep. Of course, he towered over most people who didn't dribble for a living. He was also wider than Rep. Considerably. Once straw-colored, his thinning hair now tended toward off-white, and his face and belly showed evidence of thousands of six p.m. beer calls and scores of nights in bars celebrating verdicts, or commiserating about them, or telling stories about them. But after three decades-plus of trial work, *joie de guerre* still gleamed in his eye when he thought about facing a jury again.

"For what it's worth, based on an hour or so with them," Rep said, "Lena and Ole both have sharp tongues and hard-boiled attitudes, but I think they really do love each other. I don't think it's one of those things where they just stay together out of habit or inertia. I think they've really been in love for almost fifty years."

"Did you just say 'them?'" Kuchinski asked, his voice rising in astonishment. "You mean Lena was with Ole when you talked to him?"

"Most of the time, yeah."

"So they didn't tack a no-contact order onto Lena's bail requirements?"

"If they did, someone apparently forgot to tell Lena."

"I've heard they run a pretty loose ship up there in Sylvanus County, but that doesn't sound like any attempted murder charge I ever heard of," Kuchinski said, pulling out his cell-phone and punching the speed-dial button that would get him to his secretary's voice-mail. "Excuse me for a second. I've gotta leave word for the Polish Della Street to check CCAP as soon as she gets her computer turned on and pull the actual charge against Lena off the net."

Rep waited while Kuchinski left the message.

"I hope you're right about Ole and Lena being love-birds," Kuchinski said then, "and you very well could be. But that doesn't mean she didn't knock him into the middle of next week."

"I know."

"The hardest punches I ever took came from my first wife—and I spent two years in the Marines. She loved the hell out of me, at least until the last few months before she moved out. But that didn't keep her from cracking a plate over my head once when we mixed it up. And I didn't even hit her first. I hit her *back*, you understand, which I know means I'll never be president of the Thoughtful and Sensitive Males Club, but I didn't provoke her the way they're saying Ole did Lena. It's bad enough to smack your wife in the kitchen. When you hit a woman in public, in front of her friends and neighbors, you really do something to her. You better be sleeping with one eye open for awhile after you pull that."

"I'll make it a point to avoid that," Rep said as they reached the parking ramp and prepared to part company. "Do you think you'll be able to do anything for their plebe? Or did Lena talk to you about that?"

"That one is not a trial lawyer's dream. More like a trial lawyer's nightmare. I'll need some help on that."

"Well, if I'm reading Melissa right, you might get some."

"The kid is in serious trouble," Frank Seton told Melissa around nine that evening. "I checked with a couple of buddies who are still at the Academy. He could be expelled."

"For drinking and wenching?"

"No. If we expelled midshipmen for that, the fleet would become seriously undermanned."

"Then what's the problem?"

"Problems, plural. Two. First, he managed to get himself relieved of his uniform and his military i.d. in the course of his little escapade. That caused a mini-uproar because it was the night before the Army-Navy game and the people in charge of security had to wonder if whoever took the stuff was thinking about taking a shot at the President during the game. The retired gunnery sergeant who found him and probably saved the kid's life was on that right from the get-go. Led to a lot of headaches that nobody needed."

"But that wasn't the kid's fault," Melissa protested.

"It sure wasn't the fault of the four-thousand midshipmen who *didn't* get their uniforms and i.d.'s stolen that night. But that's just background. The big issue is what looks like an honor code violation."

"Meaning he lied?"

"Meaning that the story he's told so far is the equivalent of 'the dog ate my homework.'"

"For crying out loud, Frank, he's an eighteen-year-old kid and from what Rep told me he's been through a life-threatening trauma."

"The honor code is non-negotiable, sis. The country is at war. You can handle a professor's lies in a footnote, but an officer's get sent home in a government-issue metal box wrapped in the flag."

Melissa fiercely bit her lip. She picked up a small rubber ball with her right hand and squeezed it tightly. Noticing this, Rep prepared to duck in case Melissa threw the ball against the nearest wall and he had to avoid the ricochet.

"Sorry," Frank said after the brief pause that ensued during Melissa's anger-management exercises. "That probably came off as sententious. But that's the way the folks at the Academy will look at it."

"So, bottom line, he needs a lawyer for sure, right?"

"He can consult a legal advisor at the Academy, but I think he should definitely get his own counsel. I'd say the main thing he needs, though, is someone who can crawl around down there and find out what really happened to him—and hope that maybe it bears some resemblance to what he's said."

Melissa sagged back in her chair. This didn't sound like a problem that Walt Kuchinski or anyone else could handle very well from Milwaukee.

"What about the retired sergeant?" she asked then. "Do you think he'd be willing to talk to a lawyer here, just to get the ball rolling?"

It was Frank's turn to pause. Instead of prompting him, Melissa prudently waited the seconds out. She knew that he felt manipulated, that she was exploiting his desire to impress his little sister. He had been striving to impress her for decades now, and she knew that if she just waited patiently his psyche would do all the work for her.

Chapter Six

Thursday, December 18, 2008

"Good stollen," Kuchinski told Lena Lindstrom in her kitchen as he stabbed another forkful of pastry that looked like it had arm-wrestled a fruitcake and won. "By the way, you have *not* been charged with attempted murder."

"That's what Deputy Doofus arrested me for. Attempted murder."

"Cops don't prefer charges, they file criminal complaints. District attorneys decide what charges to bring. They didn't say 'attempted murder' at your bail hearing, did they?"

"They just said some numbers. I didn't pay a lot of attention to that part. All I cared about was that Ole wasn't dead and could he get me out."

With the hand that wasn't forking German pastry, Kuchinski pushed his computer printout of the criminal complaint in *State v. Lena Lindstrom* across the almost spotless birch table. With his index finger he tapped a statutory reference highlighted in yellow on the page.

"Were these the numbers?"

Lena fished tiny, half-moon glasses from her skirt pocket and parked them on the bridge of her nose. She then leaned forward to squint at the document.

"They were, I guess. 'Wisconsin Statues section nine-forty-point-nineteen-paren-three.' If that's not attempted murder, what is it?"

"I know him," Frank said at last. "He ended his active du
career at the Academy, and his last year overlapped with n
first year teaching there." Another pause. Again Melissa wait
until her brother finally spoke again. "I guess I could give hi
a call."

"I'd really appreciate that."

"You're a spoiled brat. You know that, don't you?"

"Let's just say this isn't the first time I ever heard that."

"Aggravated battery: intentionally causing substantial bodily harm to another. What it boils down to is, you did a major number on someone and you meant to do it."

Lena studied the criminal complaint with a vaguely puzzled expression, as if it were an unusually challenging acrostic.

"Why didn't he charge me with attempted murder, do you suppose?"

"I asked the assistant DA that when I stopped by to see him before I came out here. He said he doesn't think a jury would believe you were trying to kill Ole. Besides, aggravated battery is a Class D felony. Maximum sentence of twenty-five years. That's plenty."

"I guess so. For someone my age, that's the same as life anyway."

"You'd be looking at something way south of the maximum, but there'll still be some time on the inside if you're convicted."

Kuchinski chewed meditatively on another forkful of stollen. A twenty-five year maximum sentence generally got clients' attention, but Lena still seemed to be floating serenely above the battle, as if this were happening to someone else. Amateur perps often did, at first. *People like me don't go to prison. Prison is for losers and druggies and punks in the 'hood and creeps who download kiddie-porn on their computers.* He always had to slam the cell door a few times to get their attention. So far, Lena didn't seem to be hearing the clang.

Moving away from the table, she retrieved a mug of steaming coffee from the counter next to the sink and gazed out the window at an expanse of snow and a large, cylindrical, silver propane tank in the backyard. After glancing at her watch for the fourth time since Kuchinski had arrived, she took two plastic, bottle-green pill jars down from the top shelf of the cupboard just to the right of the window. She gobbled one pill from the first jar and two from the second, washing each one down with a swallow of coffee.

"Ole and I did the 'sixties together," she said then with a quiet wistfulness. "The 'sixties didn't hit Wisconsin until about 1966, so we were a little old for it. Almost thirty. But we did them all the same. Summer of love, tie-dyed jeans, rainbow shades—all that stuff. The Milwaukee Police Department had a Red Squad back then, to keep track of lefties, and I'll bet they had a three-by-five file card on each of us. We did the drug thing, although we did it in a wholesome, Midwestern way. No speed or acid, just a little pot. I felt like fourteen kinds of fool the first time I smoked marijuana. Did the radical politics thing, did the hippie thing, did the off-the-pigs thing, marched on the Pentagon, got our silly butts arrested in Chicago in 'sixty-eight, got a whiff or two of tear gas in Madison, demonstrated outside the federal courthouse in Milwaukee when we couldn't afford a bus ticket to Washington. You know?"

No, I was busy getting shot at by the Viet Cong about that time. That's what Kuchinski wanted to say.

"I know what you're talking about," he answered instead.

"But we never did the free love thing." Lena pivoted spryly to face Kuchinski. "No nubile groupies for Ole. No radical studs for me. We really loved each other. We always have."

"You're saying you didn't conk him."

"That's what I'm saying." Lena spoke the words with weary resignation, as if she didn't really expect Kuchinski to believe her. "I've been madder at Ole Lindstrom than I ever was at Nixon—and there were times when I would've killed Nixon without a second thought if I'd gotten the chance. I've hit Ole more than once in our forty-eight years together, and I got my money's worth when I did. I've thrown ashtrays at him, and I've gone after him with rolling pins and carpet beaters and God knows what. But I'm not the one who brained him that night."

"So no pleading this one down to simple battery with a year's probation and forty hours of anger management classes."

"Not likely. And no battered wife defense, either."

"Fair enough." *Wonder if she'll feel the same way on the courthouse steps.*

It takes two hours to drive from Milwaukee to Appleburg, where Kuchinski had stopped to see the assistant district attorney handling Lena's case before driving out to Loki for his first interview with Lena. He'd spent that time trying to work out some way for the intruder theory to work. He'd needed every minute of it.

He'd started with a punk, teenage male, sixteen or seventeen, looking for easy pickings that he could turn into quick cash to feed a drug jones, or maybe just out for some thrills. This hypothetical perp figures the Lindstroms are at a bar. Saturday night in rural Wisconsin, that's a safe bet. So he decides he'll pop in for a little low-risk snatch-and-grab. Uses the back door into the kitchen. Maybe the Lindstroms left the door unlocked, so that's why there's no forced entry. Okay. He's still inside when he hears Ole come back and decides he has to hammer him to get away.

Kuchinski had hit a mental wall right there and it had taken him seven miles of Highway Forty-one to get past it. No way the hit-and-run theory works. The punk nailed Ole with a frying pan, so he had to be in the kitchen when he decided to attack, and Ole got hit in the living room. Which means the perp had a clear way out through the back door without hitting Ole and would only have increased his risk by trying to sneak up on him.

So why *did* he hit Ole instead of just running for it? Because he hadn't gotten what he came for yet and needed time to look for it. That meant this wasn't just a snatch-and-grab by some random juvenile delinquent but a hunt for something specific by someone who had a reason to believe it was there. If he didn't find it, *that* explains why nothing was missing. Plus, it would account for the perp still being there when Lena got back well after Ole did. And if the perp was looking for whatever he wanted in the club room, and panicked when Lena returned, he could have made the noise Lena said she heard while he was making his belated getaway.

By the time he saw the sign saying APPLEBURG NEXT 5 EXITS, Kuchinski had convinced himself that he might have something he could say with a straight face to a jury. He hadn't convinced himself it was true, necessarily, but he wouldn't be deciding the case so he didn't see where that entered into it.

"Any chance I can take a look around the house and yard?" he asked Lena now.

"Sure."

Kuchinski followed Lena into the dining room and stopped there while she continued into the living room. He looked around deliberately. A good two feet of hardwood floor outside each edge of the worn, beige carpet under the table and chairs. Less than four feet of clearance between the table's near corner and the china cabinet. He tried to imagine someone unfamiliar with the house coming through this room in the dark without making any noise or banging into anything.

Can't see it. Ole had been drinking and maybe he'd passed out. But if he was passed out, why would the intruder bother to hit him?

He walked into the living room. Funny looking piano. Couch and chairs and coffee table that would have looked like they came from IKEA except they also looked like they'd been made before IKEA was selling much of anything stateside. Big, flat picture window right out of *Leave it to Beaver*. TV ditto. Great big honking console in a walnut cabinet that must have weighed a ton, set flat on the floor. Was the damn thing actually a Philco?

"The television is mostly a prop," Lena said, as if she were reading his mind. "We watch in the club room if there's something we want to see. But the club room is supposed to be a home office for tax purposes, and the IRS might not swallow that if we didn't have a TV in the living part of the house."

Kuchinski's ears pricked up. He knew just enough tax law to be dangerous, but he was pretty sure you had to have a bigger income than this modest house with its forty-year-old furniture suggested to make a home-office deduction worth worrying about. That wasn't what got his attention, though. He was trying again to reconstruct some plausible version of events that night.

What do you do after you've smacked your wife in public? If you're any kind of man at all you're either so mad you can't see straight or you're awash in shame and remorse. And you're worried that this time you've gone too far and you've lost her for good. So maybe you take a couple of stiff drinks, except he didn't see a wet bar or a liquor cabinet in here, and the police file the ADA had turned over to him this morning didn't say anything about a glass on the floor or an open bottle in the room. Maybe you veg out in front of the tube just to take your mind off the whole thing. But Ole would have done that in the club room, not here.

Play the piano or whatever it was as a stress reliever? Maybe. But the deputy had found Ole lying not far from the front door, head toward the door as if he'd been facing it, standing up, when he was hit. Why?

"Was the front door open when you walked in and found Ole?"

Apparently surprised at the question, Lena squeezed her eyes tightly shut for three or four seconds and frowned.

"I think it was, now that you mention it. I don't think I even noticed at the time."

"In the middle of the night in December?"

"You're right," Lena said, "that's odd. But I remember now I didn't have to go open it to let the deputy in. He just barged right through."

"Did Ole play the piano?"

"Harpsichord. Not for twenty years. He has a perfectionist streak that keeps him from having the patience for it. Used to be he'd play beautifully for sixteen bars or so and then he'd hit a wrong note and get so frustrated he'd start cussing and stomping on the floor. He finally got to where he wouldn't play at all."

"Was the light on in the living room when you came in?"

"No. I came back to the house on full boil, ready to have it out with him. I gunned the Ford up the driveway, screeched to a stop, slammed through the back door, flipped on the kitchen light on my way through, flipped on the dining room light as

I stepped into the living room, and then turned on the light in here. That's when I saw him."

"So when he was hit," Kuchinski said, "he was apparently just standing here, in the dark, facing the open front door."

"Unless the intruder opened the front door to get out."

"But you heard the intruder make a noise in the back part of the house just before you walked in here."

"That's true," Lena conceded thoughtfully. "It doesn't make much sense, I guess."

"Sure it does. Ole opened the door so that he'd be sure to see you drive up. He left the inside lights off so he'd have a clear view outside. He might have been worried that you wouldn't come home at all. If you did come home, he wanted to be ready as soon as you arrived. I don't know if he wanted to be ready to say how sorry he was or ready for round two, but it was one or the other."

"You think Ole will remember it that way?"

When I get through with him he will. Kuchinski left this thought unvoiced. No sense giving away trade secrets.

"How about a look in the back, where you heard the noise from?"

"Follow me."

Kuchinski marched obediently behind Lena back to the club room. He saw the array of flags against the back wall and sliding glass doors. He walked over to verify that the doors opened onto a weathered deck, the boards splintered and turning gray. But only a patch of snow here and there showed up on it.

"Do you and Ole keep this deck shoveled off?"

"Ole does. He goes out there when he smokes, so it won't bother me. He keeps the deck clear so he can go out when he feels like a smoke without putting his heavy boots on."

"Does smoking bother you? The police report said that you asked the deputy for a cigarette."

"I did, I guess. I quit twelve years ago. It was my sixtieth birthday present to myself. I only cheat every once in awhile, in what you might call your high-stress situations."

"And you've gotten to where you hate it?"

"Just the opposite. I love the smell of cigarette smoke. Ole takes it outside because he doesn't want to undermine me. He knows if I had to walk around smelling the stuff all day I'd relapse."

Kuchinski went up on tiptoes so that he could glance over the tops of the flags, through the sliding door glass. A snow shovel leaned in the corner where the deck met the angle of the house.

"What was the fight about?" he asked abruptly.

"At the bar? Of course at the bar. What other fight would you be asking about?"

Kuchinski waited. He figured the question had taken Lena by surprise, and he sensed that she was stalling.

"Oh, you know," she said then. "Couples just get on each other's nerves sometimes, especially in winter. Some little irritation, you start snapping at each other, someone says the wrong thing and all of a sudden your ears are ringing and your cheek smarts."

Kuchinski nodded. Looking discreetly at Lena, he worked his hands through a couple of furled flags, found the handle for the sliding door, and pulled the door open. This knocked two of the flags over. Their staffs made a muffled, hollow sound as they hit the floor. Hollow and not very loud. Lena didn't exactly jump out of her skin—and she was standing only ten feet off, not half-a-house away from the noise. He bent down to pick up the fallen colors.

"Anything broken in here?" he asked.

"Not that we found."

"Anything missing?"

"Ole says no. He knows the room better than I do. I haven't missed anything from the rest of the house."

Again Kuchinski nodded. He walked deliberately toward the middle of the room.

"You know," he said, "there's a speech they teach lawyers to give to their clients in criminal cases. Real macho thing. Something along the lines of, 'Lie to your wife, if you want to. Lie to your girlfriend and your boss and your parole officer.

But don't lie to me, because right now I am the only friend you have.'"

Lena looked at him levelly for a couple of seconds, cool appraisal deepening her eyes.

"Boy, you are a real lawyer, aren't you?"

"What was the fight about?"

"Okay, you win," Lena said after another two-second pause. "It was about Harald."

"Your nephew at Annapolis?"

"Right. Ole was talking about how great that uniform would look in campaign photographs. I told him to just leave Harald out of the political stuff—that he had enough on his mind trying to survive plebe year without being shoe-horned into some photo-op as stage dressing. I got a little sharper than I maybe should have, I guess, and touched a nerve, so Ole got up to go away mad. I stood up and grabbed him to keep him from going. He took that the wrong way and pushed me back into my seat."

"Pushed you or belted you?"

"I can see where it might have looked like a little clop across the chops to someone a few feet away. It wasn't all that big a deal. Believe me, I got much worse from my mother for lipping off when I was a kid."

"Okay. I'll want to have someone take pictures of the living room and this room. Plus I'll need to get a detailed floor plan drawn up for the first floor."

"I don't know about the floor plan, but one of Gary Carlsen's Laurels does professional photographic work for him. She might give us a rate—and pennies count."

"I'll look into it. Will Ole be around this morning? I'd like to chat with him, too—face to face, and just the two of us."

"He won't be around here this morning, but if you hustle back to Milwaukee you might be able to catch him there. He's down there talking with Carlsen and your buddy Rep." She looked again at her watch. "I'll call him and tell him to hang around so he can buy you a late lunch, if you like."

"Right," Kuchinski said. "Pennies count."

Chapter Seven

Ole Lindstrom had just finished telling Gary Carlsen to "turn that damn thing off" when Lena's call came through. While Ole punched his cellphone and muttered into it, Carlsen obediently leaned back in his desk chair to silence a talk-radio host blaring from a boombox on the cabinet behind him. He gave Rep a good-natured, what-can-you-do? smile as silence replaced the yack.

"'Know the enemy,'" Laurel Wolf said, shaking her head and wagging her finger as she slipped what looked like a world-class digital camera over her left shoulder on a wide, embroidered bandolier strap. She walked past Carlsen's work-area toward the door.

"Is 'the enemy' me or the talk-jock?" Ole asked her.

"See ya," Wolf said. "Back at one-thirty."

"Isn't three hours a little long for a cigarette break?" Carlsen asked.

Wolf flipped off her boss while she tugged at the camera strap.

"That's right, you're the Laurel who *doesn't* smoke," Carlsen said as he snapped his fingers theatrically. "I should know that by now. My bad."

Wolf said something in a language Rep didn't recognize. She smiled while she said it. Sort of.

"Do you understand the Chenequa dialect?" Carlsen asked Rep.

"No, but I bet I can translate that."

They were on the south half of the third floor of a long red brick building on Milwaukee's near south side. The building had been a rolling mill for eighty-five years and an eyesore for thirty-five. Now, tuck-pointed, re-glazed, and otherwise spruced up, it housed an odd-lot collection of twenty-something artisans who wanted ample room and low rent: silk-screeners, photographers, web-site designers, bookbinders, commercial artists, sound- and video-recording producers, and Gary Carlsen's public relations company, Future^3 (pronounced "Future Cubed," as Carlsen carefully explained).

Rep had mentally nicknamed the premises the Carlsen Archipelago. What Carlsen called "islands" dotted an open expanse of what had once been nineteenth-century shop-floor, with no enclosures between them. Carlsen's desk and computer table and a two-drawer, lateral file cabinet formed his "work island" under western light streaming placidly through an elegantly slanted skylight. Looming at random intervals on either side were "creative islands" where people could fuss with customized digital printers and lay glossy prints out on long tables or oversized easels; "teamwork islands," defined by four conference tables arranged in a solid square, without chairs; "activity islands," featuring DVD players and layout materials; "research islands," with CD-Rom racks and file cabinets sporting very long, very thin drawers; and lesser work islands for lower ranking employees. Carlsen had explained that the island concept was "the latest thing from the coast."

"The application for copyright registration on Lena's song is filed," Rep said. "Phase two is capturing your theme in the same kind of artistic expression the song gives to your hook."

"I'll call Ms. Gephardt and tell her to get to work on a book," Ole muttered.

"Worked for Obama," Carlsen said.

"Not a book," Rep said. "Pictures, images, music. If you rip off a political idea expressed verbally, you practically have to copy it word for word before a court will even pay attention.

Your theme is that there's a new sheriff in town: bring an unsullied, energetic amateur in from outside the system to clean up the mess made by professional politicians. That's like having a murder mystery where the crime is solved by a private investigator whose cynical exterior masks an idealistic soul, working in uneasy collaboration with a gruff but grudgingly respectful police detective. It's a neat idea, but you can't copyright it. It doesn't belong to anyone. It's just part of the genre's furniture."

"So in real world terms, what am I supposed to do?" Ole demanded. "Dig up an art student to 'express' my 'concept' in an abstract painting? Or gin up five-million dollars or so and make an art-house movie out of it?"

This question hung awkwardly in the air for five or six seconds. Rep could imagine a number of answers to it, but he didn't think that any of them would strike Ole as constructive. Carlsen, meanwhile, sat absolutely still, leaning back in his chair, eyes hooded, his rigid body somehow expressing not languor but inner excitement. Then, quite deliberately, he swiveled in his chair to face his keyboard. Ole scowled, but before his mouth opened Carlsen held up his right index finger in a gesture that said, "Just chill for a second."

After tapping nimbly at the keys he mouse-clicked through screen images at a speed suggesting late-night channel surfing by a college student with attention-deficit disorder. He paused for a moment at a cartoon image showing a woman in Lincoln green, drawing the string on a bow and arrow. Shaking his head, he clicked past it as Rep noticed that it was an ad for Chesterfield cigarettes. A few more clicks and another pause, this time at an ad showing a woman at the wheel of a race car. Again he went on.

"Didn't they sell anything but cars and cigarettes in the 'fifties?" he muttered.

Another minute into the process he paused again. He looked contemplatively at the screen and then hit PRINT. The color sheet that he pulled from the muscular printer next to his computer was still warm when he laid it on the desk between Ole and Rep.

"Kinky sex," Ole said. "Great."

HELLLLO, Rep thought. *I can't wait to see where this one's going.*

"This sold a lot of Stafford Flour for General Mills in 1934," Carlsen said.

It was a full-page ad, mostly print but drawing the eye first to a bright cartoon at the center-top of the page. The cartoon depicted a comically dismayed cowboy who had stretched his torso through an open kitchen window to steal a slice of freshly-baked cake from the counter. The cook had caught him in the act and taken him by surprise. She had pinned him to the sill by pulling the window sash down tight against his waist. Now, grinning with unbecoming delight, she was smacking his rear end with a long-handled scouring brush. The tag-line said that Stafford Flour made food so good a real man would risk his skin to taste cake made with it.

Carlsen's eyes snapped open as he sketched a quicksilver smile that Rep read as saying, "I'm way cooler than you but too polite to mention it."

"So?" Ole asked.

"Comics," Carlsen said.

Rep winced. After the smile it seemed a little anti-climactic, somehow.

"Comics," Ole said.

Carlsen's arms spread wide and his face suddenly glowed with vibrant enthusiasm.

"Start with simple comic strip story-lines, circulated on-line. Aim it first at college students and cynical gen-exers. Generate a little buzz and watch it spread to alienated pink-collar twenty-somethings on cubicle farms in Dilbert-land—but make it funny enough to force attention from political reporters. Hook them with subliminal kinky sex just like General Mills did, and then hammer them with our theme snuck in between the lines. Link them to every blog we can think of. Link them to a web-site with all the policy-wonk stuff spelled out. Gephardt isn't some new dyke sheriff, she's Lara Croft with a school marm's ruler instead of a laser-gun and a big, maternal smile instead of a scowling pout. Non-threatening and reassuring, except to the bad guys. When we pass ten-thousand hits a day, we step it up."

"'Step it up' to what?" Ole asked.

"*Live action* comic strips. Human beings instead of drawings, but *behaving* like cartoon characters. Like *Ironman*, except three minutes instead of two hours, because technically *Ironman* was a live action comic *book*."

"Distributed how? Youtube?"

"Youtube, My Space, Facebook, Twitter, *et* bloody *cetera*. Count on the hook and the outside-the-box stuff to draw the attention of commercial networks and generate free media."

"The two most beautiful words in the English language," Ole said with an emphatic nod. "It could work. How do we get Gephardt to sign off on it?"

"We generate the buzz *first*, and get the theme out there *first*. Not flogging any candidate. Pure civic concern about discrimination or corruption or whatever we're worried about this week. Once we've got the brand, *then* we hook the saleswoman."

"I like this boy," Ole said to Rep.

He beamed as he spoke the words. He suddenly looked like a dad whose son had been named valedictorian and made the Olympic track team on the same day. His cranky sniping and impatient dismissals of Carlsen's comments faded in the nimbus of unambiguous esteem for the younger man. Carlsen basked contentedly in the glow of his mentor's approval.

"I'll leave the political tactics to you," Rep said. "Legally, though, if you get me ten or twelve comics panels or a handful of storyboards, I'll get you a c with a circle around it."

"Sounds like a plan," Carlsen said, taking a quick glance at the digital clock in the lower right-hand corner of his computer screen. "Let's hit the bricks with it."

Carlsen turned the boombox back on as Ole and Rep got up to leave. They made their fifteen-second walk to the door to the accompaniment of the talk-jock wrapping up a chat with a caller who apparently agreed with every word he said. The last thing

Rep heard as he opened the door to the hallway was the radio voice saying, "Great call. Now, here's a question I'd like your input on around the corner when we start a new segment after the break: Is racial discrimination by the government somehow *not* discrimination if the goodies the government is passing out are gambling licenses?"

"Now how do you suppose he managed *that*?" Ole asked, looking with twinkling eyes at Rep.

Kuchinski urged his Cadillac Escalade steadily south toward Milwaukee, glancing with anxious misgivings every ninety seconds or so at the dog-eared, white manila folder on the passenger seat. The folder held the police file on the Lindstrom investigation. He'd only taken a cursory look at it so far, but what bothered him was the way he'd gotten it. Usually you have to negotiate fiercely over disclosure of the investigative file in a criminal case. Not this time. He'd walked in to hand the assistant DA his written request, and the bored prosecutor had pulled the file off his credenza, tossed it on his desk, and said, "Tell Lois outside to copy whatever you want. Fifty cents a page."

In other words, the ADA didn't think there was a scrap of information in the file that would be the slightest help to the defense. He thought he had Lena Lindstrom cold. Kuchinski was thinking that he might have to pull something out of left field to win this case.

For forty-five miles he resisted the temptation to call Melissa. She was his link to Frank Seton. Frank was his link to Harald Lindstrom at the Naval Academy. The Ole/Lena slugfest had started with a fight over Harald—and in Kuchinski's eyes that meant the kid was now prominently standing right up against the left field wall. Trial lawyers aren't known for outstanding manners, but Kuchinski was a pragmatist. Make yourself a nuisance with people who do you favors, and pretty soon they stop returning your calls.

He made it to Allenton before his resistance collapsed and his itching fingers reached for his cell phone, nestled in the cup-holder in front of the car radio. He was just about to grab it when six bars of the theme from *Perry Mason* chimed tinnily from it.

"Kuchinski."

"Melissa. My department chair just dropped something on my desk that I think you might want to see. My last class today ends at ten to four. If you get a chance to stop by a little after that, I'll be happy to show it to you."

"I'll make time. What is it?"

"A proposed presentation for a symposium on domestic violence that Veronica Gephardt's organization is sponsoring. The title of the presentation is *The Banalization of Spousal Battery in American Popular Culture, 1930 to 1980*. Ms. Gephardt apparently isn't altogether comfortable with it, so she asked the university's English Department to vet it. I'm the designated pop culture deconstructionist and stuff flows downhill, so I'm sitting here with it."

"'Spousal battery/popular culture.' You mean like Ralph Kramden saying 'to the moon, Alice' in every episode of *The Honeymooners* and Ricky turning Lucy over his knee in *I Love Lucy* and John Wayne swatting Maureen O'Hara in *McLintock*?"

"Good examples, but it goes way beyond that. It shows up in comic books and paperbacks and even print advertising for mainstream products."

"The golden age of wife beating," Kuchinski commented.

"That's the thing. At least in popular fiction, it went both ways. That's one of the problems Gephardt has with it. Some of the examples in this presentation get in the way of the doctrine that men have a monopoly on spouse abuse. Edward Everett Horton's wife gives him a shiner in *Top Hat* because she thinks he's been flirting with another woman. Lois Lane throws dishes and rolling pins at Superman in their fantasy marriage. What made me think of you is a running gag in a 'fifties sit-com called *The People's Choice*. Every time the second banana causes a problem with some kind of kitschy shenanigans, his wife bangs him on the head with a skillet. This is invariably accompanied by a comical '*CLANG!*' sound effect and titters from the laugh track."

"I'll bet if I listen closely enough I'll also hear 'lack of intent' in the background. You're saying that a couple the Lindstroms' age could easily have the idea that a husbandly or wifely smack now and then isn't all that big a deal."

"I have no idea what a jury will think," Melissa said, "but I thought you might want to take a look at it."

"You have provoked my interest, Professor Pennyworth." Kuchinski paused artfully for three carefully timed beats before he continued. "By the way, has your brother Frank called back yet?"

"No, he hasn't. Are you actually going to try to juggle two Lindstrom cases at the same time?"

"I don't have any choice, because they just became the same case." Kuchinski briefly explained Harald Lindstrom's connection to the criminal charge Lena was facing.

"I'll email Frank and tell him that we'll call him together when you stop by this afternoon."

"Much appreciated." Kuchinski smiled broadly as he ended the call, and not because he saw a sign promising a Culvers Restaurant at an exit two miles ahead, with the prospect of a double bacon cheeseburger and a chocolate malt. Well, not only because of that.

◇◇◇

"Thanks for the early lunch," Ole told Rep forty-five minutes later as they strolled back into the office suite that Rep now shared with Kuchinski. "But Lena said Walt was going to buy my noon meal."

"You're a witness in her case. This way, if the prosecutor asks you whether Walt gave you anything in exchange for your testimony you can say, 'No, he didn't even buy me lunch.'"

"Fair enough."

"I'm guessing Walt will be back within twenty minutes." Rep glanced at his watch.

"Ten," Kuchinski's receptionist/secretary/office manager said. "He just called in that he's on I-forty-three and cruising downtown on a full stomach."

"I'll wait out here and read the *ABA Journal*, then," Ole told Rep, "so that you can get back to work registering copyrights and trademarks.

"Okay. Good luck with Walt."

As Rep passed the large, circular receptionist's desk, he spotted a pink phone-message slip on the spindle over his name. This was a bit unusual. Almost all callers just went into voice-mail these days if they didn't get through. Rep grabbed the slip and glanced at it. Someone named Randy Halftoe wanted him to call about "a new matter."

Shrugging, Rep folded the slip into his palm so that he wouldn't forget it. He wasn't as compulsive about work as most corporate lawyers, but even he knew that attorneys should always return business calls the same day they came in.

Chapter Eight

"Midshipman Lindstrom's story is that he got a text message from Ole Lindstrom telling him to meet someone named Chris Deer at that motel," Lieutenant-Commander Francis Xavier Seton said over Melissa's speaker phone at four-thirteen that afternoon. (To ascribe these words to 'Frank Seton' would be accurate, but wouldn't capture the 'now-hear-this-I'm-not-going-to-say-it-twice' timbre in his voice.)

"You mean Ole was pimping for his nephew?" Kuchinski asked. "That rascal."

"He says no." Seton's voice cold enough to chill Gordon's Gin. "He says he assumed that Chris Deer was a man working for Ole as a go-fer. He claims he was completely surprised when Deer turned out to be a thirty-six-twenty-one-thirty-two doe with waist-length black hair. According to the text message, Deer was supposed to bring a Thinkpad laptop computer that the midshipman had left with Ole. The 'password' required to boot the computer up is a fingerprint swipe with the mid's right index finger."

"Rep gave me one of those for our last anniversary," Melissa said. "The finger-swipe feature is neat, but there's supposed to be an alternative typed password that you can default into if the finger-swipe doesn't work."

"There was, but Ole claimed he couldn't make that one work."

"Someone should call the Guiness Book of World Records," Kuchinski said. "This sounds like the longest text message in history."

"That's a good point," Melissa said. "Why wouldn't Ole just call him?"

"Kid says he doesn't know," Seton said.

Maybe because Lena might have overheard, Kuchinski thought.

"And no one can check the midshipman's phone to verify the text message because it was stolen along with everything else he had, I suppose," Melissa said.

"Correct. Bottom line, though, he did go to the motel."

"Which is breaking the rules to start with, right?" Melissa asked.

"Actually, no. A plebe wouldn't ordinarily be allowed to be that far off-grounds on a Friday night, especially during the weekend of the Army-Navy game, but his company was leading in competitions and efficiency ratings, so he had special town liberty privileges."

"Okay," Kuchinski said. "He gets to the motel, meets the femme fatale—what happens next, according to him?"

"She takes him up to room two-oh-eight, he boots up the computer, and then she does a Carl Sandberg on him."

"'A Carl Sandberg?'" Kuchinski asked.

"'I have seen your painted women beckoning the farm boys underneath the streetlamps,'" Melissa quoted. "Seductive ladies have been taking the rap ever since Eve ate the apple. Why should we expect the script to change now?"

"She fixes him a drink," Seton said. "Three good swigs and it's lights out for Midshipman Lindstrom. The next thing he knows he's alone, stark naked, and in a very bad way. He stumbles into the lobby in a panic, where he collapses just in time for retired Gunnery Sergeant Mayer to save his life."

"Any chance we can talk to Mayer?" Kuchinski asked.

"You are talking to him," Seton said. "He's sitting right beside me. He's the one I got most of this information from. And he's the only one the kid has really opened up to so far."

"*Semper Fi*, Gunny," Kuchinski said.

"When did you enlist?" a gravelly, skeptical voice asked.

"I didn't. I got a telegram from President Nixon."

"'Nam, huh? *Sin loi.*"

"You got that right. Da Nang was *sin loi* and then some."

It was Melissa's turn to look baffled until Kuchinski mouthed "Vietnamese for 'tough shit' in her direction.

"So I'd say the kid has a problem," Frank said.

"I'd say he has a problem-and-a-half," Kuchinski said. "Do you believe his story, Gunny?"

"If I made up a story it'd be a lot better than that one, and he's at least eight clicks smarter than I am."

"One of the main reasons the Academy hasn't cashiered him already is that the gunnery sergeant has weighed in on his side with some key people," Seton said. "Officers who don't respect the opinions of gunnery sergeants don't last long. That and the fact that Lindstrom was indeed dosed with chloral hydrate instead of taking some recreational drug himself, and the motel clerk vaguely remembers the woman who checked into two-oh-eight maybe having a laptop with her."

"Does Lindstrom have any idea of what was on the computer that could have been worth so much effort?" Melissa asked.

"No," Seton said.

"What does Ole say about the text message?"

"No one has asked him yet."

"Well someone is about to," Kuchinski said, "because it sure didn't come up in the two-hour chat he and I just had."

"Are you representing the kid?" Seton asked.

"Yeah, at least until I can track down someone who knows more about the Articles of War than I do."

"It's called the Uniform Code of Military Justice these days," Seton said, "and for what it's worth my take on this is that rules and procedure won't have much to do with Lindstrom's case. What that kid needs is someone to pin down some facts to back his story up."

"How about it, Gunny?" Kuchinski asked. "Where should I start?"

"Well, I've done a little digging already," the gravelly voice said. "And believe me, it is rocky, hardscrabble soil. But I have one person who might have useful information and might be willing to share it if she is properly motivated."

"'She,'" Kuchinski said. "What's her name?"

"Crystal. I don't know her family name, and I'm not altogether sure she does. She was the one with me when I stumbled over Lindstrom. We have had a word or two with each other since then, and I do believe she could be helpful."

"Does AirTran have a non-stop to Baltimore?" Kuchinski asked. "I'd like to get out there as soon as I can after I've talked with Ole again."

"There's a catch," the gunnery sergeant said. "Crystal is a shy little thing. I know, I know—her line of work, how do you figure shy? But there it is. The person who talks to her is going to have to be a girl—lady, excuse me. Her idea, not mine."

"Well that's a complication," Kuchinski grumbled as Melissa looked thoughtfully at the phone, "but if I scramble a bit I might be able to gin up a work-around."

"Can you get a BA in English at the Naval Academy?" Melissa asked.

"You can't get a bachelor of arts degree in anything at the Naval Academy," Seton said. "You *can*, however, get a bachelor of *science* degree in English there. The military academies produce the only English majors in the world who've taken compulsory courses in thermodynamics, electrical engineering, four years of math, and all the hard sciences. What are you thinking, baby sister? That I have an officer-chum teaching English at the Academy who might welcome a guest lecturer from, say, UWM?"

"Two of Jane Austen's brothers were admirals in the British Navy. Until the British victory at Trafalgar, the fear that Napoleon would invade England was part of the psychological landscape in her life and the lives of everyone she knew. 'Austen and the Fleet.' The lecture almost writes itself."

"You know what, Commander?" the gravelly voice chuckled. "You just got had, brother."

Five seconds of silence ticked by.

"Not a new experience for me where this particular professor is concerned," Seton sighed then. "I'll send some emails."

Rep glanced at his watch. Two minutes after six, and no Randall Halftoe. Halftoe had called at four-forty-five, fifteen minutes after the first appointment time they'd set up, to say that he'd be running late. How about five-forty-five? Rep had agreed. New business is new business, and Melissa would be working late anyway. Halftoe still hadn't shown, and calls to his number went right to voice-mail.

This didn't particularly surprise Rep. People often get cold feet before coming to see lawyers, as if attorneys were dentists who gave you toothaches instead of curing them. Still, he wasn't going to wait all night. He started logging off his computer. That figured to take until five after six or so. If Halftoe hadn't shown by then he'd just forget about it.

The screen was just going to black when his phone rang and he answered it.

"Counselor? I am really, *really* sorry, bro. Got hung up on something and couldn't shake free to save my ever-lovin' life." His voice had a smooth, almost-but-not-quite-southern cadence and a studied, California-wannabe mellowness.

"How soon can you get here?" Rep asked.

"I'm here right now. I'm freezin' my tush off downstairs outside the main door, which is locked tighter than a drum, and I can't seem to get the attention of a security guard."

"The guard went off duty at six. I'll be right down."

Rep rode the antique elevator impatiently down to the lobby. Standing under the floodlights that bathed the pavement in front of the Germania Building's main entrance he saw a man in his early forties, hatless despite the sharp cold, sleek, ebony hair combed straight back and running a little long. The tan skin showing over the fur collar of his richly woven brown wool coat looked a lot more like, say, Fort Lauderdale in August than Milwaukee in December. He was holding an oxblood leather attaché case in his right hand and had a large, black and white vinyl/canvas carry-all hanging by a strap from his left shoulder.

Rep pushed the outside door open.

"Thanks, bro. Hold this for a sec, willya?"

Rep took the carry-all that Halftoe pushed toward him while Halftoe used his left hand to brace the door open and step into the lobby. As soon as they were inside, Rep handed the bag back to Halftoe and led him to the elevators. Halftoe spent the creaking trip up to the ninth floor apologizing again for "blowin' off two appointments," as he put it.

"No problem." *The customer is always right.*

Rep showed the prospective client to one of the guest chairs in his office, sat behind his desk, and squared a legal pad in front of him.

"Okay," he said. "What's the nature of the problem?"

Halftoe looked puzzled for a split second, then flashed an oh-I-get-it smile.

"Campaign finance regulation," he said, broadening the smile.

"That's not really my field, but I have some partners who can help you out."

"No sweat," Halftoe said. "It *is* my field."

From the attaché case he took two typewritten pages, stapled in their upper left-hand corners, and handed them to Rep. Rep found himself examining a two-column list. In the first column appeared names, addresses, and telephone numbers: Jimmy Eagle, Thomas Clay, Shadrach Bass and so forth, eight names on the first page and six on page two. The second column showed dollar amounts. All of the amounts were between fifteen-hundred and two-thousand dollars, and they all ended in zero.

"That is a list of friends and employees of Flaming Torch Chenequa Gaming and Entertainment Enterprises who support the objectives of the Paper Valley Political Education and Values Fund," Halftoe said, as if he were reading verbatim from the Code of Federal Regulations. "They have dipped into their modest personal resources in order to put their money where their mouths are. They are unsophisticated wage-earners. They don't write checks or go to thousand-dollar-a-plate dinners. They just pass the hat. That's why the donations are in cash. They have asked me to make sure their contributions get into the right hands."

"I see." Halftoe was "bundling"—turning over campaign contributions ostensibly gathered from numerous employees. In truth, the money had almost certainly come from the company's coffers instead of the employees' pockets, but by attributing the donations to them the company could evade the limits on corporate campaign contributions.

Halftoe hoisted the carry-all to Rep's desk.

"Just over twenty-thousand all told. You can count it if you want to. I wouldn't blame you if you did. No sir. I'd do it. When you're done, I have a receipt here that I'd be obliged if you would sign."

"That won't be necessary," Rep said.

"I appreciate that, sir, I surely do."

"I can't accept this money."

"You are listed as the attorney of record for Paper Valley in its recent copyright filing," Halftoe said, his bafflement entirely unfeigned. "That makes you a legally designated agent with full authority to act on its behalf."

"I'm familiar with the statutory language. If you'd like to negotiate a license to use *Come Now You People*, I'll be happy to talk with you. But I haven't been engaged to"—he almost said 'launder,' but checked himself at the last second—"run political campaign contributions through my trust account."

"This money wouldn't actually have to go into your trust account, would it?" Halftoe asked.

"Anytime I take money for a client it goes through the trust account whether the law says it has to or not."

Halftoe looked thoughtfully at the ceiling for a couple of seconds, then favored Rep with an expression so warmly understanding that Rep felt oddly like a virgin being gentled by an experienced lothario into the beginning of her sentimental education.

"This is all perfectly legal. You understand that, right?"

"I'll take your word for that," Rep said, "but this just isn't my gig. The copyright application shows Paper Valley's address. I'd suggest that you send the money there."

◇◇◇

Melissa pulled her office door closed as she steeped into the hallway and heard the lock click firmly into place. It was almost seven-thirty at night, and she would have to lead tomorrow off with an eight a.m. class. She wanted to hustle home, slip out of wool and into denim—"jean therapy," as she called it—nuke some Lean Cuisine, and relax.

"Professor Pennyworth!" an urgent voice behind her called. "I have a sin offering!"

"Why don't you just say three Our Fathers and three Hail Marys?" Melissa muttered as she turned around.

Then she saw the large, sleeved Starbucks cups the woman was carrying. Although she looked to be in her early to mid-forties, her chestnut hair bounced almost girlishly against the back of her neck as she hustled down the Curtin Hall corridor at something more than a trot but not quite a run.

"Latte or hot chocolate, your choice," the woman said. "I'm Veronica Gephardt, in case you haven't guessed. I'm the one to blame for that shit detail that got dumped on you." She lowered her voice almost to a whisper when she spoke the vulgarity, as if she were mildly ashamed about using it but feared that a prissier expression would seem stilted and out of place.

Melissa accepted the cup in the woman's left hand. *What's the point of Lean Cuisine if you can't drink hot chocolate before braving a winter's night walk to the parking lot?*

"I sent you an email about the presentation you asked to have reviewed," Melissa said. "I said that on first reading it appeared to be a competent piece of academic work that would readily stand comparison with many if not most presentations at academic symposiums."

"I read that and I appreciate your prompt response. I'd like to drill down a bit into your assessment. Would you recommend the work for publication in a peer-reviewed journal in your field?"

"Before I could answer that question I'd have to spend at least a week analyzing the piece and reviewing the underlying research." Melissa sipped rich cocoa and licked her upper lip. "So it seems like a moot point. I can't drop everything else, and I gather you couldn't wait a week for an answer even if I could. Besides, it's very unusual to evaluate symposium presentations against a criterion like that. Are you actually applying that standard to all the papers you're considering?"

"That's a provocative question," Gephardt said, her tone suggesting a playful complicity. "Might we step into your office, professor?"

Melissa toyed with saying no. When she looked at Gephardt she saw the polished self-assurance of someone on weekly speaking terms with people who routinely write seven-figure checks—someone whose first job every year was to raise the money to pay her own salary, and who brought it off, year after year. Gephardt's manners so far had been impeccable, without a hint of presumption or condescension. Perhaps unfairly, though, Melissa thought she read something different in Gephardt's unblinking gray eyes and the firm set of her mouth: a sense that Gephardt's peers were the university chancellor; that tenured faculty were hired help, and mere assistant professors drones who did what they were told without asking provocative questions.

One of the iron rules of assistant professorship is to pick your fights carefully. So instead of saying no Melissa unlocked her door.

"Thank you," Gephardt said as she followed Melissa in and found a seat. "The answer to your question is that we are *not* putting all the presentations through the peer-review wringer. If that suggests to you that I have an agenda, I do. I admire detached and dispassionate scholarship, but I don't aspire to it."

"Each to her own taste," Melissa said.

"Just so. As Kant said, approximately, the world needs carpenters as well as philosophers."

"I didn't know Kant ever came that close to common sense. I'll skip any comment about hammering away at the point."

"Good one," Gephardt said, smiling wryly with apparently genuine warmth. "I'll take the hint and cut to the chase. Presenting meticulously documented facts in a carefully evenhanded way can be meretricious. Domestic violence is a complex issue. As an empirical matter, women are indeed the physical aggressors roughly as often as men are in fights between couples. The fact remains that, on average, men do a lot more damage than women do whether they're hitting first or hitting back. Speaking in broad generalities, a man who's hit by a woman is irritated; a woman who's hit by a man is hospitalized—or sent to the morgue. I'm not over-dramatizing. Women die from domestic abuse literally every day in this country. I'm less worried about correcting gender stereotypes than I am about stopping the bleeding. That's my agenda."

"And you have every right to it," Melissa said. "Your organization is an advocacy group. You don't have to put on a studiously neutral, fair and balanced program, any more than the Catholic Church has to give atheists equal time at the pulpit on Sunday mornings."

"We're in complete agreement."

"But that doesn't mean you get cover from me. Tell the contributor that his submission doesn't meet the needs of your organization if you want to. I'll back you up from here to Sunday. But I won't say that a perfectly competent effort by one of my colleagues is substantively deficient when it's not."

"And I wouldn't ask you to do anything like that," Gephardt said. "I may not be a Ph.D, but I'm smart enough not to ask you to lie."

"Thank you."

"At the same time, though, I couldn't help noticing a damn-with-faint-praise tone in your carefully qualified comments about the proposed presentation. You said it 'appears to be a competent piece of academic work.' Fine. But as a matter of literary analysis, do you actually agree with it?"

"Not entirely," Melissa admitted. "When men are comically chastised in the examples he gives, it's because they've done something foolish or reckless—caused problems through some kind of idiotically thoughtless mischief. The implicit message is, 'If you behave like a child, you'll be treated like one.' When the women are beaten, on the other hand, it's often because they've asserted themselves and have to be put in their place. Maureen O'Hara refuses to shrug off her husband's recreational sex with a dance-hall girl, so she's not only smacked but publicly humiliated. Elizabeth Allen dares to treat John Wayne as an equal in a business negotiation and gets spanked for it. The women aren't chastised for acting like children but for acting like adults."

"And so the apparent equivalence that the presentation posits is superficial," Gephardt prompted.

"Sure—*if* you buy my argument. But it's not a breach of academic standards to disagree with me."

"Would you do me a favor?" Gephardt asked. "Would you mind putting what you just said into a presentation of your own? I'm not looking for original research. A rebuttal like the one you just gave me will do fine. The conference isn't until February, so you'd have a good six weeks to work it up. I know it's an imposition, but it would be a huge help."

Melissa aimed a carefully guarded expression at Gephardt. *'Imposition' doesn't even start to cover it. But I can't say no and you know it.*

"I'll be happy to," Melissa said, lying through her teeth. "But when the contributor finds out he'll be facing custom-tailored rebuttal, he'll probably react by withdrawing his paper."

"I fervently hope so," Gephardt said. "That will simplify my life considerably."

At just after eight o'clock that night, Laurel Wolf took a digital photograph she'd just run off on the printer next to her computer at work and brought it over to Carlsen. He turned his attention away from the *Battlestar Gallactica* trivia questions on his own computer screen and examined it.

"This will save you the trouble of waiting until I go to the john and trying to figure out which file I stored this in on my computer," she said.

Carlsen ignored the attitude and studied the print. It showed Rep Pennyworth under bright lights on the porch of the Germania Building, accepting a carry-all from Randy Halftoe.

"He's even dumber than I thought he was," Carlsen muttered.

"Are you gonna give him a call?"

"I suppose," Carlsen sighed. He offered Wolf an expression making it clear that he felt much put upon by the inadequacies of the human race, but would soldier on anyway.

"Be brave," she said mockingly. "Remember: Custer died for your sins."

Chapter Nine

Thursday, January 15, 2009

"How did your improvised lecture go?" Frank Seton asked Melissa.

She fell into step beside her brother and began walking with him down a broad corridor on the second floor of Samson Hall at the Naval Academy.

"'Improvised' is a little strong, isn't it? It took a while to set this up, so I had almost a month to prepare it. And an undergraduate paper I wrote on *Persuasion* had three paragraphs on the prize award system in the British Navy during the Napoleonic Wars. The hardest part was getting used to students answering questions by barking, 'Ma'am, yes, ma'am!'"

"Technically, they don't have to address civilians that way."

"I mentioned that to the first one who did it. He said, 'Ma'am, yes, ma'am!' So I decided not to make waves, so to speak."

They had gotten to within about ten feet of the end of the corridor. Midshipmen changing classes had been passing them at a brisk pace since they began their walk. With the corner approaching, though, Melissa reflexively braced herself. Before she took another step six plebes in her general vicinity broke into an all-out run, elbows pumping and knees churning. As they rounded the corner they yelled "BEAT ARMY!" in unison.

"That's called 'chopping,'" Seton explained. "The plebes have to do it all year."

"But the Army-Navy game was six weeks ago."

"That was the Army-Navy *football* game. We'll be playing Army in basketball or fencing or baseball or something or other until almost the end of the academic year."

Melissa bit her tongue as they headed down a staircase, but she sensed that her brother was reading her highly critical thoughts anyway. *These are some of the brightest kids America has. The average college boards for plebes entering the Naval Academy are well above UW-Madison, much less UWM. Why do we put them through this 1950's style fraternity hazing stuff?*

They came out of Samson Hall into clammy gray chill. Melissa glanced at her watch: just after two p.m. Visions of driving on unfamiliar roads through the Maryland countryside brought a small frown as she wondered whether she'd make her flight home at seven-thirty that night.

"How long will it take us to get to wherever Gunnery Sergeant Mayer and his friend, Crystal, are?"

"Depends on how fast you can walk four-hundred yards or so. Gunny has her in the Drydock restaurant over at Dahlgren."

"How did he manage that?"

"Crystal was worried that, regardless of what small bar or hotel restaurant we picked, her meeting might be spotted by someone who would tell the wrong people about it. Gunny pointed out that none of those inconvenient potential witnesses were likely to be at an eating establishment that you can only reach by showing proper i.d. to a Marine with a sidearm."

They walked past a cannon with a bulbous breach.

"That's the Dahlgren Gun," Seton explained. "Designed by the officer who had this building named after him as a result. Some people call it the gun that won the Civil War."

"I'm guessing that none of those people are in the Army."

"Not likely," Seton admitted, chuckling as he pushed through tall doors heavy with brass and varnished maple and headed downstairs to the basement. Seton stopped at the doorway of what looked at first glance like a typical college rathskeller and pointed to a booth against the far wall of the dim interior. A man in late middle age and a woman who would have gotten carded at most Milwaukee bars sat sharing a pizza. The young woman wore large sunglasses even in the subdued basement lighting.

"There they are," Seton said. "I'll wait just outside the door here. I left your buddy, Kuchinski, in the main hall upstairs when I came over to pick you up after your lecture. If you get to a point where you think you've got Crystal loosened up enough to handle him, give me a wave and I'll fetch him."

"Got it. Frank, thank you very much. I really appreciate this."

Mayer spotted Melissa before she was halfway across the room. He hopped out of the booth and with considerable ceremony introduced himself to Melissa and gestured her into a seat opposite Crystal, who offered Melissa a damp handshake and said "Hi" in a small voice. Crystal seemed petite but not frail to Melissa, reserved and defensive but not timid. Her lustrous hair was varying shades of blond, going from almost straw colored on the sides to white-gold where she had parted it on top, as if sunlight and the tanning booth variety had bleached it unevenly during hour after hour of basking and tanning.

"Thank you for taking the time to meet with me," Melissa said. "I guess you know why I'm here."

"You want to help that boy that got his bell rung and it turns out he's a mid. I think that's real sweet and I *admire* you for doin' that. I want you to know that."

Crystal spoke with an accent that becomes familiar in areas where lots of soldiers and retired soldiers live: a sort of country-southern, not quite one or the other; the kind of thing you might get if McDonalds melded deep Georgia and west Texas into a semi-homogenous dialect that it thought would sell all over the country.

"Thank you," Melissa said. "I'm hoping you know something about the woman who met with him."

"I really don't. Not all that much, anyway. You see, Speedbump—he's the guy who takes care of me and some other girls? You know?"

"I get your drift," Melissa said, nodding.

"Well, anyway, Speedbump isn't one of those guys with real bad tempers, but he doesn't like disrespect. He's not the kind who'll come down on a girl just because she has a slow night, but he won't have his girls talking back to him. You know? And I respect that. You know?"

"Sure." Melissa cringed inside and wondered if it showed in her expression.

It did.

"You look like I just said a bad word in church," Crystal said, an amused lilt coloring her voice.

"I don't want you to have the wrong impression about Speedy Tarrant," Mayer said, "which is what Speedbump's mama calls him. He's not one of these wire coat-hanger types you see in the movies. Besides, he knows about a little game I sometimes play called 'gunny roulette.' Speedbump is not gonna mess with Crystal."

"I'm sorry. I'm out of my depth here. I guess I'm one of those ivory-tower professors who come off like sissies when people talk about stuff like this."

"You're a professor?" Delight brightened Crystal's voice. "What are you a professor of?"

"English."

"Really?" Crystal pulled her sunglasses off and leaned farther toward Melissa. She had so much make-up on her eyelids that layered flecks were clearly visible.

"Really and truly," Melissa confirmed.

"Look, could you help me with something?"

"I'll try."

"I'm taking this course? At Baltimore County Community College? In, like, literature?"

"That's great," Melissa said.

"Crystal here wants to be a paralegal," Mayer drawled.

"Right," Crystal said. "Because lawyers make, like, a *lot* of money. I don't mean I won't marry for love. I will, I truly, truly will. But it's common sense you're gonna fall in love with someone you spend a lot of time with, so I figure when I've finally got some skills I might as well spend my working time with guys who do real well financially. You know?"

"Makes sense to me," Melissa said.

"BCCC is making Crystal clear up some gaps from high school before they'll enroll her in paralegal training," Mayer said.

"And in this one course, the teacher gave us a list of topics we could write about. And I couldn't even *pronounce* most of them, so I just picked one about the steeplechase metaphor in *Anna Care-ah-KNEE-na*. And I'm like, I can't find that in *Monarch Notes* and I don't even know what he's talking about."

It took Melissa less than a second to make two decisions. First, she wasn't going to correct Crystal's pronunciation of *Anna Karenina*. And second, she wasn't going to quibble about helping Crystal cheat on her homework.

"You read about Colonel Vronsky in *Monarch Notes*, right?"

"Right." Crystal nodded earnestly. "He's, like, her boyfriend, and they're doin' it."

"Right. Vronsky is a cavalry officer. One of his favorite horses is a mare that he rides in a jumping exhibition in his unit of the Russian Army."

"Like jumping over water and hedges and fences and things? That's 'steeplechase?'"

"Yes. When Vronsky is taking the mare over one of the jumps something goes wrong. The mare falls and breaks her leg, and Vronsky has to kill her himself, with his own service revolver."

"Oh, God, that's so terrible!" Crystal wailed. "That poor horse!"

"Right. Well, that's the steeplechase metaphor. Because—"

"I get it! The horse is, like, Anna. And Vronsky 'riding' her is them doin' it, even though she's married and all her friends will think she's, like, a slut because she's sleeping around. And then she's gonna end up dead, isn't she?"

"Yes."

"I knew it! He knocks her up, doesn't he?"

"Yes."

"I knew it! I *hate* it when guys do that and then don't take responsibility. I can't *tell* you how much of a help this all is. I was sittin' there, staring at my computer screen with fu— uh, with *nothing* and now I'm gonna get a A."

"Glad to help."

"Your turn to be helpful," Mayer told Crystal with an elbow nudge.

"Uh, right. Okay. Like I said, it's not much. Like, maybe, a couple of weeks before Champ and me tripped over that mid in his birthday suit, there was a story going around among the girls about a special gig that would pay a little more. Now, usually, that means you're gonna have to do something creepy? Which I don't like to do? But the story was this wouldn't be that way."

"Did you ask Speedbump what it was?"

"Well, we didn't really get that far. I talked to Speedbump about the story, and he just chuckled like a guy whose AIDS test just came back negative and said, 'Baby girl, they want someone who's blond-haired and blue-eyed, so I don't think this is your gig.' And I'm like, I don't understand. 'Cause I have blond hair and blue eyes? But I didn't ask any questions because I didn't want to disrespect him. I just said, you know, 'Okay, Speedbump, whatever you say goes, you know that.'"

"I wouldn't get too upset about it, darlin'," Mayer said, putting an almost brotherly comforting arm around Crystal's shoulder. "I think Speedbump was just trying to say in his own tactful way that the talents called for by this particular job weren't in your skill-set."

"Anyway, it lands up that Speedbump didn't take the job at all."

"Which is interesting," Mayer said. "Speedbump's line of work being what it is, his gag reflex isn't what you'd call overly sensitive. There aren't too many things I can think of that he wouldn't do for the right price. But bein' that he lives here and all, one thing he for damn sure wouldn't get his fingerprints on is walkin' off with a military i.d. and a uniform."

"Which suggests that what happened to Midshipman Lindstrom is a good candidate for the job Crystal heard about— and that backs up Lindstrom's story."

"HOO-raw," Mayer said, while Crystal seemed to shrink into the corner of the booth.

Melissa closed her eyes for a few seconds so that she could concentrate. She took a deep breath, and when she let it out the exhalation was louder than she'd intended.

"What are the chances that I could talk to Speedbump?" she asked Mayer.

"Those would be slim and none," Mayer said. "Speedbump ain't no genius, but he's not certifiable, either. Far as he's concerned, talking to you is the next thing to talking to cops, and no way he's talking to cops, whether they're FBI, NCIS, or some other initials."

"I'm betting I can't smoke in here," Crystal said. "Am I right about that?"

"The Chief of Naval Operations can't smoke in here, darlin', and he outranks you."

Without thinking about what she was doing, Melissa reached out and squeezed Crystal's right hand.

"Don't worry," she said. "No matter what happens, your name stays out of it. It took a lot of guts for you to tell me what you know, and I'm not going to give Speedbump any reason to… be disappointed in you."

"Oh, Speedbump isn't the one I'm worried about," Crystal said, eyes widening and lips bowing into a surprised oval. "It's the other girls. You see, it's like we're our own little Las Vegas. You know? That's the way we think of it. 'What happens here stays here.' You know?"

"Yes," Melissa said. "I know."

A black rivulet started down the outside of Crystal's right nostril as her eyes teared up. When she spoke she shook her head quickly back and forth and her voice choked.

"If they thought I'd washed some dirty laundry outside the family, I wouldn't have a friend left in the whole world. 'Cept Champ."

"Like Anna Karenina," Melissa murmured. "Well, they won't hear it from me. Good luck on your paper. Gunny, thanks for your help."

"Professor, thanks for caring about a mid. And remember, there's generally more than one way to skin a cat."

On that note, Melissa scooted out of the booth and rejoined her brother.

"I didn't see a signal," he said as he led her toward the stairs.

"I didn't make one."

"You learn anything?"

"I learned that I walked in here like an arrogant *bourgeoise* with a head full of clichés that would make a romance writer blush, and as a result I almost blew the whole thing. But I lucked out and got something. It's not everything I came for but it's worth the price of admission." She told him what she'd picked up.

"You hit a clean double, baby sister. Don't beat yourself up because it wasn't a home run."

They reached the upper level and Melissa saw Kuchinski about twenty yards away, pacing back and forth in front of a glass and mahogany display case while he talked in low tones into a mobile phone. His face was purple.

They strolled over. While she waited for Kuchinski to finish his call, Melissa glanced desultorily at the artifacts mounted behind the display case's glass. One drew her eye. It was a facsimile of a handwritten letter. As she examined the sloping, old-fashioned script, she saw that it was written during the Revolutionary War by John Paul Jones, addressed to an agent of the Continental Congress who proposed to buy a merchant vessel that Jones could convert into a warship. Jones' rejection of the proposal was stinging: "I want nothing to do with a ship that will not sail fast; for I mean to go in harm's way."

"That's why we do this stuff," Seton said. "If someone comes up with a better way to get kids in their twenties to stand to their posts under fire and run up hills with machine guns shooting at them, we'll use it. Until then, we do it the way we do it."

"You were reading my mind. At least you didn't tell me to drop down and give you fifty."

"Stay tuned. The afternoon is young."

Kuchinski snapped off his mobile phone and shoved it angrily into his shirt pocket.

"Ole?" Melissa guessed.

"Nope. Ole hasn't found time to return my calls since he told me that he didn't know the first damn thing about any text message—although he did verify that the computer Harald left with him is still ensconced in that den/office/political clubhouse of his. But he's been a little bit scarce since then."

"So who was making you so mad?"

"The assistant DA in Sylvanus County. He's going to amend the charges against Lena to add attempted murder."

"What does that mean?"

"That means he thinks he's found a motive."

Chapter Ten

Walt Kuchinski didn't like anything about airplanes but he disliked exit rows less than he disliked everything else. On the AirTran flight from Baltimore to Milwaukee that night he and Melissa managed to get seats in one, across the aisle from each other. His long legs stretched out luxuriously in front of him. The battered investigative file from the Outagamie County DA's office lay bristling with Post-It notes on his tray table and the tray table of the seat beside him and the seat itself. Pinched carefully between the thumb and the first two fingers of his left hand was twelve dollars in fives and ones, representing the exact change required for two mini-bottles of Johnny Walker Black. He'd tell the flight attendant not to bother with ice in the cup; the way he felt right now, in fact, he might tell her not to bother with the cup.

He gazed at three overlapping eight-by-ten photographs laid out across the top of the file material in front of him. They showed in panorama the edge of the deck off the clubroom at the Lindstroms' home and six feet or so of the snow bordering it.

"You don't look happy," Melissa said, pulling out a copy of the *Milwaukee Journal Sentinel* that she'd picked up on the way to the gate that morning and hadn't gotten a chance to look at yet. "And I guess I don't blame you. That's not exactly a virgin mantle of wedding gown-white snow out of a Hallmark Christmas card, but I sure don't see any boot prints in those pictures."

"Black and white prints of a monochrome surface in bright sunlight," he muttered. "You lose a lot of perspective and depth-perception."

"To the point of not being able to spot a single hint of sole pattern in snow seven inches deep?"

"Might be hard to sell to a jury," he conceded. "Having an expert come in and yap about it won't be enough. We'll have to go out there and videotape a demonstration." He stroked his chin with the thumb and forefinger of his right hand as he considered the issue. "Put twenty-five pound weights in a pair of waffle-stompers and drop the things in the snow. Then take a picture of it and see if it looks a lot like this one."

"Do you really think it will?"

"Depends on who takes it." Kuchinski grinned slyly. "Our hypothetical intruder's lack of footprints doesn't bother me all that much. I have more of a problem with the timing."

"What do you mean?"

"The Lindstroms live in the second right-hand house west of a T intersection with County Highway M. Cul de sac at the other end. Lena says she heard the intruder make a noise in the back of the house, and that's why she hustled out of the kitchen. In mid-hustle she stumbles over Ole's body and screams. Carlsen calls nine-one-one because he hears the scream as he's pulling up. There's not enough time for the intruder to make his getaway before Carlsen is there."

"He didn't notice anyone running by, I take it," Melissa said.

"You take it correctly."

"Okay, as long as we're making stuff up, let's hypothesize a smart intruder. He parked his car on the other side of the road, maybe eighty feet up or down the street, where Carlsen wouldn't necessarily have noticed it. When he spots Carlsen on the street he just lies low by the side of the house until Carlsen goes inside. Then he hikes to his car and takes off."

"I like that, but it means our intruder has to travel something like, hell, I don't know, square of the hypotenuse, call it maybe a hundred-eighty feet from the Lindstroms' house to this parked car we just conjured up. He has to get this trip done in the three or four minutes before the hard-working Sylvanus County constabulary has a deputy on the scene. Now, that deputy might not be Sherlock Holmes, but I think he would've noticed a car high-tailing it down the Lindstroms' street or along County M while he was on his way, and his report says he didn't."

"I guess the timing is a problem, at that," Melissa sighed. "I can understand why you're a bit glum."

"Oh, that's not what has me down. That problem is just a day at the office. What's bumming me is I'm wondering whether I can keep on representing Midshipman Lindstrom."

"Why couldn't you? I thought we made some real progress today."

"We did." *That's the problem.*

"If Ole can corroborate anything that we heard today, that might get the kid off the hook all by itself."

"That's true." *It might put Lena in the slammer for about seven years, too.*

"Then what's the problem?"

"Can't get into it, I'm afraid."

A beverage cart sandwiched between two flight attendants came in between them, interrupting the conversation. Ninety-three briskly efficient seconds later Kuchinski was thoroughly supplied with undiluted scotch and the cart had moved on. Looking back over at Melissa, he saw her frowning as she studied her newspaper. Her right fist, resting on the tray table, was balled and squeezed tight. He took this as an infallible sign of irritation.

He was right.

"You're not honked off at me, are you?" he asked.

"What?" She looked up abruptly. "Oh, no. Of course not. I am quietly furious with Vernoica Gephardt."

She handed him the front section of the paper, folded to *No Quarter*, the political gossip column on the upper half of the second page. Kuchinski couldn't remember ever reading anything in this column that he didn't already know, but there's a first time for everything. He guessed, correctly, that the third paragraph was what had aggravated Melissa:

> The Republicans have never gotten traction on their efforts to make an issue out of campaign contributions from Indian gaming interests linked to sweetheart casino licensing deals agreed to by Democrats. The Dems, though, may soon be catching flak on that issue from their other flank. Insiders hint that political neophyte and goo-goo ("Good Government") activist **Veronica Gephardt** is on the verge of launching a long-shot maverick campaign for Attorney General, seeking nomination as a Democrat. Indications are that she will jump on exclusive tribal gaming pacts as a wedge issue, tied to a general clean-house theme attacking the corrupt wheeling-and-dealing that she'll say has become business as usual in Madison. Don't be surprised by an announcement in the next two to three weeks.

"I don't know about jumping on a wedge," Kuchinski said thoughtfully. "Seems like that could be an uncomfortable proposition."

"That is a particularly unhappy metaphor."

"But that's not what you're upset about, I'm guessing."

"No. An announcement 'within the next two to three weeks' would put her uncomfortably close to the end of the domestic abuse conference she has set up."

"That's the one she's talked you into doing a cameo at so you can do some dirty work for her?"

"Yes. Helping her finesse a delicate problem is one thing. Being used as a political pawn is something else."

"I've been knee-deep in the campaigns of half the people on the Milwaukee County Circuit Court. If you're gonna be hatin' on politics, break it to me gently."

"'Hate' is way too harsh," Melissa answered. "To me politics is like smoking. It doesn't appeal to me personally, but I'm not a prig about it. I don't mind if other people do it, and if someone wants to do it around me I generally say okay. I just don't want to be involved in it without being asked."

"Well, I'd say you have a right to be upset, then. Because it looks to me like you are getting a lungful of second-hand politics."

Rep was surprised. The rule of thumb in Milwaukee is that hookers start west of the river, and he was just east of it.

"Hi, tiger. Want some action?"

The young woman who posed this query pronounced "action" "ACK-*shawn*." He looked up from his cheeseburger and got a second surprise. The lass could have passed for a Renaissance madonna if Renaissance madonnas had gone around flourishing unlit cigarettes—and for a moment Rep had the mischievous thought as he took her in that that might not have been such a terrible idea. Her lustrous blond hair spilled out from under the hood of a white parka that had been built for looks rather than warmth and that did little to conceal the appealing aspects of a slender, well-rounded body. She was only five-four or so, but the poise of her runway-ready stance, combined with violet eyes that seemed to be laughing at him, made her seem taller.

Rep glanced at his watch: six-fifty-five local time, making it almost eight o'clock in the east. He couldn't know that Melissa and Kuchinski were deep in conversation, but he knew they were airborne.

"I have to pick my wife up at the airport in about an hour-and-a-half," he said.

"You're Rep Pennyworth, the lawyer, right?"

"Yes."

"I'm Laurel Fox."

Right. "Ack-shawn."

"Pleased to meet you."

She acknowledged that with a smirk as she raised her mobile phone and punched a speed dial button.

"I found him," she said into the phone. "Not Ole, the lawyer. He's at Safe House on Front Street....Sure, I'll put him on." She tendered the phone to Rep. "Gary needs to talk. He's about to have kittens, so pretty please."

Rep took the phone.

"What's up?"

"Carlsen. Sorry to bother you. Really. But I need, like, a super favor."

Rep suddenly knew what it meant to hear someone sweat. The cool, bantering tone was gone. A sense of urgency verging on panic permeated Carlsen's voice.

"What do you need?"

"It'll make more sense face to face. I'm on my way right now. Can you give me five minutes?"

"Sure. It'll give me an excuse to have some dessert."

Returning the phone to Fox, Rep gestured toward the chair on the other side of his table. She sat down and shrugged her parka off. A waitress appeared almost instantly.

"What would you like?"

"An ashtray." Fox looked dubiously at the waitress' frown. "And coffee, I guess."

"The smoking area is outside, twenty feet north of the door. I'll get your coffee."

"I'm not supposed to let you out of my sight until he gets here," Fox said to Rep as the waitress strode away. "I don't suppose you'd like to wait outside?"

"No."

Fox sighed theatrically and buried the cigarette in her right hand.

"This is gonna cost him," she muttered. "When did he say he was going to get here?"

"Five minutes."

"In the over/under, I want the over."

"No bet."

He should have taken her up on the wager. Carlsen appeared four minutes and twenty-seven seconds later. His bearing in person matched his voice over the phone. Something had dialed his coast-cool persona down about two clicks. There was a jerkiness in his movements, and his lips were almost white.

"I can't find Ole," he told Rep.

"If he's not at his home, I don't know where he'd be."

"In half-an-hour he's supposed to be meeting with Vernoica Gephardt—and he absolutely must not do that."

"Okay, if you say so, but I don't see how I can help."

"Let me call him on your phone. I think he's ducking my calls. When he sees my number on his screen he just doesn't answer. If he sees your number, maybe he will."

"Sorry. I don't have any idea what his issues with you are, but I can't help you fake out my own client."

"You don't understand," Carlsen said, bending forward and reaching out almost desperately toward Rep. "It's Lena. She's been arrested. Again."

"What for?"

"Bail jumping. One of the conditions of her release on bail was that she not leave Sylvanus County."

"And the cops caught her leaving?"

"No. They caught her coming back. About an hour ago."

Rep took his phone out and thumbed Ole Lindstrom's number into it. Six rings took him to a voice-mail prompt.

"Rep Pennyworth," he said after the beep. "Calling a little after seven in the evening. I have something important to talk about with you, concerning Lena. Please call me back as soon as you can." He recited his number and ended the call.

"You can have my seat while you wait," Fox said to Carlsen. "I'll be outside freezing my fanny off and polluting my lungs. On second thought, give me your keys and I'll kill myself in the warmth of that gas-guzzling road-hog you drive."

"I have a better idea," Carlsen said. Glancing at the check the waitress had left on the table, he carelessly tossed down more than enough currency to cover the charges and a decent tip. "Gephardt's office is at UWM, and that's at least ten minutes from here. If we head over there right now we might be able to intercept him in person in case he doesn't call back."

"Good luck," Rep said, staying firmly in his chair.

"Keys, tiger," Fox said, producing an impressive crack as she snapped her fingers. "Laurel needs a fix."

With a shrug worthy of a Yiddish expletive Carlsen dug a key ring out of the left pocket of his ski jacket and tossed it to Fox, who was already halfway to the door and had her cigarette once again fully deployed.

"I need you to come along so I can talk to Ole right away in case he calls you back," Carlsen said to Rep.

"If Ole calls me back I'll tell him about Lena and let him know you want to talk to him," Rep said, shaking his head. "I'm picking my wife up at the airport at eight-thirty. By the time we got to UWM, I wouldn't have more than ten or fifteen minutes there before I'd have to leave anyway."

"The airport is only a twenty-minute hop from downtown Milwaukee."

"I always drive at the posted speed limit so that I can help conserve America's vital natural resources."

Carlsen opened his mouth, but whatever came out was lost in an ululating howl that sliced effortlessly through the modest door separating the Safe House Restaurant from the outside world. Eyes snapping wide open, Carlsen dashed for the door. Rep followed at the more sedate pace appropriate to nibbling on a cheeseburger as he moved.

Front Street, such as it is, runs about two-hundred-fifty paces, from Wells to Mason. Roughly halfway along this modest distance, just past the Safe House entrance, it stops pretending that it's a real street and admits that it's really just a wide alley. Unless you're driving a delivery truck, you're not supposed to park there.

Carlsen had. By the time Rep got outside, Carlsen had reached the open passenger-side door of his SUV and was gaping at the interior. Fox stood a few feet away, vacant eyed, seemingly oblivious to the cold and to the cigarette—now lit—hanging from the first two fingers of her drooping left hand.

Halfway expecting to see a body inside the SUV, Rep walked over. Instead of a body, he saw a Buck hunting knife. Its satin

Chapter Eleven

Joe Sieman jogged into the north end of Juneau Park on the east side of downtown Milwaukee just after seven the following morning, as pale, dawn-pink light was giving way to more robust sunshine. Unconsciously he picked up his pace a bit. The south end of the park at Mason and Prospect lay only about a third of a mile away, and that's where he'd finish his three-mile run, across the street from the Cudahy Towers Condominiums where he lived.

He wore a Green Bay Packers-logo stocking cap and a gray hooded sweatshirt, but made no other concessions to the twenty-five-degree weather. No gloves, and his shorts left his legs bare from well above his knees. Under-Armor and Thinsulate hadn't existed when he'd done his Army stint forty-plus years ago, and he wasn't going to deck himself out in wimp-gear like that with the temperature over twenty and no real wind coming off the lake.

Breathing hard now, he ran past a replica of Solomon Juneau's log cabin, the first permanent European structure in what Indians called "the Gathering Place of the Waters"—which had sounded to Juneau like "Milwaukee." Someone so inclined could have thought of the cabin as the first small footprint of white imperialism in Wisconsin, but Sieman wasn't much given to introspection and he didn't.

Twelve healthy strides beyond the cabin brought him to a statue of Leif Erikson. This was a concession to Milwaukee's Scandinavian black hilt picked up highlights from the street lamps shining through the windshield. Four inches of gleaming steel blade glinted in the eerie glow of blue and green lights on the dash-board. The blade's other four inches were buried in and under a folded newspaper that the knife pinned to the passenger seat.

Pressing closer, Rep saw that the paper was turned to the upper left-hand side of an inside page. The only words he could make out were in boldface: **Veronica Gephardt.**

community, which insisted that the Vikings had gotten here first, even though they hadn't bothered building log cabins and, in fact, had pretty much just passed through. The sculpted Leif looked oddly feminine, even gay, in a micro-mini skirt and with no weapon but a dinky little curved knife that no self-respecting Viking would have bothered to loot from a slain enemy.

Perhaps a hundred yards past Leif stood the park's namesake, Solomon Juneau himself. That was a little more like it. Juneau basked in French grandeur on a massive stone pedestal, with his musket gripped firmly in his right hand and his eyes gazing confidently west.

Still twenty yards away from the Juneau statue, Sieman frowned. His eyes weren't what they used to be, but he could make out something on the ground in front of the pedestal that bothered him. It looked like a big American flag lying in a heap, and if that's what it turned out to be Sieman was going to be pissed off. You don't like the war, don't like NAFTA, don't like the World Trade Organization, don't like this or that, fine: hunt up a picket sign and parade around outside the federal building or city hall; chant some slogans; slap a bumper-sticker on your car; write a letter to the editor. But leave the flag out of it. People had died for that flag, and some of them were friends of his.

Shifting into the closest thing to high gear he still had at sixty-six, he hurried toward the red-white-and-blue bundle. He pulled up short as he got there, for the flag wasn't just lying on the ground. It was wrapped around something—something big and lumpy.

After a moment's hesitation, Sieman squatted and pulled back the top fold of the flag wrap. He wasn't squeamish. He'd been a farmer and a soldier before he went into sales and finally started making money. Grisly stuff happened on farms and around heavy weapons. Whatever was here, he was pretty sure he'd seen worse.

He was wrong.

In a few seconds he found himself looking at what was left of Ole Lindstrom. He was dead. And he'd been scalped.

Chapter Twelve

If Milwaukee ever was the placid, crime-free place that people like Siemen think they recall from a memory-gilded past, it isn't anymore. But it isn't Detroit, either. A mutilated corpse found across the street from the priciest condominiums in the state qualifies as breaking news.

The news broke into the banter of Jagler and Mueller, WTMJ's morning guys, at seven-thirty-six a.m. Melissa heard it as she was pulling into her UWM faculty parking space. Rep had told her about the knife through the newspaper, so the reporter's solemn intonation about "the brutal murder of an elderly man from rural Wisconsin just discovered on Milwaukee's east side" sent a premonitory shiver through her gut. The reporter confirmed her fears in his next sentence, when he gave Ole Lindstrom's name. The story wrapped up with a promise of "more at the top of the hour." Melissa turned the radio off and thumbed Kuchinski's speed-call number on her mobile phone.

"Have you heard the news?" she asked after his voice, echoing through cyber-space with a highway-hum in the background, answered her ring.

"Yeah. Lena's back in jail. I got messages from Rep and her both last night while I was driving home from the airport. I've been on my way to Appleburg since before dawn."

"That's not what I mean." She told him about Ole.

"Whoa. Scalped?"

"That's what they said."

"Wow. Okay. Hmm." Eight silent seconds followed these distracted syllables before Kuchinski spoke again. "Listen. Thanks. Sometime in the next forty miles I'm gonna have to put this all together, and I'm not real clear on how to do that."

"All right. Good luck."

As Melissa ended the call and got out of the car she saw Veronica Gephardt about forty feet away, striding briskly toward Janssen Hall and looking rather elegant in winter blue against the gray-white, featureless sky. She was wearing overlarge sunglasses and walking with her head down, as if deep in not very happy thoughts. Melissa wondered whether Gephardt had read her icily polite email, sent just before bed last night. She'd had to go through four drafts to ratchet the thing down from angry to bitchy to grumpy and finally to just chilly. Impulsively, she hustled to intercept Gephardt.

"I picked up your message on my Blackberry last night," Gephardt said in a flat, featureless voice as Melissa approached. "You should know better than to believe everything you read in the papers, but I understand your feelings. And of course I respect your decision."

"I've changed my mind," Melissa said, falling into step beside the other woman. "I'm willing to stay on the program and make the presentation."

Gephardt stopped and looked at Melissa. With the sunglasses hiding a good part of the upper half of her face, only a minuscule upward tug at the left corner of her lips hinted at any emotion.

"Even though I'm 'using you to promote my pursuit of public office,' as you put it?"

"Your political ambitions are your own business. If I'm being used—well, I'm a big girl. I can take care of myself."

Gephardt resumed walking as she spoke again.

"Thanks, then. That eliminates one headache for me. Just out of curiosity, why the change of heart?"

The truth wouldn't do. *The guy pushing your candidacy just got killed, he was my husband's client, and this mess has been hassling me like a low-grade fever for a month. Walking away suddenly doesn't seem like such a hot idea*—that would definitely qualify as excessive candor. So Melissa pretended to be out of breath as she rifled her brain for a genteel lie. She came up with something she hoped was plausible.

"The homily I heard at mass last Sunday mentioned a poster that Kofi Annan had in his office when he was UN secretary general. It showed an eight-year old girl in Africa who was starving to death. The caption read, 'She would love to have your problems.' It seemed like an admonition to keep personal irritations in perspective, so I've been trying to do that."

"I wouldn't have taken you for a church-goer." For the first time in the conversation Gephardt's tone was at least companionable, if not quite friendly.

"It's a fairly recent thing."

"Husband?"

"Student. It's a long story."

"Well, it's none of my business," Gephardt said. "I shouldn't be prying."

They had reached the overhang outside the main entrance to Janssen Hall. Gephardt continued toward the door while Melissa stopped. As Gephardt stepped into the deep shadow, she kept her sunglasses on. For just a moment, catching Gephardt's profile in the changing light, Melissa thought she glimpsed the border of a red and purple bruise peeking out from underneath the edge of the right lens.

Kuchinski actually needed just twenty miles to re-map the legal landscape radically altered by Ole Lindstrom's murder. Once he'd accomplished that, visiting Lena Lindstrom dropped to number two on the day's agenda. Just past Fond du Lac, keeping one eye on Highway 41, he went to the GPS system touchscreen on his dash and changed his destination from the Sylvanus County

Justice Center to the Lindstroms' home address in Loki. The sultry female voice provided by the system's computer chip petulantly acknowledged the new instructions.

◇◇◇

"Remember me?" the woman asked Rep at eight-twenty-five as he strode toward the Germania Building's elevator lobby. "I'm the Laurel who doesn't smoke."

"Sure. Photographer for Future-Cubed, right?"

"Yeah. Do you have a couple of minutes?"

"Of course. Come on up to my office."

"That's okay, we can talk down here." She held out a large brown envelope. "Gary wanted me to give this to you."

"What is it?"

"A picture of Randy Halftoe handing you a bagful of money."

Rep gave her a blink and a puzzled frown. He didn't take the envelope.

"I know you didn't accept the cash and that you made him take the bag back. Gary knows that too. Randy isn't the sharpest tomahawk on the rez, but he's not dumb enough to play games with walking-around money. He explained what happened and got the delivery right on the second try."

"Then what's the point of giving me the picture?"

"It's Gary's way of saying he made sure there weren't any misunderstandings. He just wanted you to know."

"Okay." Rep shrugged and took the envelope. "Thanks."

"Listen. Gary told me about that thing last night. With the knife and everything. Would that be, like, attorney-client privilege or something?"

"No. He's not a client, and last night I wasn't an attorney. I was a witness."

"So if the cops ask about it, you'd have to tell them?"

The question didn't quite stun Rep, but it surprised him. In the second or two that it took to recover, he realized that she must not have gotten the news about Lindstrom yet.

"I guess you haven't heard, and I'm sorry to have to be the one to break it to you," he said. "Ole Lindstrom's body was found this morning. He was murdered and then scalped. If the police don't call me by nine o'clock, I'm going to call them. I'd be willing to bet that Lindstrom spent most of his last day on earth chatting up political contacts—like the reporter who wrote the Veronica Gephardt item that ended up pinned to Carlsen's front seat with a knife."

Wolf's right hand went to her throat and then to her mouth. Her eyes darted in apparent confusion to her right.

"Listen," she said, her voice sounding tentative and confused. "Maybe we should go up to your office after all."

"Okay."

Rep escorted her up to his quarters. For the fourth time that week he noticed that the third shelf on his book case was still sagging a half-inch or so at the near end, even though he'd moved *Nims on Copyright* and a couple of other weighty tomes to the bottom shelf. For the fourth time that week, he made a mental note to buy a new pair of shelf brackets over his lunch hour.

Then he remembered he had a guest. He turned to offer to take her coat, but Wolf had already shrugged out of it and sunk uninvited into a chair in front of his desk.

"Do you know what the expression 'pay to play' means?" she asked.

"If you have to deal with politicians, it helps if they've written notes thanking you for your campaign contributions. Am I close?"

"Yes. That applies pretty much across the board, but Indian gaming is heavily regulated and politically touchy. So the casinos write lots of checks. Tribal casinos are a favorite whipping boy for a lot of people. When casinos get what they want, people assume it's because of the checks."

"Imagine that."

"It isn't fair," Wolf insisted. "The casinos don't make the rules. They're just playing the game the same way everybody else does. But that's the way it is. It's sitting right there in case some politician is looking for an issue."

"Ole Lindstrom, for example—with Gary Carlsen's help. They were setting Veronica Gephardt up to run on exactly that issue."

"Sure. But that wouldn't really bother the casinos. A state attorney general isn't that big a deal. No one is going to outlaw Indian gaming, even if they could. People love to gamble and it makes tons of money for the government. The Gephardt stuff is just par for the course."

"You're saying the campaign issue would just be out there to fool the rubes and no one would kill Lindstrom to nip it in the bud."

"Right. And no casino thug would have done that knife thing to warn Gary off."

"They'd just shovel some money at Lindstom's political action committee," Rep said. "As they tried to do through me."

"Like I said," Wolf shrugged, "that's the way the game is played. So what this looks to me like is that someone killed Lindstrom for some other reason and is trying to lay it on the tribes. I'll give you four to one the talk-jocks on rant-radio are screaming about it right this second."

"I'd double-down," Rep said, "but in the long run the house always wins."

"*I'm* not a casino girl," Wolf protested.

"It's just an expression," Rep said. "Sorry."

"I work for Gary and I like him a lot. That California cool act of his gets a little old, but he has real talent and he's built a thriving business in a tough market. Plus, he can be sweet when he wants to be, and he's straight with me."

"Fair enough. So why did Gary send you to shut me up about the knife warning?"

"He said it would just be a distraction. He was even afraid people might think he'd staged it himself to try to bring attention to Gephardt's candidacy."

Rep leaned back in his chair and folded his arms across his chest.

"I saw him when he got a look at the knife sticking out of his front seat. His shock and fear looked real enough to me—but maybe he's just a good actor."

"If he's that good then he's hiding his talent under a bushel in Milwaukee. He should be in Hollywood. Still, the police can be skeptical about…things like this."

Rep thought he heard *things like…insinuating pictures* implied in her tone. He wondered if he were imagining things.

"Can't be helped," he said. "I'm going to tell the police about the knife business. I'd suggest that Gary do the same thing."

"I'll pass that on," she said as she stood up and folded her coat over her arm.

She didn't thank him for his advice.

Sylvanus County tends to be a little anal about speed limits, but even so Kuchinski managed to reach the Lindstrom home before nine-thirty—just in time, as it turned out.

"Morning!" he called genially to the cops—one in uniform and two in civvies—who were fussing around with the front door as he jumped out of his car.

They didn't try to hide their irritation, but one of detectives worked up a passable smile while Kuchinski mushed across the front lawn snow from the curb where he'd parked.

"Good morning, counselor," the smiler called. "If you're wondering about a warrant, we have one." He flourished an unfolded sheet of legal-sized bond.

"To search for evidence of bail-jumping?" Kuchinski asked as he approached the porch. "What would that be, I wonder? Rand-McNally maps? Passports?"

"Got it," the other detective said as the front door swung open.

"You don't mind if I tag along, do you?" Kuchinski asked.

"We weren't expecting you," the first speaker said.

"Don't worry about it," Kuchinski said, weaving through the three men and sidling into the house. "My feelings aren't hurt."

The cops shrugged. All three of them. At the same time.

Kuchinski could tell that they knew what they were doing. They got the search done in less than forty-five minutes. As far as he could see, they didn't miss anything and they didn't find much, bagging up only a few bulging, window-envelopes from a mail-sorter on the kitchen counter. They weren't looking for the same things Kuchinski was, he figured, but he didn't find anything either. No fresh blood stains on the living room carpet, no heel marks from a body being dragged through the kitchen or across the garage floor, and he couldn't see anything different in the club room: electronics still there, flags still there, chairs and tables still in place. If anyone had scalped Ole Lindstrom in this room, they'd made a pretty neat job of it. He accompanied the cops to the front door, doing his best to look sympathetic.

"Don't sweat the slim pickings, guys," he said. "That warrant is a crock. You could have found Osama bin Laden lying under Jimmy Hoffa's body and it wouldn't have been admissible anyway."

"No problem," the detective Kuchinski now thought of as the spokesman said. "We're not working on commission."

◇◇◇

A little after one-thirty that afternoon, when Laurel Wolf saw the guy and the gal standing so close to her Ford pick-up that their white-puff exhalations could have fogged the passenger side window, she knew what was up. She continued walking steadily toward them, but she punched a quick number into her mobile phone and raised it to her head as she did so.

"I'm about to be arrested," she said. "Downtown, so I'm guessing they'll be taking me to the Safety Building instead of one of the substations." She clipped the phone back to her belt and smiled at the pair by her car. "Hi. Admiring my ride?"

"Laurel Wolf?"

"Yep."

"You're under arrest for malicious destruction of personal property with a value exceeding five-hundred dollars, namely, the leather seat cover of a vehicle owned by Gary Carlsen. You have the right—"

"No sweat, I'm lawyered up. You have to cuff me?"

She had already turned her back to them and put her hands behind her back with her wrists parallel. She knew the answer.

Chapter Thirteen

"I know," Lena Lindstrom said in a resigned monotone. "One of the deputies told me. I guess he was trying to get a rise out of me."

Those were the first words out of her mouth when the matron finally showed her into the interview room where Kuchinski was waiting at one-fifty-three p.m. They came as no surprise. The deputies at the Justice Center had jerked him around for over two-and-a-half hours after he'd gotten there, fussing about visiting hours and the shift being short-staffed because of this big semi wreck on County Highway M and a lot of other stuff he knew was nonsense. This meant that sometime during his drive from Loki, Sylvanus County had gotten the news about Ole.

"I'm sorry," Kuchinski said. "Words aren't much good when something like this happens, but I am sorry."

"Thanks. Much obliged."

She sat down on the window side of a square wooden table and turned sideways, so that she could lean her right elbow on the back of the chair. Her eyes were dry, and a poker player would have admired her face. A stranger to the upper Midwest might have thought her stoic. Kuchinski knew better. She had the vacant eyes of someone who senses something inside them ebbing away and fears it will never come back. A palsied tic he hadn't seen before twitched almost imperceptibly at the bottom of her right cheekbone. He waited.

"Well," she said briskly, "you didn't drive all this way to watch me feeling sorry for myself. Let's get to it."

"We don't have to do this now."

"No, let's get at it. It won't get any easier."

"Fair enough." Kuchinski sat down across from her. "Yesterday, before Ole's death, the DA got me word that he was going to upgrade the charge against you to attempted murder. That means he thinks he's found a motive."

"I thought the motive was that Ole slapped me around a little."

"Unless I miss my bet, he's working on a more complicated theory now. Something that goes way beyond a little spur-of-the-moment spousal flare-up."

"What are you saying?" Lena demanded. "What's the new and improved case against me?"

"It's guesswork, but I'm good at guessing. Ole pulled something that made you want to kill him. This is the DA talking now, not me. So you picked a fight over Harald to provoke him into the slap. That way, you could carry out a killing you'd planned for other reasons, and sit in the dock as a sympathetic defendant facing an involuntary manslaughter charge."

"Are you serious?" Lena's eyes suddenly gleamed with the remembered spark of an old activist, spoiling for a fight and looking forward to every second of it. "You think he's going to tell a jury that my husband beat me *and I had it coming?* That's quite a reach, even for Sylvanus County. Every woman who isn't a Stepford Wife will be picketing the courthouse. Every crime commentator on cable news will have him on toast."

"Except Nancy Grace."

"Maybe not Nancy Grace, you've got a point."

"Unless he's actually found something," Kuchinski said. "He thinks he has. We have to talk about what it might be."

"It might be anything, I guess. I don't have the first damn clue what, though."

"They executed a search warrant at your house this morning. The only things they took away looked like bills or bank statements or something. Any idea what they might have been?"

Lena looked sharply at him, the bravado evaporating from her expression. What it left behind wasn't fear, exactly, Kuchinski thought. More like very unpleasant surprise. She turned her face away from him and directed her next words at a Blaine's Farm & Fleet calendar on the wall.

"Why'd they have to kill him?" she asked in a reedy voice as she shook her head slightly. "He wasn't going after the money. He didn't care about it. He wasn't going to bleed anybody. All he wanted was one more time at bat. One more bunch of all-night strategy sessions in war rooms, one more season on the edge of the limelight. One more statewide campaign. One more victory lap."

"Not much to ask."

"No."

"Is there anyone you want me to tell? Clergyman or something?"

"No. Ole wasn't much of a one for church. Me either. They wouldn't let me call Harald, but I wrote him a note. I have a friend, Sarah Flanagan, who's been through some wars with me. She's coming in to help, so I can talk to her about the arrangements."

"Okay."

Kuchinski waited. No sense going back to investigation of criminal charges yet. Not 'til Lena was ready.

"Do you think they'll let me out to attend the...you know?"

"I'll work on that."

"Much obliged." She turned her attention back to the wall calendar.

He felt like walking around the table and putting a comforting hand on her shoulder, letting her cry on his chest if she wanted to. He didn't do it. He sensed that she'd despise pity, lash out in anger at him and herself. He sat there as unobtrusively as someone his size could sit anywhere, shifting his position just a bit from time to time as minutes seeped by. Finally, turning her whole body around in the chair, she folded her hands and put them on the table.

"All right, you wanted to know about the envelopes."

"We can give it a while longer, if you like."

"No, it's better for me to face it. I need something to work on. Something to set my mind to."

"I'm ready," Kuchinski agreed.

"I handle the household checking accounts, but Ole took care of the political action committee accounts. He spread them around, mostly among banks in the Fox River Valley."

"Okay."

"He kept one account, though, at the Mercantile Bank in Milwaukee. One of the things he had there was a safe deposit box."

HELLO, Kuchinski thought.

"Two keys?" he guessed.

"Right. We kept one here. Harald had the other."

"Must have been a pretty special box."

"It held the family jewels, as far as Ole was concerned. A few thousand in ready cash, but more important the money list. The real contacts who could get serious checks written at unions, organizations, corporations—"

"Indian tribes?" Kuchinski suggested.

"Those too."

"Okay. Tell me what happened."

"Yesterday morning I stumbled over the statement for December. It must have come in January, but I hadn't paid any attention to it. There was a safe deposit box access charge on it."

"Why was that a big deal?"

"The access was for Harald Lindstrom. Ole had shoehorned that boy into some fundraising scheme that was way over his head, when he knew I didn't even want Harald's picture taken for a campaign brochure. That's why I jumped bail. I went down to Milwaukee to have it out with him."

"Got it," Kuchinski said. He said this as if Lena had just told him that she'd put the brakes on as soon as she saw the yellow light but just couldn't stop before it turned red—as if he were fighting a six-point citation in traffic court instead of possible life without parole.

"I got to his hotel room about three in the afternoon. He always stays at the Pfister, and he always leaves a key at the desk for me in case I come down."

"Did you have it out with him?" Kuchinski asked quietly.

"No. He wasn't there. I had it out with *her*."

"'Her' being?"

"Gephardt. She was in the room, and she wasn't dressed for a board meeting, either. I'm not the girl I used to be, but I got in one good punch and a first class backhand. Then I called Ole and reamed him a new one with a message on his voice-mail. After that I headed back."

"The police report says the highway patrol stopped you just short of the Sylvanus County line at seven-forty-two. So that has you leaving Milwaukee at, what? Five-thirty? Six?"

"Not long after five, actually. Traffic was bad going north 'til I got out of Milwaukee County."

"Did you stop for gas along the way?"

"No. Why?"

"I don't know what time Ole was killed. But whatever time it turns out to be, I'd really like you to have an alibi for it."

About forty-five minutes south of Appleburg, when Kuchinski called in to check his office voicemails, the longest one was from Rep. After listening to it twice, he dialed Rep's number and managed to reach him on the first try.

"How sure are you that the news of Lindstrom's murder really came as a shock to Ms. Wolf?"

"As close to a hundred percent as you can get without losing the minimum lawyerly skepticism required under the ABA by-laws. She said she wasn't 'a casino girl.' We could check that."

"You've got a point there. She's not necessarily the only Native American with a tomahawk to grind in this powwow. The casinos have plenty of skin in the game, so to speak."

"I thought everyone agreed that Lindstrom's act was just a nuisance at worst—that there's zero risk of Indian gaming being outlawed in Wisconsin."

"That's absolutely right. But *expanding* gaming so that even palefaces can run casinos is a different proposition altogether. The Chenequa feel like they have more than enough competition from the Potawatomie and Ho-Chunk tribes already, without whitey getting into the act."

"Maybe," Rep said dubiously. "Anything you'd like me to do until you get back?"

"Just transfer me to Her Serene Highness."

Kuchinski waited impatiently through the five seconds it took Rep to patch the call through to the tart-tongued, vastly competent woman who for thirty years had worked as Kuchinski's receptionist/secretary/office manager/apparatchik.

"What is it now?" she bawled.

"Memo to the Brady Street Ski Club," he said, listening to her keyboard clack as she addressed an email to Rudy Markowski, Splinters Marcinski, Vince Topolewski, and Harry Skupnievich (honorary member). "Gentlemen: Need to know ASAP whether one Laurel Wolf, Native American living and working in Milwaukee, is known to the police, including the FBI and anyone else who carries guns on the job around here, and if so how, and for how long, and for what."

He paused. He figured he'd have to ask the group for something else pretty soon. He'd want Mercantile Bank's surveillance tape for the first Saturday in December, and he didn't expect Mercantile Bank to cough it up voluntarily. When it refused he'd have to use the Brady Street Ski Club for creative motivational purposes. That was bound to happen eventually, so why not just do it now?

No, he decided, he'd at least give the bank a chance to do things the easy way.

"Anything else?"

"Not for now," he said. "Just add 'Regards, K' and send it out."

Chapter Fourteen

"Sarah told me that Lena wanted 'a tame Lutheran who's not a Republican,'" the Reverend Thor Soederstrom said with a self-deprecating smile to Rep, Melissa, Kuchinski and Sarah Flanagan, the friend who had taken charge of memorial service arrangements at Lena's request. "I'm as close as she could come. I'm a born again non-denominational, but I got one of my degrees from the rock-ribbed Lutherans at Concordia University and I've voted for more Clintons than Bushes."

"Works for me." Kuchinski scowled as he looked—again—through the Schaeffer Funeral Parlor's large south window at the governor of the state, who was—still—talking to television cameras in the parking lot. The service was at least half-an-hour behind schedule, and the first premonitory hints of winter twilight were beginning to challenge the bright afternoon sunshine.

"Getting impatient?" Melissa asked.

"It's bad enough that they held Ole's body for over a week while Milwaukee County and Sylvanus County arm-wrestled over jurisdiction. Now they're holding up the memorial service to make sure the governor finishes his photo op before Lena shows up in handcuffs."

"At least they're letting Lena come," Flanagan said, eyes glinting behind gold wire-rims.

"Oh, they *want* her to come," Kuchinski said. "Cops love to watch spousal suspects pay their last respects to victims. Once in Milwaukee a husband suspected of killing his wife threw himself on the casket sobbing, 'I'm sorry, honey, I'm so, *so* sorry.' You better believe the jury heard about that. But today oughta be about Lena saying goodbye to the man she was married to for almost fifty years, not about proving a murder charge they might never bring in a county where it might never be tried."

"You mean they haven't decided yet where the murder was committed?" Rep asked.

"Nope. They know the body was moved after death and they know the scalping was post mortem too. No surprises there. But they haven't pinned down where he got killed yet, and they're a little shaky on when as well."

"Didn't you say the Lindstrom home looked pretty clean for a murder site?" Melissa asked.

"Yeah, but cause of death was blunt force trauma. If you hit someone hard enough on the head you can kill him without necessarily splattering a lot of blood around. Even so, if Ole got killed in that house my prime suspects are Martha Stewart and Felix from *The Odd Couple*, because whoever did it found a very creative way to clean up the mess."

Soedertstrom folded typewritten notes into a leather-bound book that was way too thin to be a Bible and stuck it under his right arm. A very light brown beard marked his cheerfully pudgy face, and sparkling blue eyes lent his features a look of serene contentment. He wore a caramel colored, corduroy sport coat over an open-necked white shirt and a black sweater-vest, as if he were trying to seem vaguely clerical without rubbing anyone's nose in it.

"How about the original charges against Lena for braining Ole with that frying pan?" he asked Kuchinski. "Is Sylvanus County going ahead with that prosecution?"

"They're stalling," Kuchinski said. "They stepped that one up to attempted murder. An acquittal on attempted murder would make it tougher to convict her of actually murdering him even if they stumble over some evidence—which they haven't, by the way."

With that he sketched an *excuse-me* nod and broke away from the group. A glance through the window told Rep why. The governor's SUV and chase car had just pulled out of Schaeffer's parking lot onto Christiana Avenue, while flashing red and blue lights cleared downtown Appleburg traffic from the path of a Sylvanus County Sheriff's patrol car that was swinging in. Kuchinski was going to meet his client.

"I'll have to remember to be discreet about Mr. Kuchinski's comments," Soederstrom said, self-deprecating this time with a chuckle instead of just a smile. "Spreading his remarks around could influence potential jurors."

"I'm sure that's the last thing Walt would want," Rep said, resisting the temptation to wink. "I see Gary Carlsen over there near the door. I'd better go have a word with him before he gets buried too deeply in his Blackberry. I heard that Laurel Wolf was arrested after she talked to me and I'd like to find out how she's doing."

With grudging admiration, Melissa watched her husband's deft getaway. She knew that Kuchinski had recently told Rep a lot more about Laurel Wolf than Carlsen would be likely to impart.

She surveyed the room while Soederstrom took up the conversational thread with Flanagan. Most of Loki seemed to be milling about uncertainly. The vague expressions on many faces suggested that the people felt they ought to be there but weren't sure what they should do. There was no food, so this wasn't a wake. Instead of a casket and a cross there was an urn full of ashes with a flag and a bunch of political pictures around it, so it didn't seem like a visitation, either. There was no grieving widow in place yet to receive their condolences. They couldn't eat, pray, or commiserate, and their experience hadn't equipped them with any variations for this type of occasion.

Huddled in the room's far corner, beyond the urn and display, Melissa saw six elderly men, the youngest in his late sixties and the oldest past eighty. They were talking with each other. They occasionally threw an appraising look over the rest of the crowd, but their body language shut everyone else out. In the diagonally opposite corner near the intersecting outside windows, Melissa surprised herself by spotting Veronica Gephardt, standing with two other people and listening instead of talking.

She didn't bail out with the other politicians before Lena showed up. Give her credit for that.

"We're doing selections from John Donne for the service," Soederstrom was saying then in a confidential tone, tapping the leather-bound volume. "Sometimes religious sentiments go down more easily if they come from a poet instead of a priest."

"John Donne was both," Melissa pointed out. "And he was doing riffs on Saint Paul when he wrote *Death Be Not Proud.*"

A modest stirring in the crowd and a collective inhalation signaled Lena's entrance, uncuffed but between two beefy cops in mufti. Dressed in her own clothes instead of jail orange, she still moved with the hesitant jailhouse shuffle of someone who'd gotten used to walking irons. It took a few seconds for the deer-in-the-headlights look to leave her eyes as she came deeper into the room. The cops walked her past rows of folding chairs up to the front and stationed her on the window side of the room, perhaps ten feet from the urn display and at a right angle to it. Flanagan scurried over to give her a quick hug and stand as close to her as the cops would allow. Medium brown hair in a gentle, right-parted cut framed Flanagan's oval face, and a smile of sisterly concern softened her features. A wary gleam in her eyes, though, suggested that if the cops pushed Lena too far they'd get some push-back from her.

Lena glanced uncertainly at each of the cops, as if asking permission. Then she turned her face to the room with a look of uncertain expectation and stood, waiting.

Nothing happened.

The quiet buzz of low-key conversation had stopped. Everyone was looking at her, but for something like thirty painful seconds they all seemed frozen in place. Her neighbors,

people who had known Ole and her for decades, stood in inde-
cision, paralyzed by the anomaly of a widow who was also a
suspect and a receiving line that was fifty percent stone-faced,
foot-shuffling cops. Fidgeting, Soederstrom looked toward the
podium near the urn, apparently thinking of doing something
to force the issue.

Before Soederstrom could act on this instinct, Melissa saw a
disgusted, *the-hell-with-THIS* expression darken the face of the
man nearest her in the elderly group. He strode across the room
with his arms swinging briskly at his sides, twenty years seeming
to drop from his age as he made the trip. A dozen determined
paces brought him to Lena.

"I don't know if you remember me, Ms. Lindstrom," he said,
firmly enough for everyone in the quiet room to hear him. "It's
been many years. I'm very sorry for your loss."

"Of course I remember you, Tom Koehler," Lena said, taking
his right hand in both of hers as her eyes came alive and her face
suddenly seemed to glow. "You were there when we elected Bill
Proxmire to replace Joe McCarthy. You truly were present at the
creation. It means so much to me that you could be here, and
I know it would mean a lot to Ole too."

The others in the elderly group came over to line up behind
Koehler. Slowly but with steadily growing conviction, the Loki
contingent moved toward the lengthening queue.

As Koehler finished his condolences and began to move away,
the cop on Lena's right took her wrist and pulled it toward him so
that he could see the inside of her hand, in case Koehler had snuck
something to her. Flanagan bristled. Koehler turned back, con-
tempt and amusement competing for control of his features.

"You're quite right to be careful with this formidable lady,
officer," he said—or, rather, boomed. "During the police riot
at the Democratic Convention in 'sixty-eight I saw her go toe-
to-toe with a couple of Chicago's finest, and she gave them all
they wanted."

A titter skipped lightly along the line. The cop glared but
had the good grace to blush as well.

"Excuse me," Soederstrom said then, touching Melissa lightly on the elbow. "Now that the line is finally moving, I think I'd better go up and make a brief announcement about the peace tree."

She had spotted the "peace tree" earlier. It was a twenty-inch abstract sculpture of a Wisconsin birch, with jagged iron spikes for branches. Slips of paper holding Bible verses and preprinted prayers on peace themes lay at the base. Those attending the service would be invited to pick one, add something to it if they wished, and impale it on one of the spikes. Melissa nodded at Soederstrom and sidled toward Koehler, who was heading for the back of the room.

"That was really quite wonderful, what you just did," she said after introducing herself.

"We liberal antiques have to stick together," he said. "In the early 'fifties the Wisconsin Democratic Party consisted of a handful of fossilized old hacks who figured the farmers would always vote Republican, so why break a sweat in a statewide campaign? Their idea of electioneering was to sit around waiting for Roosevelt or Truman to win the presidential election and then pick up Wisconsin's share of the patronage crumbs. Ole and Lena were in the trenches with people like Tom Fairchild and Bill Proxmire and John Reynolds who decided to change all that. My cronies and I came along a little later to ring doorbells and pitch in on lit-drops, but they were the real heroes, not us."

"You must have known them very well."

"I did, and it was a privilege," Koehler said with a fervor that was oddly wistful. "Lena was always more of a true believer. Ole was in it as much for the fun of the game as any policy stuff."

"He must have been good at it."

"He had a natural instinct for it, even in his twenties. I was talking with Lena about Ole's tiny little gem-like role in helping Jack Kennedy get the presidential nomination in 1960. I still get a charge just thinking about it."

"I remember my husband describing a personally inscribed picture of President Kennedy when he told me about the mementoes in the club room at the Lindstrom home," Melissa said.

"There must be a hundred pictures in that room, and there's a great story behind most of them."

"Do you live here in Appleburg?"

"No, I'm down in Milwaukee. Professor Emeritus of Civil Engineering at MSOE."

"It was very nice of you to come all this way."

"It wasn't really that much of a strain. I'm retired now. About the only things on my calendar for the next three months are this event and some boondoggle at a Brewers game that they couldn't find anyone else to cover."

"Not that Ask-the-Professor promotion?" Melissa asked.

"That's it. I'm not looking forward to it."

"Not much of a baseball fan?"

"I love the game but I'm not into the minutiae. I'm no good at 'what pitcher gave up Robin Yount's three-thousandth hit?' and stuff like that. I'm hoping for trick questions along the lines of, 'What's the major league record for put-outs by a left-fielder in a single inning?'"

That sounded like minutiae to Melissa until her memory inexplicably coughed up the trick answer.

"Three, right?" she asked.

"*Very good.* Each team gets three outs per inning. There are nine innings in a game, and there are only nine positions that can get credit for any of the outs that are made. The major leagues have been playing twelve-hundred to two-thousand games a year for over a hundred years. Statistically, there must have been many times in those literally millions of opportunities when the same fielder was responsible for all three outs in the inning. You can sometimes win a bar bet with that one, if it's late enough at night—but if it's a working class bar you'd better have the engine running on your car outside when you try it."

Rep at that moment, and for many moments leading up to it, was watching Carlsen's thumbs dance with dazzling rapidity over his Blackberry's keypad. When Carlsen finally glanced up from the miniature screen, Rep nodded to get his attention.

"Oh, hi," Carlsen said. "Sorry. This thing is more addictive than nose candy. I feel like a *schlub* fooling with it here, but it's like CDO. Do you know what CDO is?"

"No."

"It's OCD, except in alphabetical order."

"I'll remember that one. How is Laurel doing? The one who doesn't smoke."

"Oh, she's fine. Very, very fine. She was in custody a grand total of thirty-seven minutes."

"She must have a good lawyer," Rep said.

"The best wampum can buy, but what sprang her so fast is that I refused to press charges. Cops weren't happy about it, but what could I do? I just flat don't think she did it."

"The cops apparently disagree."

"Well, they said they found a clerk at Laacke and Joys on Water Street who thought he remembered selling her the knife. What does that tell you?"

What this told Rep was that inside dope the Brady Street Ski Club had patiently collected for Kuchinski over the past week during off-hand conversations with cop acquaintances in locker rooms and bars was right. Members of Wisconsin's Native American community felt that the tribes were getting excessive attention from the government, especially in areas related to money of uncertain and suspicious provenance. Some feds thought that "elements" in that community were ready to move from occasional civil disobedience to violence in their expressions of displeasure about this. This concern ratcheted up several notches in a very big hurry when Midshipman Lindstrom's mugging suggested a Wisconsin connection to a possible presidential assassination attempt. So far, however, the key individuals mentioned in the FBI's discreet reports had been identified only as FNU LNU—"First Name Unknown Last Name Unknown."

Kuchinski thought the quick collar after the knife incident meant that someone was ready to fill in one of the FNU LNU blanks with "Laurel Wolf." Rep agreed. He was more interested in learning things from Carlsen than in sharing information with him, though, so he responded with calculated vagueness.

"It seems like pretty ambitious police work for a ho-hum crime against property."

"That's one way to put it." Carlsen said. "A cynic might think the cops showed up with Laurel's picture and gave the clerk a little hint."

"It wouldn't be the first time that ever happened. What have they got against Laurel?"

"Oh, she goes way back with Wisconsin cops. She's a passionate Native American rights activist. Has more arrests than I have parking tickets. All non-violent protests, though. No weapons or rough stuff. So I don't buy the idea that she was doing dirty work for the casinos."

"She delivered a picture for them."

"That was for me."

"That's what she told me," Rep said. "But I'm having trouble buying it. You didn't have her take the picture, did you?"

"No, she did that on her own." Carlsen paused, taking a few seconds to read the skepticism on Rep's face before concluding that he couldn't leave it there. "The casinos give mucho jack to tribal causes that Laurel feels are a lot worthier than blackjack and poker. The way she sees it, that's not charity; it's conscience money that the casinos *owe* all Native Americans. She likes to let Randy and the other bagmen know that she's keeping an eye on them, just in case they have their own agenda."

"I see," Rep said. "Thank you. That was very helpful."

About a quarter of the way through the condolence line, the senior of the two cops guarding Lena decided that one deputy trained in armed and unarmed combat and equipped with a nine-millimeter pistol and a can of Mace was probably equal to the task of preventing a seventy-two year old woman from escaping. He granted himself permission to leave the irksome detail in the hands of his subordinate and wandered out front for some air.

This didn't come as a surprise to Kuchinski, who was already outside, gulping fresh air and watching the pale winter sun touch the western horizon. The cop offered a wary response to Kuchinski's jovial greeting.

"Say," Kuchinski said then, as if they were talking about the Packers' upcoming draft, "do you think you could get a message to the DA for me?"

"You wanna get a message to the DA, give him a call."

"I've been doing that, but he's far too important a man to talk to the likes of me. Also, he seems to have other things on his mind. Thing is, though, it's kind of important. See, he's had my client facing a felony charge for over two months now without doing anything about it, and now he's got her rooming with that bunch of stoners and barflies that pass for criminals in Sylvanus County. If I don't hear from him before noon tomorrow, I'm going to have to file a motion."

"To get her out on bail?" the cop asked, guffawing. "Good luck with that, counsel. She *jumped bail.*"

"Oh, I won't be moving for bail. I'll be wanting to set a trial date and do it in a big damn hurry. Fish or cut bait kind of thing. The DA thinks he has a right to keep her in jail and I think she has a right to a speedy trial. I kinda like my side of that one."

"Is that supposed to be a threat?"

"Yep, that's supposed to be a threat. Now, I can be a reasonable man. If the DA isn't sure what he wants to try her for, I can understand that. Maybe wants to polish off the rough edges on his order of proof, dot an i or cross a t here and there—well, sure, no need to get all Harvard Law School about this constitutional rights stuff. But if I'm gonna back off my speedy trial motion I'll need him to tell the judge he agrees with me about letting her out on bail. Pass the word, willya?"

The cop gave Kuchinski a long, less than friendly look.

"I'll think about it," he said.

"I'd appreciate that."

The last of the mourners had almost reached Lena when Kuchinski strode back into the funeral parlor's visitation room. He took a quick, mildly concerned look at his watch. He had expected the cop to tell him to go to hell. "I'll think about it" meant that he'd taken Kuchinski's threat seriously, which suddenly introduced a whole new level of urgency into the afternoon.

Gephardt was job-one. He spotted her and began to move in her direction, but then he saw Soederstrom approaching the podium and realized that something liturgical was in the offing. With a resigned shrug he found a folding chair in the back row and waited patiently for Soederstrom to read *Death Be Not Proud* and excerpts from *An Essay on Dramatic Poesy*, sandwiched around some of the more presentable Ole anecdotes he'd been able to find.

Soederstrom did this quite smoothly, like a guy who'd been there before and knew his business. When he wrapped things up with, "Send not to ask for whom the bell tolls; it tolls for thee," someone actually said, "Amen."

Well done, Rev, Kuchinski thought.

He stood up while thinking this, looking anxiously for Gephardt and retreating toward the door to intercept her in case she had her heart set on a quick exit. As the bulk of the attendees began to file out, however, he spotted Gephardt in front, standing next to the peace tree. Carlsen, equipped with a camera, was standing about six feet from her. As Kuchinski made his way toward them, Gephardt chose a prayer from the base of the tree and spiked it on one of the iron branches. Carlsen snapped half-a-dozen shots. Twelve feet away, both Lena and the cops with her looked up in surprise at the electronic flashes.

" 'Afternoon," Kuchinski said. "Should be a good shot. Like they say, I guess there is no off-position on the genius switch."

"I like the symbolism," Gephardt said casually. "Would you like me to put a peace prayer on for you?"

"Depends. Is there one there that says something like, 'Lord, please help the US and allied forces bring eternal peace as soon as possible to the terrorists murdering innocent people in Iraq and Afghanistan?'"

Gephardt snapped her head toward her left shoulder and Carlsen scooted away. When she looked back at Kuchinski, he couldn't tell whether he read anger or admiration in her flinty blue eyes.

"You are a piece of work, aren't you?" she said, not without appreciation.

"So I've heard. That shiner of yours is healing up nicely. No sunglasses and yet I wouldn't even have noticed it under the makeup if I hadn't known it was there."

"I think we're done here."

"That's up to you," he continued. "I've heard one story about how you got that boo-boo. I'd like to hear yours."

"And I'd like an end to world hunger. But that isn't going to happen either."

"It's no big secret how you try a murder case for the defense," Kuchinski said thoughtfully. "You offer the jury as many alternative suspects as possible—as many people as you can think of who had motive and opportunity and did something that maybe doesn't pass the smell test. I'm no Karl Rove, but it seems to me that speculation like that in a highly publicized trial could have an impact on those tracking polls."

"Are you seriously talking about including me in your parade of imaginary suspects?"

"Getting your clock cleaned by a man is surely motive enough for someone who cares as much as you do about battered women."

"*Ole?*" Gephardt demanded in a harsh whisper. "Someone told you that *Ole* hit me?"

That wasn't what Kuchinski had said, but he felt that this wasn't the time for excessive clarity.

"Like I said," he shrugged, "I'd like to hear your version."

No ambiguity clouded the look Gephardt gave Kuchinski now. It convinced him that if she were elected attorney general it would be a long time before he got another traffic ticket fixed.

But the rational circuits in her brain hummed with brisk and monotonous efficiency, and when she spoke again it wasn't her emotional reactions that did the talking.

"Ole didn't hit me," she said with resigned disgust. "Lena did."

"And not in a barroom fight over a sports bet, I'm guessing."

Gephardt sighed and rolled her eyes.

"Ole had set up a meeting for me with a potential major donor—the kind who makes you think about skipping public financing. No, I'm not going to tell you who it is. I was flying back from D.C. that morning. The plane was supposed to land at ten o'clock-something but there were delays and it didn't get in until past noon. It was Midwest Airlines. You know the date and you can check. I'd had to get up very early, I'd spent most of the day hassling with airport stuff and plane stuff, and when I finally met Ole at the Pfister Hotel I was frazzled and looked like hell. There wasn't time for me to go home to River Hills and change. He gave me the key to his room and told me to go up, take a hot bath, and freshen up."

"So you did."

"So I did. Lena popped in at what you might call the worst possible moment. She found me in her husband's hotel room, stark naked and trying to make myself look presentable."

"One of those 'it's not what you think' kind of things."

"Right, like some lame screwball comedy from the 'thirties." Gephardt's throat rattled with a brief, bitter laugh. "Lena punched my lights out and screamed a few epithets that in a pre-feminist age would have been called unladylike. Then she left, looking like she was after some more blood. You have a very violent client on your hands."

"That doesn't exactly set a precedent with me," Kuchinski said. "Thanks for your help."

He realized that he was moving with unseemly haste as he hustled away, but he had to catch up with Rep and Melissa before they left the parking lot. The Gephardt interview had taken longer than he'd expected, and only a brisk and incongruous trot through the funeral parlor's front door and down the sidewalk got him to their Taurus just as they were climbing in.

"Got a big favor to ask," he panted.

"Shoot," Rep said, pausing as he was about to duck into the passenger seat.

"I need to be at the mausoleum with Lena when they deposit Ole's ashes, but I turned over a rock while I was chatting with one of the county mounties. I'd like you to drive my Escalade to Loki and park it outside the Lindstrom house while I hitch a ride with Melissa."

"Okay, I guess. But why?"

"I think I left the deputy with the idea that Lena might be loose on bail again as early as tomorrow morning. He and his chums might decide to take one last look around the Lindstrom estate before she gets back. Seeing my car there might remind them to play it by the book."

"I love Rep to pieces," Melissa said, "but it's getting dark and one of his few faults is that he's navigationally challenged."

"The Escalade has a world class GPS."

Rep knew that he should have thought things over before saying yes, but he didn't. Back in the sixth or seventh grade, when he'd first gotten the idea that he wanted to be a lawyer, clicking through cases in LEXIS on-line or plugging reservation-of-rights clauses into trademark licenses wasn't what he'd had in mind. This kind of hustling, bluffing, street-law stuff was. He'd gotten bravely over all that intellectually, but boyhood fantasies die hard. So after securing Melissa's resigned nod—a nod that meant not approval but acquiescence—he agreed. Kuchinski tossed him the keys and he scurried with unbecoming eagerness to the Escalade's parking spot, two spaces away.

After all, he figured, *how complicated can it be?*

Chapter Fifteen

"Turn left in…one mile."

Rep drew immediate comfort from the digitized female voice, even though it managed to make "mile" into a two-syllable word: "my-ull." The voice spoke with quiet confidence, its tone authoritative but not domineering, like a patient elementary school teacher trying to help a dull student. Driving through the dark along the unlit and unfamiliar bleakness of Sylvanus County Highway M, Rep had started to fear that he had somehow overshot Loki—it was, after all, easy to miss—and was now moving steadily *away* from his destination toward the trackless (to him) reaches of northern Wisconsin. He told himself that if he started seeing Royal Canadian Mounted Police he'd turn around for sure.

But the voice and its left-turn warning reassured him. He wasn't lost after all. Yet.

He decided to roll down his window so that he'd have a better chance of spotting Veblen Street when he passed it. The intersection of Veblen and County M pretty much defined downtown Loki, and he remembered that Ole had walked home from there after smacking Lena at the Northwest Ordinance Tavern. It was the last landmark he had before Ole and Lena's street—or now, he guessed, just Lena's.

Unfamiliar with the Escalade's door-mounted controls and unwilling to take his eyes off the highway where the snow had been packed down rather than plowed, he fumbled blindly until he hit something that produced a *clunk*. Whatever it did, it didn't roll down the window.

"Relatch the…door," the voice said.

He fumbled again. The window rolled down just in time for him to spot "VEBLEN STREET" in white on green at the top of a street post illuminated by the glowing Miller Genuine Draft sign on the Northwest Ordinance Tavern.

"Relatch the…door."

"Okay," Rep muttered distractedly.

Before he could try to comply, he heard a siren somewhere behind him. He saw nothing in the rear-view mirror and 34 on the digital dashboard speedometer, which meant that he was less than five miles over the limit. So what was the siren all about? Cops carrying out a discreet and unofficial search wouldn't drive up with their sirens blaring. Would they?

"Turn left in…one…half…mile."

Okay, time to start paying attention.

He hunched forward in his seat and squinted through the windshield. He heard the siren again, still faint but nearer. This time he saw red and blue lights flashing when he checked his mirror, but they were mounted much too high for a patrol car and they were more than half-a-mile away.

"Turn left in…one…quarter…mile."

Headlights on bright, Rep peered into the blackness in search of the street where he was to turn. He thought he saw it, nothing more than a change in the shadow pattern on the snow—but that was enough for him.

"Turn left…now. Destination on your…right in one… hundred yards."

He flipped his turn-signal on and eased the steering wheel to his left, wary of the icy surface but anxious to complete the turn before the flashing lights got too close.

About thirty degrees into the turn he slammed on his brakes. His headlights picked up a small figure in dark clothes gliding skillfully on skis across the Lindstrom property and then the property of the house next door to it. No elegant *schusses,* for there was little slope to the land. This was cross-country skiing, arms working the poles with fiercely labored intensity and legs thrusting hard and fast.

That in itself wasn't bad, necessarily, he thought. Just odd. But two men appeared out of the shadows around the Lindstrom home. They were chasing the skier, and one of them had drawn a pistol. That was bad. Really, really bad.

The two men were at least twenty yards behind the skier when Rep first saw them, and they were losing ground every second as they ran through the deep snow the skier was skimming over. An accomplished cross-country skier can out-distance a horse in deep snow, much less a human being. As the skier scooted from the last front yard on the block onto the hard-tamped, tire-shredded snow on the street, Rep figured the pursuers didn't have a chance.

On the other hand, Rep reflected, their bullets might. Because the skier now seemed to be headed almost directly at him, Rep found this thought unsettling. Time to close the window and get flat.

He hit the door control panel again. He heard a lighter *thunk* and then, instead of the window going up he saw the door swinging open.

"Close…the…door."

"Not now," Rep said, as the skier suddenly seemed to fill his field of vision.

"SON-OF-A-*BITCH!*" the skier yelled in a mask-filtered voice that was unmistakably female.

Rep understood her sentiment, for the door he had inadvertently opened was swinging directly into her path. She swerved nimbly, raising her left leg high, leaning far to her right, and cutting through the snow on the far edge of her right ski. The bottom of the left ski scraped the door's edge, but she recovered her balance and quickly got both skis back on the snow.

In an instant she had slipped behind the Escalade and was off the highway and snowplowing aggressively up the embankment that led to open ground on its far side. She moved sideways up the slight hill, going almost parallel to the highway but sidestepping with a forward push, alternately lifting one ski and thrusting with the other in almost perfect rhythm, so that she was moving forward and up at the same time. The pursuers were now within ten yards of Rep but by the time they reached him the skier was up the hill and skiing forward again at a steady, confident rate across the vast expanse of open ground that lay beyond. By the time the two cops had run past Rep the skier's lead was back to twenty yards or so and darkness was closing behind her.

Against the ululations of the ever approaching siren, Rep heard the dull thuds of running steps as one of the pursuers came back to him. He knew from a dozen action-adventure movies what was coming next: *Sir, police officer! I am commandeering your vehicle!*

"Need your truck, bub," the guy said instead, flashing a badge.

Hollywood gets it wrong again, Rep thought sourly as—with considerable physical encouragement from the cop—he exited the Escalade. He had taken off his overcoat and hat before starting the trip so that he wouldn't get overheated in the SUV, and he deeply regretted them now.

"Close...the...door."

"You tryin' to be smart with me, bub?" the cop demanded as he vaulted behind the wheel.

There's a snappy comeback for that question but Rep didn't use it. The guy was doing his job, his job was a lot harder than Rep's, and he didn't deserve aggravation from people whose idea of occupational hardship was the espresso machine going on the blink. Besides, the siren's wail would have drowned out any impudent riposte.

The cop slammed the door, smashed the Escalade impatiently back into gear, and began turning in an ungainly oval to circle back toward the embankment. He apparently hoped to pursue the skier cross-country by muscling the SUV up the embankment and into the countryside abutting Highway M.

This strategy was plausible enough, but it reckoned without the fire engine, which was what the flashing lights belonged to and which was now closing in.

"Look out for the truck!" Rep yelled as he scurried for the far side of the highway.

The Escalade's brakes squealed as the cop frantically tried to turn away from the suddenly looming monster. With a foghorn reinforcing its klaxon, the pumper truck swerved clumsily toward the center of the highway. The Escalade nosed over the edge of the highway and into the bottom of the embankment. Rep heard a loud pop inside the SUV and saw what looked like a quick, white balloon burst. Slipping repeatedly on the snow but falling only once, he hurried to the Escalade and opened the driver's side door. The cop was shaking his head like a flanker who'd just gotten his bell rung by a cornerback. Blood streamed profusely from his nose.

"Recalculating…Make a…legal U-turn as soon as… possible."

"Where are we supposed to be going?" an exasperated voice yelled from the fire truck.

"Where's the fire?" Rep demanded of the guy in the Escalade, realizing with a guilty shiver that he had *always* wanted to ask a cop that question.

"Back of the house," the cop said groggily. "This side."

Club room. Had to be.

"How badly are you hurt?"

"Nothing broken, I guess." The cop's voice was dull and detached.

Rep hustled over to the fire engine and pulled himself up on the running board.

"There's a police officer in that SUV. The airbag deployed. He needs help."

Without hesitation, one of the firemen swung out of a club cab behind the front seat with a first aid kit in hand and ran toward the Escalade. Rep pointed at the Lindstrom home around the corner and up the street.

"There!" he yelled. "Go up the driveway, and I'll show you from there!"

The siren cranked up again, the lights seemed to flash faster, and the pumper lurched forward and turned onto the intersecting street. Rep hung on as the wind blew his hair straight back and billowed his suit coat. When he started for Loki half-an-hour ago he had been acting out a twelve-year old's fantasy of a street-smart Perry Mason. Now his fantasy life had regressed to six: he was playing fireman.

"As far back as you can go!" he yelled as the pumper careened onto the Lindstrom driveway.

The truck chugged to the end of the driveway, just beyond the turn-in to the garage, which sat at a right angle to the back of the house.

"This way!"

He jumped off and began running around the garage toward the club room on the far side of the house's back. He was wearing a wool Hickey Freeman suit and Allen Edmonds Park Avenue oxfords. Neither was designed for running through seven inches of snow. He floundered as if he were trying to run in clown feet. The snow seemed to cut his shins like an icy knife. By the time he reached the deck in back of the club room one of the firemen, in full gear and lugging a large fire extinguisher on his back, had passed him.

Rep pointed through the patio doors, now unblocked by either curtains or flags, at a glowing heap in the middle of the club room floor. The mound was over a foot high, with the top layer, at least, consisting of American flags unfurled and laid in overlapping layers, suggesting a grotesque parody of a patriotic patchwork quilt. Flames leapt from it. They flickered as well on the surrounding carpet, where they went out and then flared again.

The fireman grabbed Rep's right arm in a grip that reminded Rep of a blood pressure cuff at systolic peak. He pulled Rep backwards, away from the deck.

"Stay right here!" he barked. "Stay *away* from the glass!"

Rep nodded. The firefighter clumped forward onto the deck and through the partially opened patio door into the club room. Then he closed the door to cut off the draft of winter air fanning the flames—in the process, of course, blocking his own retreat from the crackling blue and yellow flames consuming the middle of the room. Rep caught his breath at courage like that, displayed unthinkingly, in this casual, day-at-the-office manner.

The fireman swung the battered black fire extinguisher around, pointed its cone at the flaming mound, and began spraying something that looked cold and white at it. The flames retreated without disappearing. Gray-black smoke that had been gathering near the ceiling now seemed to move menacingly downward.

A second fireman came running up to Rep, dragging a heavy fire hose behind him. Body tensing, he looked into the club room for three or four seconds. He apparently saw something that Rep didn't. When he spoke his voice had a *this-is-serious* tone to it.

"We're a man short because our number two hose-jockey is helping Deputy Hairston," he said. "Do you think you can hold a hose?"

"I can try."

"Try real hard. If you let go, you're the one who's gonna have to inform my next of kin."

The fireman stepped forward onto the deck. Rep grabbed a healthy section of the fire hose, full and heavy but still static. He tried to imitate the grip the fireman had on his section, wrapping his right arm around the thing until he had buried it in his armpit against his body, with the fingernails of both hands digging into the hose's fabric cover.

The fireman banged the hose's long brass nozzle on the glass in the patio door. His colleague inside the club room turned around. The fireman on the deck made an emphatic *get-out!* motion with his right hand. He pointed to where flames had leapt from the mound and were dancing hungrily up the east wall.

The fireman inside nodded, crouched, and plunged through the smoke toward the club room's inside door.

"Get ready, now," the guy on the deck yelled at Rep. "Don't panic when it flares."

With conscious finesse, almost gently, he used the nozzle to nudge the patio door open, creating an aperture barely wide enough to let the nozzle itself through. Even that minimal width sucked in enough air to produce a brilliant burst of upsurging flame that seemed for an instant to fill the room. Rep started to jump back on pure reflex, but then tightened his grip on the hose and managed to hold his ground.

"Okay, here it comes!" the fireman on the deck called. "Hang onto that hose like it's your—"

"That's okay!" Rep yelled. "I'll make up my own simile!"

With an emphatic twist the fireman turned an L-shaped valve key mounted on the back of the nozzle. The hose came alive. Writhing like a pain-crazed python it slammed Rep's armpit and then his ribs and then his forearm, all in less than two seconds. His palms burned as if he'd scalded them. He squeezed his eyes shut as he felt his face contort in pain and heard something simultaneously inarticulate and unambiguous escape from his mouth. But he didn't let go of the hose.

The guy on the deck directed a powerful stream of water at the center of the mound and then moved the gushing liquid in controlled and gradually widening circles. In less than thirty seconds the mound and the surrounding carpet looked like nothing but cold ashes.

Without pausing he then pushed the door open wider and charged into the room. He played the water on the walls and now the ceiling that the flames had reached, literally pouring it on until all trace of fire had disappeared and only the acrid smoke remained. Then he turned the hose back to the smoldering mound, saturating it.

At that point he twisted the nozzle valve back and the length of hose in Rep's arms gave up its fight. He crept warily toward the mound, as if stalking dangerous prey. Rep heard *galumphs* through the snow and glanced over to see the fireman who had exited through the house approaching.

"How ya doin'?" he asked jovially.

"Still breathing," Rep answered.

"Looks like you came through it all right, I guess. Want me to grab a piece of that snake so you can go count your fingers?"

"I love that plan."

The fireman stepped in front of Rep and got a good grip on the hose. Rep gratefully let go. The fireman inside was cautiously peeling layers of the mound away with the toe of his boot. As he cleared the third or fourth layer, Rep saw a gust of smoke spurt from the middle of the mound, where a dull, orange-red glow suddenly appeared. The guy inside glanced at his colleague, who nodded. One valve-twist later the nozzle was bathing the mound at point-blank range in another high-pressure stream of water. Only when pooling water lapped over the insteps of his boots did the firefighter stop the flow.

Sagging slightly, as if a bit let down by the end of the fight and the sudden adrenaline drop, the firemen retreated onto the deck. Rep came up there to get out of the snow and join them.

"Arson, huh?" one of them suggested.

"Sure wasn't careless use of smoking materials," the other said.

Rep wasn't sure which said what because he was gazing transfixed at the wreckage of what had once been Ole Lindstrom's club room. The firefighters had saved the house, but the room looked like a total loss. Five decades of political memories and partisan booty—the sum and substance of two human lives, for all practical purposes—lay in smoking ruins.

"What's your name, anyway?"

Realizing that the question was directed at him, Rep turned to the fireman who'd taken the hose over from him.

"Rep Pennyworth."

"'Rep Pennyworth?' The hell kind of a name is that?"

Rep recognized the good-natured locker room josh, the jock towel-snapping the equipment manager.

"It's the one Mr. and Mrs. Pennyworth gave me. I didn't have a vote."

"Well, Rep Pennyworth, after a deal like this on a cold night a smoke-eater gets his choice of coffee or brandy. Which will it be for you?"

"Brandy."

"That's the right answer."

They stepped off the deck and began trudging back toward the pumper. As they walked, the firefighter gave him a little pop on the bicep with his fist.

"You did all right, bub."

Chapter Sixteen

"Arson, huh?" Kuchinski asked.

"That's what the firemen said."

Rep leaned against the side of his Taurus next to Kuchinski as the two of them gazed at a bevy of cops and other emergency personnel swarming around the Lindstrom home. He shifted his hips a little. He hoped that some sense of feeling would return soon to his rear end, which like his feet and legs was now penetrated by a chill that even Korbel brandy couldn't reach.

"That would make the skier you had a close encounter with the prime candidate for arsonist," Kuchinski said.

"She certainly is."

"'She'? I'd raise my eyebrows to indicate surprise, but they're frozen in place."

"She yelled something at me while she was skiing past. It was a woman's voice."

"So a woman comes around at nightfall to burn the place down. The cops show up for one more look, just in case Lena returns tomorrow. They surprise the arsonist, who leads them on a merry chase and escapes—but not before one of the cops trashes my ride."

"There's an interesting nuance I picked up while I was walking around trying to avoid hypothermia before you and Melissa got out here. I overheard the deputy who *didn't* trash your Escalade using a wireless digital dictaphone to call his report in to a computer back at headquarters."

"Digital dictation? Is Sylvanus County going metrosexual on us? I figured deputies up here still typed their reports with the hunt-and-peck method on Royal Underwood manuals." Kuchinski paused to take a breath. "What did you accidentally-on purpose overhear while you were sorta standing around, ready to be useful if they asked you?"

"He said they had 'effected entry' through the front door and had just gotten inside when they were 'alerted by a noise of indeterminate origin from the vicinity' of the club room. They 'initiated investigation immediately,' but by the time they got back there 'the perpetrator had fled, the fire was in progress,' and after they called in the fire they 'initiated pursuit' of the perpetrator outside."

"A noise of indeterminate origin."

"Right."

"Just like Lena heard."

"Right."

"But in the *maybe* ten seconds it would take them to get back there," Kuchinski said, "assuming they didn't stand around for awhile polishing their badges, this talented perp gets outside, slips into a pair of cross-country skis, and sprints out to a twenty-yard head start."

"Which I don't buy," Rep said. "Have you ever put on a pair of cross-country skis?"

"I'm more of an *après*-ski guy myself. I skip the out-in-the-cold-where-you-could-break-an-ankle part and just go straight to the sitting-around-a-fire-at-the-chalet-sipping-Tom-and-Jerrys part."

"Well, I've done it twice. There's a sort of flexible tab that extends beyond the toes on each of your boots. It has three small holes in it. You have to fit tiny pegs on the bindings into the holes and then clamp the bindings shut over the toes. No way anyone this side of the Olympic biathalon team gets that done in less than eight seconds—and that's from when she has the skis flat on the deck and is standing right beside them."

"So the arsonist had to be already outside and pretty much on her skis when the cops heard the noise."

"Yep."

"Hmm," Kuchinski said.

"Who's that fella with a goose-down parka pulled on over his three-button suit who looks like he's thinking about heading this way?"

"Stan Keegan, the duly elected district attorney for Sylvanus County. He's not a bad guy. But him still being in office duds this time of night means he was sitting at his desk waiting for a report on the follow-up search when he heard about the fireworks display out here. So don't believe him when he tells you the cops were acting on their own."

"There's one more thing before he gets here," Rep said. "In the minute or two that I was in the club room, I noticed something about the cabinets that seemed odd—but I can't put my finger on what it was."

"Maybe I'll manage a look myself before the night is over."

"Here he comes. I wonder if he's going to chew me out."

"You'll know in about four seconds."

"Are you Reppert Pennyworth?" Keegan asked as he reached the two men.

"I am."

"Well I'd like to shake your hand. I don't know what the hell you thought you were doing when you just happened to show up here around the time some hardworking law enforcement officers were conducting a lawful search on their own initiative, but getting help for the wounded officer before you worried about anything else was the right thing to do."

"Thank you."

"Walt," Keegan said then, "don't forget the receipts when you send the county a bill for any damage to that truck of yours. Now if you've got a minute I'd like to talk about how you're so hot to go to trial all of a sudden."

"I've got all the time in the world for you, Stan," Kuchinski said, moving toward the house. He held up a finger to keep Keegan's attention and turned back to Rep. "Thanks for your help, buddy. Next time I'm expecting a knife fight in a dark alley

I'll remember to have a trademark lawyer watch my back. They tell me the Escalade is drivable, so you and Melissa can head on back if you want to."

"Good idea. I'll see you tomorrow."

"So let's talk," Kuchinski said then to Keegan as he resumed his progress up the driveway.

"Don't get too close to the house. It's a crime scene, you know."

"It's been a crime scene since December and that didn't stop your boys from dropping by without an appointment. Anyway, I'm not gonna discuss important legal stuff while I'm standing around out here in the cold."

Shrugging, Keegan began hiking up the driveway next to Kuchinski.

"Here's the thing about that motion, Walt. If I take Lena to trial and lose—well, those things happen. But if I stipulate to bail and she runs off with a possible murder charge hanging over her, I could show up on *The O'Reilly Factor*, running away from that punk of his who does ambush interviews. That could have a negative impact on my job security."

"She's a seventy-two year old woman whose only living relative is a plebe at the Naval Academy. Where's she supposed to run?"

"I don't know. Cuba? North Korea?"

"*Cuba?* She's a *Democrat*, not a Communist. There's a difference."

"There is?" Keegan nodded at a cop standing at the front door as he and Kuchinsk stepped into Lena's living room. "That was a joke, by the way."

"Stan, you've been prosecuting criminal cases for twenty-some-odd years. How many times have you seen a premeditated spousal murder using a blunt instrument without facial mutilation?"

"You're right, that's rare. It's like some frenzy gets hold of them. But maybe that's what the scalping was all about."

"The scalping was either the point of the murder or an attempt to frame Indians for the crime. Either way, it wasn't a frenzied, primal impulse."

"So what's your point? That Lena couldn't be the killer? Because your hook is too short for that long a reach."

"My point is that no one is really sold yet on Lena being the murderer, including you and the cops in Milwaukee. I can't let her sit in jail while you fellas think things over. Let's just chill things until you've got your act together enough to accuse someone of the real crime here."

"We seem to have reached the famous club room," Keegan said. "What are you looking for?"

"I'm not sure yet. I'm hoping that I'll know it when I see it."

They sloshed into water still standing on the floor. Everything he saw that wasn't charred or singed was sodden and water-ruined. Kuchinski waded around the room, examining hulks that had once been televisions and computers, and dripping wrecks that were all that was left of furniture and cabinetry.

"At least give me a hint," Keegan said as he smoothed remnants of brown hair that the parka's hood had ruffled..

"I'm looking for whatever made the noise that Lena heard last December—and that your cops heard earlier tonight."

"Fool's errand," Keegan said. "If the arsonist didn't take care of it, the arson did."

Kuchinski looked steadily at the drawers and storage cabinet beneath the shelving built into the south wall. He shared Rep's frustration. His mental radar was pinging but he couldn't find the dot.

"You got the American Jurisprudence Book Award in Constitutional Law at UW," he said to Keegan, "and I didn't even make law review at Marquette. So you must be smarter than me. There's something wrong with this picture, but I can't put my finger on it. What is it?"

Keegan looked around.

"The doors on that cabinet underneath the drawer are open. I don't know why that seems odd, but it does."

Kuchinski focused on the gaping cabinet. An internal shelf had slipped off its brackets at one end and now sat at about a thirty-five degree angle with what looked like a decade's worth of the hard-bound Wisconsin political directories called *Blue Books* bunched at the fallen end.

And just like that, he had it.

"Look at the books," he said.

"What about them?"

"They're bone dry, that's what."

"So what?"

"So it wasn't a high-pressure stream of water from a fire hose that knocked that shelf down, that's what."

"Ah," Melissa said about twenty miles south of Appleburg on Highway 41, "*there's* the magic word."

Rep stirred from a damp and uncomfortable half-sleep and peered through the Taurus' windshield. The only words he could see were in garish pink on black, giving the name and a summary of the wares offered at a squat store built with bright pink cinder blocks.

"Which word? 'Naughty' or 'Nice' or 'Adult' or 'Playthings'?"

"'Vacancy.'" Melissa pointed at the sign for something called the Sawlog Motel, about a hundred yards beyond the smut shop. "It just winked on, about five seconds after an SUV peeled out of the parking lot and onto the highway."

"Probably a couple of teenagers who have to get back before curfew. That looks like the kind of place that has vending machines selling condoms in the men's rooms."

"As long as it has clean sheets, indoor plumbing, and hot water in the showers. You are *not* going to spend two more hours riding back to Milwaukee with your frozen body in wet clothes. We're going to get you a hot shower and a good night's sleep and then finish the trip in the morning."

Rep felt he should object, if only for form's sake.

"I can make it."

"I wasn't introducing a topic for debate, dear. My mind is made up."

"So how are you going to get sure enough about your suspicion to decide whether to share it with Walt?" Melissa asked.

"The only idea I've come up with so far is to talk to Laurel Wolf again. Face to face."

"I don't like that idea very much."

"Neither do I. I'm hoping I'll come up with something better if I sleep on it."

"Why don't you just tell Walt you thought that maybe it sounded like her voice but it's no better than fifty-fifty and you could certainly be wrong?"

"That's a last resort. As soon as I raise the issue, Walt has to go after her. Until Lena is cleared, he needs alternative suspects. And if Walt is going after her, that means I have to tell the police as well."

"Which would be a rotten thing to do if she's actually spending tonight in Milwaukee peacefully playing with Photoshop or wiggling her hips under Gary Carlsen," Melissa said.

"Yes it would. I have a feeling I'm about to be scolded again for copping mock-heroic attitudes."

"Not at all, dear. As we've talked this through, I've realized that you aren't actually in any real danger."

"That's comforting, but why?"

"Because if Wolf isn't the arsonist she'll have no reason to harm you. And if she is, you'll never talk to her because she'll be long gone by tomorrow morning."

He gratefully acquiesced.

Half an hour or so after they had checked in, a fresl
ered Rep lay in bed over a towel while Melissa spong
hot, damp face cloth at a combination of lacerations th
like welted rope burns and deep, purple bruises on
forearm and right ribcage, where he had held the hos

"This is wonderful," he murmured.

"I have to admit, I do feel rather saintly at the n
she said distractedly as she concentrated on her mini
"When I get over the spasm of saintliness, however, I
little cross with you."

"Why?"

"You know very well why."

"Because instead of being a bashful and reluctant h
actually having the time of my life when I caused all
and inconvenience?"

"Exactly. To be fair, though, if you hadn't gone off
juvenile frolic you wouldn't have found out that the sk
woman, and so you couldn't have passed that helpful
tion on to Walt."

"There's some more possibly helpful informatio
her that I haven't passed on to Walt yet, because I'm
about it. All I have to go on is my recollection of what
sounds like."

Melissa stopped in mid-dab.

"You think you might have heard the voice before?"

"Yes."

"One of the Laurels?"

"Let's just say I'm really glad she didn't have a knif
when she skied by me."

Melissa pressed the damp, steaming cloth against a
larly nasty scrape and held it in place. Rep winced but
tongue. If he said, "That hurts," she would reply, "Of
hurts." He didn't think that such an exchange would hel
at the moment.

Chapter Seventeen

"She's gone," Carlsen told Rep just after eleven the next morning in a voice so listless it seemed to shrug.

"Oh."

"All of her photography stuff is gone. Cameras, everything. Wiped everything off of her computer. No answer on either of the phone numbers I have for her. She's history."

"Got it," Rep said.

He paced a bit, trying to glance around the interior of Future^3 without being obvious about it. The place seemed to be cruising along in laid back normality. A handful of people went about engaging tasks in unhurried calm. A mop-headed kid who couldn't have been much out of high school, wearing a large pair of padded earphones, tapped at a desktop computer keyboard. A young man and young woman with matching pink and blue hair bent over a table-sized layout, flourishing grease-pencils. Rep spotted Laurel Fox across the room, headed for the door and fitting what looked like an antique telephone-answering machine into a powder blue backpack. The thing was at least a foot square, and Rep counted four black levers across its face. Except for Carlsen himself, it didn't look like Laurel Wolf's disappearance had caused much of a ripple yet at the company.

"I have no idea what happened," Carlsen said. "I thought we were going along great. Then this."

"Any clue about where she went?"

"There are several thousand square miles of Native American reservation land in Wisconsin and Minnesota. She could be anywhere in there. For that matter, she has a portable skill and a salable ride. She could be halfway to a dozen big cities by now. If she's emotionally upset about something, though, I'd bet on the rez."

"Tracks are done, tiger," Fox called from the door. "See ya." The door closed behind her before Carlsen could have responded even if he'd wanted to.

"This has to be tough on you," Rep said quietly. "I know how much you liked her, and she thought the world of you."

"She is someone very special," Carlsen said, shaking his head. "Not sure how I'm going to handle it. I'm having a tough time processing all this."

"Well, I'd be surprised if she doesn't get back in touch with you at some point. For whatever that's worth."

"Thanks. But between us, right this minute it ain't worth much."

Rep waited until he reached his car before he called Kuchinski.

"How's Lena doing?" he asked.

"Bail hearing tomorrow morning. We'll spring her. Her buddy, Flanagan, has some friends and neighbors doing what they can to clean up the fire and water damage. Where are you, by the way? It's not like you to take the morning off, even after a rough night."

"I just left Future Cubed. Laurel Wolf has disappeared. It has all the earmarks of a hasty but carefully planned exit."

"Whoa," Kuchinski said. "That does make the cheesehead more binding, as my sainted mother would have said if she'd thought of it. Why do you suppose she flew the coop?"

"Because she's the one who set the fire, and she's afraid I recognized her voice."

"How sure are you about that?"

"Last night it was a coin-flip. Right now I'm about eighty percent certain."

"Sure enough to tell the police, in other words."

"Yeah," Rep said, "but I thought I'd tell you first. If they're still grilling me next week when Melissa is scheduled for Gephardt's conference, I'm hoping you'll drop by UWM and explain where I am."

"You kidding? You just dropped a twenty-four carat alternative suspect in my lap. For that I'd get to the conference early and help them with their Power Points. And don't worry about the cops overdoing it. I still know how to spell '*habeas.*' I'm not sure about '*corpus,*' but I can look it up."

Chapter Eighteen

Thursday, February 5, 2009

"So Melissa's panel is next?" Kuchinski asked Rep a little after four as he swirled pink punch in a stubby plastic cup with sloping sides.

"Right after this break, according to the program."

Rep fingered a glossy, four-color, saddle-stitched brochure with **SILENT CRISIS/ PUBLIC CONSCIENCE: A SYMPOSIUM ON DOMESTIC BATTERY** splashed in satin black over vivid yellow across its cover. As the cover design suggested, the program brochure wasn't exactly a model of academic understatement. Color pictures illustrated more than half of its forty-two slick pages—in which, by Rep's count, Veronica Gephardt's name appeared thirty-seven times.

"I bet you could recite Melissa's presentation yourself by now," Kuchinski said.

"Close. She's done several run-throughs with me. I'll listen to her diligently, though. If I blow this off she might slap me around when we get home."

"Careful, boy. Earnest true-believers are immune to irony. If one of these tightly wound activists overhears a crack like that, you'll find yourself brought up on heresy charges."

Rep felt a squeeze on his right elbow. He looked over his shoulder to see Melissa.

"This is a surprise," he said. "I thought you'd be busy making final edits or something."

"I probably should be, and I need to talk to Professor Ibish about some stage business he has in mind to start his presentation. But I want you to do something for me."

"As long as it doesn't involve fire hoses or tomahawks, I'm game."

She handed him a folded sheet of pale blue loose-leaf paper.

"If I nod at you during the question-and-answer period, ask me the questions on this page."

Rep looked skeptically at his wife's green-flecked brown eyes. He saw a mischievous glint that he knew very well.

"What are you up to, minx?"

"Just follow directions, darling." She pecked him on the cheek. "Try to sound sincerely indignant."

"And I thought she just wanted me here for moral support," Rep said to Kuchinski as Melissa strode away.

"I'd get moving if I was you, boy. The break is over in two minutes, and you're gonna want a seat near the middle, on the aisle."

This sounded like good advice and Rep took it. Seven minutes later (symposium schedules are notoriously approximate), when Gephardt appeared at the podium and began half-apologetically urging everyone to "please find a seat, so we can get our final panel under way," Rep was sitting on the center aisle, twelve rows from the front, less than four feet away from the nearest audience mike.

Like every panel on the program, this one—"He-hits/she-hits: The Comedic Banalization of Inter-Gender Aggression in Popular Culture"—consisted of three people. As with every other panel, one of those people was Veronica Gephardt. On this one, the other two were Melissa and the genial-looking, thirty-something chap whom Melissa had just identified as Professor Ibish. He wore a three-piece set of green-tone Harris tweeds set off by what Rep could tell was a clip-on bow-tie. The program said his first name was Harold and that he taught American

Studies at Case Western Reserve University. He wore a game, bring-it-on smile. Rep thought he'd probably like the guy if he'd just learn to tie his own bow-ties.

"Do you notice a pattern in the make-up of these panels?" Kuchinski whispered to Rep as he thumbed through the pages.

"I haven't really studied it."

"On each one you have a certified lefty, a right-winger from central casting, and Gephardt right in the middle as the voice of reason between the two extremes. I don't know how this dog-and-pony show measures up as a scholarly conference, but as political theater it's a masterpiece."

"If she's typecasting Melissa in the role of lock-step ideologue, she's in for a surprise."

Gephardt began to introduce Ibish. She started in a deliberately low voice, which stopped the lingering chatter and caused people to lean forward and strain to hear. That was a pro move, and Rep admired it.

Ibish rose to the podium, thanked Gephardt for the introduction, and then turned toward Melissa.

"Professor Pennyworth?"

Still seated, Melissa raised what looked like a thick, narrow board about two feet long in her right hand, drew it back over her left shoulder, and whacked Ibish back-handed on his right bicep. A startlingly loud and very emphatic *SMACK!* echoed through the room. At least half the audience jumped and a healthy minority reflexively laughed. Unfazed by the seeming assault, Ibish reached out his hand and Melissa gave the club to him.

"Thank you, Professor Pennyworth," he said, raising the instrument. "The technical term for this little prop is 'slapstick.' As you can see if you look closely, it consists of two very thin pieces of wood sandwiched over a thicker piece of rubber. The wood is attached to the rubber at the handle end but not at the business end. When you hit someone with it, the rubber at the unattached end smacks against the wood on one side, and the wood on the other side smacks against the rubber. The result is a dramatic noise but no real harm to the target."

Rep glanced around. The prop and the stage business had done their job. Ibish had the crowd's attention.

"This simple device and its immense popularity on stage since at least the sixteenth century," Ibish continued, "is the reason that we call almost all physical comedy today 'slapstick.' Long before Punch and Judy, for at least five-hundred years and probably a lot more than that, women hitting men and men hitting women has been making people laugh in every country in the western world—as it did just now, in this room."

"He's pretty good," Kuchinski whispered to Rep.

Ibish then ran through twenty crisp minutes of Power Points drawn from movie and television comedies and a few over-the-top print advertisements, interspersed with polysyllabic commentary. The clips showed decades of inter-gender battery in American and English comedy, with women the victims and the aggressors in roughly equal proportions. The audience reacted at first with occasional gasps, embarrassed chuckles, and a kind of low, indeterminate hum that might have been puzzled or angry. From roughly the halfway point, though, once the shock had worn off, the listeners responded mostly with silence. Ibish's last clip showed Anne Hathaway slapping Steve Carrel in the movie version of *Get Smart!*, with Carrel asking in exasperated bafflement, "What was that?"

"Some insist that popular culture is an engine," Ibish concluded, "shaping who we are and what we do. Some claim that it is just a mirror, reflecting us as we have always been. Whichever side is closer to the truth, it would appear that, at least in the world of laughter, spousal battery is an equal opportunity vice and a gender-neutral phenomenon."

"Right," Rep whispered to Kuchinski under cover of the polite applause and scattered hisses that followed. "And after they smacked their wives for serving stale coffee at breakfast like that guy in the Chase and Sanborn ad he showed, American men in the 'fifties shot guns out of bad guys' hands on their way to work."

"Is that line from you or Melissa?"

"Me. Melissa liked it, though. She said she'd try to squeeze it in."

"Thank you, Professor Ibish," Gephardt said, in a tone of studied neutrality. "The next time I see *I Love Lucy* or the Marx Brothers, I'll look at it with different eyes. And now, as our final presentation for the day, I'd like to ask Professor Melissa Pennyworth, who teaches in the English Department here at UWM, to provide us with her take on what Professor Ibish just dubbed 'the he-hits-she-hits issue.' Professor Pennyworth received her undergraduate degree from the University of Michigan and her master's and doctoral degrees from Stratton University. Her most recent publication is, 'Vladimir Lenin and Jane Austen's Snuff Box: The Problem with Facts in Deconstructionist Literary Theory,' which appeared this past fall in *GRAIL: The Graduate Review of Academic and Interdisciplinary Literature*. Professor Pennyworth?"

Enthusiastic applause greeted Melissa as she stood up, for the audience understood that her role was to refute Ibish and had therefore decided she was right before hearing the first word out of her mouth.

"Apropos of engines and mirrors," she began, "it may be well to recall Lord Palmerston's admonition: 'Half the wrong conclusions at which mankind arrive are reached by the abuse of metaphors.' Neither Hollywood nor Madison Avenue is in the documentary business." She followed with Rep's crack about shooting guns out of bad guys' hands.

This produced raptures. Rep figured she could coast from there if she chose.

She didn't choose. She told the audience in twelve minutes what she had told Gephardt in less than two several weeks ago. She didn't try to dress it up as searing insight, presenting her comments instead simply as common sense with footnotes. The audience didn't care. A few would clearly have preferred a ranting jeremiad against Ibish and all of patriarchy, but even they seemed happy enough. In the collective view of most attendees, Melissa was on the side of the angels and they would have offered her their contented approval if she'd read the UWM staff directory to them.

"In short," she said with a nod at Gephardt, who had already heard the comment she was about to make, "once you get past the slap and down to the stick, he-hits and she-hits aren't quite so equal after all. We can say with only a slight risk of oversimplification that men get hit in comedies for behaving like children, whereas women get hit for behaving like adults."

"Thank you, Professor Pennyworth," Gephardt said, once she could be heard over the applause. "Are there any questions for our panelists before I offer my concluding remarks?"

Rep saw nothing ambiguous in Melissa's nod. He leaped up and bounded to the microphone.

"This question is for Professor Pennyworth," Rep said, getting a Vulcan death-grip on the mike. "After Agent Ninety-nine slapped Maxwell Smart in Professor Ibish's clip from *Get Smart!*, Smart asks, 'What was *that?*' In terms of your theory, what was it?"

"The same thing it was when Shakespeare used the same trick in *The Taming of the Shrew* and Cole Porter imitated it in *Kiss Me Kate!*," Melissa said. "Sex. The slap is a clichéd suggestion of the sexual tension that's supposedly crackling between these two characters already, even though they think they loathe each other. It wasn't particularly fresh when Shakespeare had Katherine and Petruchio trading punches and it's pretty shopworn by now, but apparently it still works."

Rep glanced at the loose-leaf paper for the next question he was supposed to ask.

"And so that's why we think domestic battery is funny?" he demanded. "Sex?"

"Exactly," Melissa said as dead silence replaced the murmur. "Comedy is darker and much more serious than drama. The point of drama is to help us purge the tension created by powerful emotions like love, hate, and terror. The point of comedy is to let us experience the thrill of satisfying desires so depraved and forbidden that we can't even admit to ourselves that we have them."

"*Like beating up your spouse?*" Rep asked, virtually frothing now in over-the-top indignation.

"Like beating up your spouse," Melissa confirmed with an emphatic nod. "If you've been married to someone for five years without ever wanting to slug him—or her—then you might have a companionable relationship, you might have a successful relationship, you might have a joyful relationship. But you don't have a passionate relationship. Wherever you find real sexual passion, violence isn't very far below the surface."

"Thank you," Gephardt said then, rather quickly and in a voice that was oddly distracted. "That's all the time we have for questions."

Thank heaven for that, Rep thought.

He sat down as Gephardt launched a bit hastily into her concluding remarks. Their explicit point was that domestic abuse wasn't just aberrant, lower-class behavior but a society-wide phenomenon deeply rooted in social attitudes and constantly reinforced by everything from rap music to clothing ads, making it important to "invest resources"—that is, spend money—not just on "remediation" but also on education and "pre-event intervention." The subtext, unstated in Gephardt's remarks but quite clear, was that if you wanted someone to do something about this, Veronica Gephardt was your girl—er, *woman*.

Contrasting with the skill and verve she had shown earlier, her delivery seemed a bit flat and anti-climactic. Even so, she got a standing ovation. Rep saw people throughout the room drop legal pads and programs on the floor and clinch Bic pens between their teeth so that they could raise their hands over their heads and clap 'til their palms throbbed.

Never mind attorney general, Rep thought. *In this room she could run for messiah.*

He and Kuchinski let the crowd file out ahead of them while they waited for Melissa. It took her a couple of minutes to gather her things and shake hands with Gephardt and Ibish, so most of the crowd was near the exit when she finally came up to them.

"Nice work, lover," she said. "I'd slap your fanny like football players do, but under the circumstances that might be misconstrued."

"Thanks, but I'm still not sure what you were up to. What was the point?"

"Ask Walt."

"What was the point?" Rep asked, turning to find Kuchinski gaping at him.

"Weren't you looking at Gephardt when Melissa did her little riff on passion and punch-outs?" he asked.

"Certainly not. I was giving Melissa my undivided attention."

"Gephardt turned beet red and at first she squirmed like a third-grader who's been sent to the principal's office. She got it back under control, but she had to work at it."

"Do you really suspect Gephardt of *crime passionel?*" Rep asked his wife.

"I don't know about that. After her reaction just now, though, I'd bet my nineteenth century edition of Emily Dickinson's poems that Gephardt and Ole had an intimate relationship."

"But doesn't that tend to put Lena's neck in the metaphorical noose?"

"Not if Ole and Gephardt were mixing business with pleasure and stumbled into a conflict of interest in their professional relationship," Kuchinski said. "Look at this."

He turned his program to the inside of the back page and showed it to Rep:

A SPECIAL THANKS TO OUR DONORS

The Wisconsin Policy Project wishes to express its deepest appreciation to the following sponsors, whose generous support has made this vital conference possible and advanced the work of the organization:

Twelve names followed. Two were large law firms, one was a utility, one was an insurance company, four were major

Milwaukee manufacturers, and three were foundations. The top name, however, was the one that caught his attention: **THE TORCH BEARERS (CHENEQUA GAMING ENTERPRISES, INC.).**

"Okay, I see the connection," Rep said. "But I thought the gambling issue Ole was ginning up was mainly smoke and mirrors. Even if the Torch Bearers' donation is indirect influence peddling, how do we get from there to Ole scalped and wrapped in the flag?"

"According to Huey Long, before he got shot back in the 'thirties," Kuchinski said, "an honest man is one who, once he's been bought, stays bought. An organization with important political interests can't afford to be blown off by politicians who've supped at its table and drunk from its cup, so to speak. You're supposed to stay bought."

"So the one you're fitting the noose for is Laurel Wolf."

"Or Veronica Gephardt. I'm not particular—as long as it isn't my client. This is just a start, though. We're gonna need something a lot more substantial than a comely blush and Melissa's intuition to get the cops interested in Gephardt."

Rep was still digesting that observation when they caught up with the back of the crowd halfway down the hallway outside the auditorium. The rear guard consisted of a young couple, apparently friends and colleagues rather than spouses or lovers. The male's dress and grooming screamed "graduate assistant" from his slightly overlong, sort-of-but-not-really unkempt hair to his scuffed-but-not-dirty Clarks walking shoes. The woman was only a bit less stereotypical.

"I didn't even know Jane Austen *used* snuff," the woman said.

"I have *got* to see *Get Smart!* again," the guy said.

Chapter Nineteen

Monday, February 9, 2009

"Professor Pennyworth, what you're asking for is absolutely out of the question."

"I know that it's highly irregular," Melissa stammered.

Robert Yi Li, general counsel for the University of Wisconsin-Milwaukee, picked up a miniature Lady Justice paperweight from his desk and thumped it decisively on top of a pile of agreements authorizing the use of the black-on-yellow UWM Panther logo on hooded sweatshirts. He fingered a lapis lazuli fountain pen in the upper right-hand pocket of his charcoal gray pinstriped vest. He grinned incongruously, apparently in grudging admiration of Melissa's sheer *chutzpah*.

"No, professor, your request is not 'highly irregular.' Asking me to sodomize the chancellor in front of your class to illustrate some obscure passage in an e.e. cummings poem would be 'highly irregular.' What you're asking for is outrageous by several orders of magnitude beyond that."

"I wouldn't ask if it weren't extremely important."

"So I assume. But it would have to be a matter of life-and-death—as in someone bleeding from two veins who can't get a tourniquet without these data—before I could even consider it."

How about, my husband is a potential witness against people with a penchant for really short haircuts, and I can't expect the police to get interested unless I have something beyond subjective impressions?

No, she decided, she wouldn't say that. She bit her lip. She couldn't remember feeling this nonplussed before an authority figure since the last time she'd gotten a detention, when she was fifteen years old.

"Let me try to explain," she said.

"Save your breath. There is nothing you could possibly offer me that would get me to go along with you on this. You can't bribe me because I have all the money I want. You can't entice me with promises of sexual favors because infidelity is unthinkable to you, as that idiot physics professor found out last semester. And you can't threaten me with a false charge of sexual harassment because you have too much integrity. You just don't have any chips."

Stress sometimes induced free association in Melissa, and so it did now. *Chips. Chipper. Chipper Jones. Atlanta Braves. Baseball.* Bingo.

"Mr. Li," she said in the most shamelessly winsome voice she could manage, "have you found anyone yet to represent UWM at the Milwaukee Brewers promotion?"

From all appearances, Li couldn't have been any more shocked if she'd flashed a breast at him. He snapped back in his chair, eyes wide and mouth gaping.

"Professor, that is the most cynically opportunistic bargaining ploy I've ever heard—and I went to Harvard Law School."

"Well, one does what one must."

"You should be ashamed of yourself."

"I am, Mr. Li. Deeply ashamed indeed. I can scarcely imagine that such depravity lurks in my heart. But there it is."

Li rocked forward now to a more normal sitting position. He reached for the pen again and this time pulled it out and uncapped it. He picked up a note pad near the front of the desk. He put it in front of him. He began writing on the pad, deliberately and in a rather elegant hand. As he wrote he spoke to Melissa while keeping his eyes fixed on the page.

"Within twenty-four hours, I will find out for you the total dollar amount of funding provided to the Wisconsin Policy Project over the last year by tribal gaming interests. Ditto the portion of total funding represented by tribal money. We will not, however, write that promise down here, as it's probably a felony and could get us both fired even if it isn't. We'll limit the written part of this contract to *your* promise."

Picking the pad up with his left hand, he tendered it to Melissa. With some trepidation she took it and read what Li had drafted:

From the Office of:

Robert Yi Li, General Counsel

I promise on my honor as a doctor of philosophy that I will do the baseball thing. No backsies.

_____

Elizabeth Seton Pennyworth, Ph.D

"This is admirably concise and free of jargon," she said as she signed the document and returned it to him.

"Harvard Law students are taught to strive for pithiness and avoid technical language."

He checked her signature before tearing the signed sheet off the pad, folding it carefully, and putting it in his lower right-hand vest pocket.

"Thank you," Melissa said then, shaking the hand that he rose to offer.

He looked at her warily over the handshake, as if concerned about her next move.

"Couldn't you have just said no to the silly ass from the Physics Department?" he asked, almost plaintively. "Did you *have* to spill coffee in his lap?"

"It wasn't all that hot. I'll look forward to your call."

Chapter Twenty

"Tribal $ to WPP FY08 = 140k = .3 of total $ funding," Rep typed twenty-two hours and thirty-seven minutes later. He did this with his telephone receiver wedged between cheek and shoulder so that he could listen to a lawyer whose client wanted a trademark license from one of Rep's clients.

"Actually," Rep said while repeatedly clicking IGNORE ALL on the Spell-Check box, "vertical minimum price-fixing agreements are *not* per se violations of the Sherman Act these days. Things have changed since 1919."

"What? Are you serious?"

"Entirely." Rep verified Kuchinski's name on the TO line and clicked CONFIDENTIAL from a drop-down box.

"What about the *Colgate* doctrine?"

"Overruled." Rep hit SEND.

"That's outrageous."

"I completely agree. But the Supreme Court didn't consult me when it decided the *Leegin* case a couple of years back. Bottom line, minimum price points are a deal-breaker for us. My guy doesn't want to see his logo in Wal-Mart."

"What was the name of that case?"

"*Leegin.*"

"I'll take a look at it and get back to you."

"I'll wait to hear."

Rep hung up. Eight seconds of vigorous massage had just about restored normal feeling to his left ear when the phone rang again. Rep brought the receiver to his right ear. He heard Kuchinski's voice.

"Thanks for the dope," he said.

"Thank Melissa. She dug it up. I just translated it into legal-speak and passed it on."

"Thirty percent of total funding is a big number. Gephardt was in a bet-your-job situation."

"I smell motive."

"So do I. I've got a call coming in from the lawyer for Mercantile Bank. Stay tuned."

Kuchinski pushed a button that ended his call to Rep and connected him to Ronald LaPlace, Esq. Ronald LaPlace, Esq. was not happy.

"Don't tell me you're not behind this stunt. I know you are."

"Depends on which stunt you're talking about," Kuchinski said.

"I'm talking about every slacker with a video camera or a picture-phone skulking around inside Mercantile Bank taking pictures of goofs coming into the bank in Santa hats and Christmas sweaters like it's early December instead of the second week in February. When our guards politely suggest that they take a hike they start whining about the First Amendment and the guards have to explain that it doesn't apply to banks. It has gotten very annoying."

"Nothing to do with me. The offer I put out is only for a picture that already exists and that was taken on the first Saturday in December, 2008."

"And because nobody has any of those just lying around, you've got a bunch of people trying to fake pictures to sell to you—as you damn well know."

"Don't worry your pretty little head about *that*, Ron. I appreciate your concern, but they're not gonna sneak a fraudulent photograph past Walt Kuchinski."

"I am *not* worried about you," LaPlace said, the exasperation in his tone unmistakable. "I'm worried about my client, whose customers and employees are getting freaked out by this low-rent street theater."

"Well, Ron, I wanna be helpful. I really do. Tell you what. Get me that tape I asked for and I'll cancel the offer."

"Suppose I threaten to sue you *and* file a complaint with the Board of Attorneys' Professional Responsibility instead?"

"You'll get your butt kicked and it won't solve your client's problem. If you get me the tape, you won't get your butt kicked and you will solve your client's problem. Your call."

He hung up.

◇◇◇

Instead of staying tuned to the Lindstrom case, Rep kept his mind firmly on trademark licenses until mid-afternoon. He had work to do for clients who, unlike Ole Lindstrom, were still able to pay for it. A little after two-thirty, he shifted his gaze from the screenful of print on the computer centered on his credenza to the hard copy of a draft license agreement folded over next to his computer. His client had scrawled "METRIC!" in the margin of the hard copy next to the best-efforts clause. The annotation did not refer to liters or centimeters. It meant that the client wanted an objective, numerical sales quota, not a vague aspiration to try hard.

Rep viewed "metric" as a mindless MBA buzz-word, but he could see his client's point. If the licensee was just going to sit there waiting for the phone to ring, then why bother with the hassle and cost of administering a license agreement? On the other hand, all Rep's client was providing was a world famous name. The real financial risk was on the licensee, who actually had a product and would surely be out there hustling to cover his own costs and maybe make a shekel or two himself. No one else had a product this good, so why risk scaring this guy off?

But "METRIC!" still sat there, staring at him. A bit irritably, he pulled a legal pad onto his lap, picked up a pencil, and started scribbling something with a number in it that wouldn't come across as too intimidating. After about five minutes—one-tenth of a billable hour, rounded up—he thought he had some language that might work. He tossed his pencil over his shoulder and got ready to plug his draft into the text.

He had just gotten his fingers on the keyboard when a dull thud behind him broke his concentration. Startled, he swiveled around. The far end of the bloody bookshelf had fallen. Improbably, his pencil had hit one of the DVDs, tipping it over along with the three next to it. That minor shift in weight—a matter of ounces—had apparently been enough to knock the sagging shelf off its brackets.

More curious than aggravated, Rep bounced from his chair and walked over to the bookcase. Squatting, he pulled the DVDs and tapes off the shelf. He lifted the fallen end. He had to pull two volumes of *Nims on Copyright* off of the shelf below the fallen one in order to find the two small shelf brackets.

Both were intact. Each had a tiny peg at one end that fit into the hole in the bookshelf and a flat piece at the other end to support the shelf. Rep frowned. At least one of the brackets had to be broken, right? Otherwise, why had the shelf fallen?

He went from the squat to his knees, bent his torso sideways, and peered at the bracket holes. On the near one, he saw a tiny speck of white wood at the bottom of the circle that the hole formed. A minute amount of the finished wood had been worn away to reveal the raw pine underneath. That sent him to the far hole. More white—two or three times as much as on the first hole. He probed the far hole with the spike on the cap of his Bic pen. He thought he could feel a tiny, v-shaped depression at the bottom. Now that he knew what to look for, he put his head as close as he could and examined the hole. No question about it: the depression was there, only millimeters deep but unmistakable, running from the outer rim of the hole to about halfway into it.

In a cartoon, a light bulb would have come on over his head. Overloading the shelf had forced the peg half of the rear shelf bracket against the bottom of the bracket hole, eating into the soft wood. Eventually, the bracket was just resting *in* the hole instead of being held *by* the hole. The pressure of the excess weight had finally forced it out. That put more weight on the front bracket, pulling it out as well and causing the shelf to fall. Even the minor vibration and slight change in pressure produced by the tap of the falling DVDs was enough to knock it out.

Lost in thought, he walked on automatic pilot back to his chair. The more thoroughly he thought this incident through, the more interesting the implications seemed. Before going back to the license agreement he was drafting, he called Kuchinski, who answered on the first ring.

"What's up?"

"I think you should set up a videotaped demonstration in the Lindstrom's club room."

"That might take some time and effort. What do you have in mind?"

Rep told him. Kuchinski whistled thoughtfully.

"That's worth some time and effort, all right," he said.

Ronald LaPlace, Esq., caved at four-thirty-two. Kuchinski downloaded the digital transmission of the surveillance tape at four-forty-five. At six-ten, Rep and Melissa were watching it with him.

Melissa, who had approached the exercise with considerable excitement, found the procession of grainy, gray images anti-climactic. Mercantile Bank's surveillance cameras focused on the tellers' windows and the ATM machines, where robbery attempts were most likely. What happened in the hallway out-side the tellers' area was a sideshow, glimpsed only incidentally by one camera's lens. At irregular intervals one or two figures would flit by at the far right edge of the frame. In most cases she couldn't even tell what race or sex the figure was, much less pretend to identify a face.

"That's as good as it's gonna get, I'm afraid," Kuchinski muttered. "This isn't *Law and Order*. I can't push some buttons and get three freeze-frame enlargements that end in a close-up of Ole Lindstrom's face."

"Or Lena's," Rep said. "Or Gephardt's, or Carlsen's. Or, I suppose, Halftoe's or Laurel Wolf's."

"Wait!" Melissa said. "Stop the tape and back up!"

"What did you see?" Kuchinski asked as he obeyed her instruction.

"A uniform." She pointed at the skittering screen. "Right there! Stop it and run it forward."

Kuchinski did so. For six seconds they saw what looked like a man in a Naval officer's service dress blues—navy blue double-breasted coat and slacks, white shirt, navy blue tie, black-visored white hat—walking past the teller area. He carried an attaché case in his right hand. The tape began with a three-quarter frontal view of the man, diminishing to profile and then disappearing. His face—possibly even her face, Rep thought—was deeply shadowed under the visor and scarcely visible.

"I'm not even sure whether that's a man or a woman," Rep said.

"Neither am I," Melissa said. "All I can say for certain is that whoever it is, he—or she—is an imposter. The uniform is a disguise."

"Why do you say that?" Rep asked.

"He's carrying the attaché case in his right hand."

"Maybe he's left-handed. He carries the thing in his off-hand so that he can use the favored hand to open doors. That's what I do."

"That's what I do too," Melissa said, "but we aren't soldiers. Frank told me that midshipmen are all trained to carry bags in their left hands, whether they're right-handed or left-handed, so they can salute with their right hands if they meet a superior officer."

"So whoever is in that picture isn't a random officer who happened to be visiting Mercantile Bank in Milwaukee the day after Harald Lindstrom got mugged," Rep said.

"Nope," Kuchinski agreed. "But at least we can stop saying 'he or she.' That has to be a man."

"I know you're setting me up, but I'll oblige," Rep said. "Why?"

"Because I can't see a woman trying to pass herself off as 'Harald Lindstrom.' And the reason Lindstrom got mugged was to steal his uniform and i.d. and pretend to be him."

"Don't bet anything you couldn't stand to lose on that," Melissa said. "The military i.d. would just say 'H. Lindstrom,' and the photograph might well be none too sharp. I'd stick with 'he or she' for the moment."

Chapter Twenty-one

Wednesday, March 4, 2009

"All right, let's get on with it," Stan Keegan, the Sylvanus County District Attorney said.

Eight people had taken up positions in a rough semi-circle in the club room at the Lindstrom home. Keegan and one of his assistants stood next to a court reporter, who sat on a folding chair next to her machine, prepared to transcribe the proceedings. Behind her and to her left stood a youngish, bearded man behind a digital movie camera mounted on a large, sturdy tripod. He was wearing earphones and gazing at the camera's viewfinder, as if he were getting ready to direct Gloria Swanson's close-up in *Sunset Boulevard*. To his left stood Rep, Lena, Kuchinski, and Sarah Flanagan, the woman who had overseen the efforts to clean up the Lindstrom home after the fire.

"Do you want me to swear the witness?" the court reporter asked.

"No," Kuchinski said. "This is a demonstration, not testimony."

"Whatever it is," Keegan said, "let's get it done. It's taken us over three weeks to get this arranged, and I'd like to get it over with before another three weeks have gone by. Believe it or not, this isn't my only case."

"Ms. Flanagan," Kuchinski said, "nod at the camera so we'll all be able to remember which one you were when we look at the tape."

The woman complied a bit diffidently, as if she weren't entirely sure she should be there.

"Did you take part in cleaning up the mess in here after the fire a while back?"

"Yes. Two friends and I. We spent the better part of two days doing what we could."

"Did you find the bookshelf down in that cabinet over there?" Kuchinski helpfully pointed at the cabinet, and the camera lens obediently swung in that direction.

"Yes."

"What did you do about that?"

"We put the brackets back in place and replaced the shelf."

"Did you buy new brackets, or use the old ones?"

"We used the ones that we found on the floor of the cabinet. They weren't broken. They had just fallen out."

"All right, Reppert. It's your theory. You're on."

Keegan opened his mouth to demand that Rep identify himself for the record, but Rep anticipated him, stating his name and address as he walked toward the cabinet. The heaviest key he'd been able to find was the one for his bike-lock. He took it out of his pocket and glanced over his shoulder, to be sure the camera could follow what he was doing. The camera operator nodded slowly. Kuchinski ostentatiously pulled a digital running timer from his coat pocket.

Rep gently pulled open the drawer above the cabinet doors. He pulled it out about four inches. He dropped the key into the drawer and pushed it brusquely shut. Kuchinski pushed the START button on the timer.

Nothing happened for five seconds. Then nothing happened for three more seconds. Keegan scowled. Rep began to sweat. Kuchinski kept a poker face. Lena and Flanagan looked puzzled.

Then a dull *CRASH-THUNK!* sounded from inside the cabinet. Rep pulled the cabinet doors open. One end of the bookshelf had fallen.

"Eight seconds," Kuchinski said, holding the timer up so that the camera could record its face, and then passing it on to the court reporter.

"What's that supposed to prove?" Keegan demanded.

"If those footsteps in the hallway are any clue, I think we're about three seconds from finding out," Kuchinski said.

Two seconds later, a uniformed cop who had been guarding the front door stuck his head into the club room.

"What was that noise?" he asked.

"Did you get that, madam reporter?" Kuchinski asked. "'What was that noise?' Let the record show that this question came from a trained law enforcement officer who was standing at or near the front door of the house at the time of the noise in question."

"All right," Keegan said. "Off the record."

"Off the record," Kuchinski agreed.

"So connect the dots for me."

Kuchinski nodded at Rep.

"There have always been two puzzles about the night Ole was hit," Rep said. "The first was why nothing was taken if there was an intruder in the house. The second was how the intruder got out without anyone seeing him and without leaving any footprints in the snow in back of the house."

"I'd say those are both still puzzles," Keegan said.

"Suppose the intruder wasn't here to take something. Suppose he was here to put some things back."

"Like what?" Keegan asked.

"Like a laptop computer and the key to a safe deposit box at the Mercantile Bank. Ole and Harald each had a key, and you needed both keys to open the box. We know that whoever mugged Harald took his key, and we know that someone accessed the safe deposit box the next day. Therefore, whoever it was must have had Ole's key as well. But he—or she—had to get that key back before Ole missed it. Therefore she—or he—came back to the Lindstrom home on Saturday night to return the key."

"Just call the intruder 'he' from now on and have all the feminists send their emails to me," Kuchinski growled. "We'll posit that it covers both sexes, like it did in the old days."

"Fair enough. The intruder is interrupted first by Ole's return. The intruder hasn't gotten back to the club room yet. He's in the kitchen or the dining room, and when he hears Ole coming in he hides as best he can. It's dark, and Ole is in no condition to spot him as he storms through to the living room. The intruder stays out of sight until he gets a clear shot at Ole from behind and then brains him with the frying pan."

"I'm keeping up so far," Keegan said when Rep paused for breath, "but it seems to me like you're a long way from home."

"With Ole unconscious, the intruder goes back to the club room. He's feeling his way carefully, because he's not sure how long Ole will be out. At the same time, he's scared stiff because he thinks he might have killed Ole instead of just knocking him out. Then he hears Lena's car pulling into the driveway. He hears the door slam. He knows he's running out of time. He drops the key back into the drawer and hurries out the front door just as Lena is coming in the back. The shelf falls just as he reaches the front porch and Lena reaches the kitchen. He skedaddles over the walkway and driveway, where no one is going to notice one or two more footprints."

"Why didn't Carlsen spot the intruder when he drove up?" Keegan demanded. "Carlsen drove up just in time to hear Lena scream. That's why he called nine-one-one. If your theory is right, the scream couldn't have been more than four or five seconds after the intruder was out the front door."

"He had a winter landscape on a dark December night to hide in when he saw Carlsen's headlights approaching," Rep said. "Once Carlsen heard Lena's scream, he hurried into the house. He had no reason to believe he should be looking for fugitives on the way."

Silence hung heavily in the room for fifteen to twenty seconds.

"Back on the record?" the court reporter asked then.

"No." Keegan said.

"So, Stan," Kuchinski said. "Whattaya think?"

"You know what I think?" Keegan said. "I think Ole Lindstrom was murdered in Milwaukee County, that's what I think. They're all college boys down there. Let them worry about this mess."

He walked out with his assistant and the cop trailing behind him.

"Will you be wanting a transcript?" the reporter asked.

"Yep. Just in case."

"This was good news, I guess," Lena said.

"It's as good as news can get at this stage," Kuchinski said, "which ain't saying much, but I guess we'll take what we can get."

Chapter Twenty-two

"So Lena's off the hook?" Melissa asked Rep that evening.

"Only in Sylvanus County. Milwaukee County officially has Ole's murder now, and they're nowhere close to clearing her."

"I don't think she murdered him in either county." Melissa poured two glasses of chilled Chardonnay and gave one of them to her husband.

"Neither do I, but I'll bet that's a minority view down at the Safety Building," Rep said. "Statistically, she's the most likely suspect. And the way they look at it, if she didn't do it, who did?"

"I'm coming up empty on that one, I'm afraid."

"So am I. But whatever the answer is, but I'd say there's a fifty-fifty chance that part of it is located in Annapolis, Maryland."

"I think you're right," Melissa said after a moment's thoughtful contemplation of her wine. "This mess didn't start with the arson in Loki or with Ole Lindstrom's murder or with the burglary of the Lindstrom home last December. It started with Harald Lindstrom being drugged and mugged near Annapolis. This isn't a series of isolated felonies. It's a mini-crime wave focused on the Lindstrom family—and half of that family is Annapolis."

"Which unfortunately will be of only marginal interest to the police—thanks in part to me."

"Because you fingered Laurel Wolf for the arson, based on the sound of her voice through a ski mask."

"Right. As far as the cops are concerned, that makes her the most convenient suspect for Ole's murder after Lena, with Veronica Gephardt a distant third. Until they find Laurel and work her over, they're not going to be thinking about tracking down a connection to some plebe getting caught with his pants down on the East Coast."

"Three suspects in a brutal murder, and all of them are women," Melissa mused. "It seems a little—"

"Sexist?"

"For now let's just say a little curious. It's not that women can't be criminals. We seem to commit a disproportionate number of embezzlements, for example. It's not even that women can't be murderers, at least with firearms."

"'God created man, and Colonel Colt made him equal,' as they used to say in the Old West."

"But when you're talking about crimes committed with tomahawks and blunt objects instead of shotguns or computers and checkbooks, you'd expect the male sex to be less feebly represented. It's a bit like field hockey versus ice hockey."

"Speaking of sexist, I think you're skating pretty close to the line with that simile," Rep said. "Anyway, you've convinced me. The under-investigated connection is Harald Lindstrom in Annapolis. So what do we do about that?"

Melissa took a quick sip of wine and looked levelly over the rim of the glass at Rep.

"Why should we do anything about it? Aside from the facts that nobody else will and Ole was your client and Walt's our friend and you feel shaky about identifying Laurel Wolf?"

"I think that pretty much covers the list of reasons. What do you think we should do?"

"I think we should finish our wine and have something vaguely nutritious for dinner," Melissa said. "Then I think we should flip a coin to decide whether we put Brubeck or Bach on the Bose. Once the music starts playing, I think we should wait for Frank's call. I left him a voice-mail asking him to give us a ring tonight."

"You rascal. Showing initiative and a gift for alliteration in the same evening."

"Next I'll have you eating salad without complaining about it."

"As long it's not the entrée."

"It is. Consider yourself lucky that it isn't dessert."

They were listening to *Blue Rondo à la Turk* about forty-five minutes later when Frank called. Melissa had won the toss, but out of sheer perversity she'd chosen Brubeck, just to contradict gender stereotypes.

"You're right about the attaché case," Frank said after they'd described the video they'd watched. "I've never seen an officer in uniform carry anything in his right hand. It gets to be pure reflex."

"So maybe one of us should try to get our hands on a first-hand account of Midshipman Lindstrom's adventure," Rep said.

"Good luck with that," Frank said.

"What are the chances of getting a look at the Academy's investigative file?" Melissa asked.

"Zero."

"How about if we could somehow gin up a special request from a judge with a fancy title on it like 'Letters Rogatory,' stamped with an embossed seal and decorated with a couple of ribbons?" Rep asked.

"Unless the judge is the Chief Justice of the United States Supreme Court, you won't get past the marine at the Bilge Gate with it. Military investigative reports are so secret they make grand jury testimony look like the lead story in the *National Inquirer*."

"Then maybe one of us should just talk to him face to face," Melissa said. "Then we can write our own investigative report."

"Even that might be a pretty good trick. He won't be leaving the yard for the rest of his plebe year."

"Why?" Melissa asked. "Hasn't he been pretty much cleared? We've corroborated his story, even if we haven't accomplished much else."

"He's been cleared of lying about voluntarily taking drugs and recklessly provoking a huge security snafu. So he won't be expelled. But one of the things he didn't lie about was drinking alcohol. He was up front about that. That's a conduct violation."

"Okay," Melissa said. "You're the expert Frank. Is there some way we could talk to him on the yard, but in private?"

"Tall order. I have one idea. It's a long shot, but I'll see what I can do. It won't happen overnight, but I might be able to get something set up for three weeks or a month from now."

"Thanks, bro."

"Don't thank me until you hear the idea—and until I've brought it off."

◇◇◇

"April Tenth, in the evening," Frank said when he got back to them four days later.

"Oops," Melissa said as she scrolled deftly through her PDA.

"Why 'oops?'"

"I have a conflict. I'm supposed to be at the Milwaukee Brewers baseball game that evening."

"A *baseball game?*"

"It's a long story."

"Can't you get someone else, or just back out of it?"

"Nope. I gave my word."

"That's okay," Rep said, jumping in when Frank and Melissa paused simultaneously for breath. "I can go."

"That's sweet," Melissa said. "You're being heroic."

"No," Rep said, "answering baseball trivia questions in front of forty-thousand people is heroic. I'm just being practical."

Chapter Twenty-three

Friday, April 10, 2009

At seven forty-five a.m. on the tenth of April, Rep began driving toward Appleburg, Wisconsin. Not quite ninety minutes later he exited Highway 41 about twenty miles south of the city and turned into the parking lot of the Sawlog Motel. Judging from the number of cars and semis parked next door in the gravel lot of Naughty But Nice, the purveyor of "adult playthings" was already doing a brisk business.

In the motel office a man with scattered skeins of hair only slightly grayer than his face looked up from an adding machine—*not* a calculator but a mechanical, tape-fed old-school adding machine—to turn incurious eyes toward Rep.

"I'd like a room."

Rep had expected an argument about check-in times, but the man just nodded and reached up to put a five-by-seven card on the narrow counter above his desk. Rep scratched data hastily into blanks on the card and slid it back with his American Express card on top. The man raised scraggly gray eyebrows at Rep's credit card.

"Usually pay cash," he muttered apologetically. For well over a minute he fussed in unpracticed clumsiness with multi-carbon charge receipts and a slide-rolling card-printer. Still without standing up he fetched a key—a literal key: brass, on a silver ring attached to an elongated green plastic diamond with 107 printed on it in white—and handed it to Rep. "Sixty-five dollars. Fifteen back if you check out in less than three hours."

"I'll take you up on that." Rep accepted the key with a vaguely queasy feeling that he was joining Harald Lindstrom in the dubious-adventures-in-cheap-motels club. He slipped it into the side pocket of his suit coat. He wasn't wearing an overcoat. The temperature was in the mid-forties, and he had learned during his first spring in Wisconsin that after winter officially ends only wimps wear overcoats for anything north of thirty-nine.

On the way to his room he passed a round-faced woman with Hispanic features, dressed in jeans and a flannel shirt but identifiable as a maid by a white apron and cap. She smiled shyly at him from behind the service cart she was pushing, but didn't hint that she saw anything unusual about someone checking in before nine-thirty in the morning. Entering his room and shrugging off his suit coat, Rep was pleasantly surprised to find a touchtone phone instead of the black Bakelite 'fifties-era rotary phone he had half expected. He consulted the itinerary for his Annapolis trip, where he'd written the telephone numbers he'd need.

He punched Veronica Gephardt's number into the motel phone first. He waited patiently through four rings and her message prompt and then spoke at the beep.

"Hi, this is Rep Pennyworth, Professor Pennyworth's husband. I understand the police are still looking for Laurel Wolf in connection with Ole Lindstrom's murder, and I've just gotten some information that I think might be helpful to her. I need to talk to her before I can go to the police with it, though, and I don't know how to reach her. It's a long shot, but I thought you might have a tribal contact that could get through to her and have her give me a call. I'm on the road today. I'll be staying at the Loews Hotel in Annapolis tonight. If you come up with someone, I'd really appreciate it if you'd have him call me there. Here's the number." He read the Loews telephone number from the itinerary and broke the connection.

He called Randy Halftoe and left the same message. When he called Gary Carlsen he varied the script slightly, dropping the reference to "tribal contacts" and replacing it with a generic hope that Carlsen would find some way to get in touch with Wolf.

He broke the connection for the third time and, with the receiver held pensively in his left hand, stared at the phone for about five seconds. Call Lena too? No, he decided. He wasn't going to contact Lena behind Kuchinski's back, and there was no way Kuchinski would fall for this scam even if Rep were willing to try it on him. He hung the phone up.

The look on the elderly proprietor's face when Rep returned the key three minutes later combined surprise and perhaps a hint of respect.

"Quick work," he commented.

"Practice makes perfect."

"Perfect," Robert Yi Li said to Melissa in her office at two-thirty that afternoon. "It looks exactly right."

"Please don't rub it in." Melissa made a half turn to get an idea of how the hem of her academic gown swirled.

"If you taught at Oxford you'd have to wear that during Michaelmas Term."

"I think it's only sub-fusc instead of the full cap and gown, and I think it's only the first day of the term. Oh, well, whatever. I feel like an idiot, but a promise is a promise."

"Absolutely right. I trust that you've prepared diligently for the event."

Through hooded eyes Melissa shot a sidelong glare at the university's general counsel.

"You be the judge," she said. "The lead-off batter in the top half of the first inning singles, the second batter triples, the third doubles, the clean up hitter singles, the number five hitter triples, and the number-six hitter makes the first out on a pop-up to second. No men score in the inning. How is this possible?"

Li puzzled over the query for a few seconds, looking steadily and with undisguised suspicion at Melissa.

"It's not possible," he said finally. "It's a trick question."

"It's entirely possible," Melissa said as she removed her cap and hood and began unfastening her gown, "if the game was played in the All American Girls Baseball League back in the 'forties."

Instead of sputtering in indignation, Li grinned with delighted surprise.

"I'll have to pull that one on Assistant Dean Mignon in the Office of Inclusiveness Affairs. If he blows it, he'll be too embarrassed to send out any memos on sensitivity to diversity concerns for at least three weeks."

At three-fifty p.m., Rep landed at Baltimore-Washington International Airport and started on the odyssey that would eventually bring him into contact with a rental car. He wasn't looking forward to the drive that awaited him. Annapolis, Maryland was laid out not quite four-hundred years ago for the kind of horsepower that comes on four feet rather than four wheels. And if while creeping along its narrow, crowded streets you get State Circle and Church Circle mixed up, you can find yourself face to face with Chesapeake Bay without the slightest idea of how you got there.

But he couldn't rely on cabs. He thought he might be in a hurry when he left.

At four-thirty p.m., the company duty officer for Sixth Company, Second Battalion, First Regiment at the United States Naval Academy looked over the twenty-seven plebes in the company who were standing at attention in front of him.

"Ladies and gentlemen, we have sea trials in a little over six weeks. Are we ready for sea trials?"

"Sir, no sir!" they shouted in unison.

"That is correct, plebes, we are *not* ready for sea trials. And I would not be counting on Friday night liberty until we are."

"Sir, yes sir!"

"Tonight, however, will be an exception. Because all fish-eaters are directed to report to the Catholic chaplain at nineteen-hundred. He apparently wants to chew you out for not saying enough rosaries or some goddamn thing. So there will be no sea trials preparation for any plebe in sixth company this evening. Is that clear?"

"Sir, yes sir!"

"Even you, Henderson?" The CDO strode over to a tall, rangy plebe, moving closer and closer until their noses were just short of touching.

"Sir, yes sir!"

"You understand that, even though you do eat fish, you are not a 'fish-eater' for purposes of this directive because 'fish-eater' is a jovially slang term for Roman Catholics and you are a Baptist—right, Henderson?"

"Sir, yes sir!"

"Very good." The CDO returned to his original position. "Dismissed!"

At ten to five Rep checked into his room at the Loews Annapolis Hotel. His heart rate ratcheted up a couple of notches when he saw the red light on the room phone blinking. Leaving his TravelPro at the door, he hustled over to the phone to retrieve the message.

Messages—plural—as it turned out. A digitized voice apparently provided by the twin sister of the woman who vocalized the GPS on Kuchinski's Escalade informed him that two people had called him.

"Veronica Gephardt, returning your call," the first recording said crisply. "I'm not sure what 'tribal contacts' you think I have, but I certainly don't know anyone who could locate a fugitive. Please do *not* call me again."

Not the first girl I've heard that from, Rep thought with a mental shrug. *But why did she bother to call?* Without deleting that message he pushed the one-button to play the second. The sultry voice advised him that it had come in "at four-thirty *p*.m. from an unknown number."

"This is Joseph Yellowfeather," a gravelly voice that sounded as if it had a lot of years on it said. "You don't know me. I am Laurel Wolf's uncle. I am calling at three-thirty local time. I will call again on the hour and then on the half-hour if I don't reach you. That's white people's time, not Indian time." Rep heard an ironic chuckle at the racial stereotype before the recording stopped.

He looked at his watch. Four-fifty-six. Yellowfeather's next call was due in four minutes. Rep took off his coat, undid his bow tie, and unbuttoned the collar button on his shirt. He retrieved his itinerary from one of the coat's inside pockets and opened it on the bed near the phone. He lifted his Travelpro to the bed, unzipped it, and began unpacking. He had gotten his socks put away when the phone rang. Pulse racing, he answered it.

"I don't know where Laurel is," the voice on the other end of the line said. "But I may be able to communicate with her. In a sense—a sense that you may not understand, but that has its own truth."

"Okay."

The caller sighed—the eternal sigh of the enlightened at the uninitiated who always mistake their uninformed skepticism for wisdom.

"I have had a dream. If that sounds like savage superstition to you, that is something I cannot help."

"I said okay. My wife is the smartest human being I know, and every Sunday she prays for faith to believe things that make dream-seeing seem like laboratory science. As long as I talk to Laurel Wolf, I don't care how it happens."

"But you're a lawyer. If you find out where she is, you would have to tell the police."

"Yes, I would. For that matter, I'd have to tell them if I were a plumber. I assume she won't tell me where she is if she doesn't want the police to know."

"Calls can be traced. Even from mobile phones."

"So I've heard, but I don't know how to do it and I won't be tracing any."

"You're asking me to take your word for it."

"I don't have any choice," Rep said. "If you want an affidavit signed by the pope and notarized by the chief rabbi of New York, I'm out of luck."

Seconds of silence crawled by. Rep resisted the temptation to ask Yellowfeather if he were still there.

"How long are you going to be at this number?" Yellowfeather finally asked.

Rep glanced at his watch and then put his left index finger carefully just below the sixth line of handwriting on his itinerary, where he had scrawled "Federal House Bar & Grille" during a conversation with Frank.

"I have to leave for an appointment in about ninety minutes. That will tie me up for an hour or so, maybe two. Then I'm going to a bar and grill called the Federal House to get a bite to eat. I should be back in the room by ten-thirty or eleven my time."

"'Federal Club'?"

"Federal House. 'Federal House Bar and Grille.' It's a place down by the docks that a friend recommended. He said that anyone in downtown Annapolis could tell me how to find it."

"You taking a client there or something?"

"No, my client meeting is tomorrow."

"All right. I'll see what I can do."

Around five-thirty central time—six-thirty in Annapolis— Melissa found her way into a small room deep within the bowels of Miller Park, garishly lit with flickering fluorescent beams that did their best to brighten walls of finished cinderblocks painted blue and gold. A blasée and effortlessly pretty blonde in gray sweat shorts and top and purple leg-warmers took a Miller Genuine Draft from a mini-refrigerator and tossed it across the room to a similarly clad and equally attractive colleague. Neither of them had seen nineteen yet, much less twenty-one.

"Want me to nuke a brat for you, as long as I'm over here?" the first asked.

"Not before I dance."

A perky brunette in slacks and a blazer with the Milwaukee Brewers script M monogrammed on its breast pocket carefully did not notice this evidence of under-age drinking. She turned a very big smile toward Melissa.

"Okay!" she said. "Everybody's here! Do you all know each other?"

"Professor Pennyworth, good to see you again." Tom Koehler, whom Melissa remembered from Ole's memorial service, stepped forward and shook her hand warmly. "Do you know Glen Watkins from Marquette and Denise Quaid from Alverno College?"

"We've never met," Melissa admitted, shaking hands in turn with the other two academics.

"You *do* know each other!" the brunette in the blazer squealed. "Okay! First, thank you all for coming! We think this will be a great promotion!"

A smattering of murmured "you're welcomes" responded, but her verbal momentum carried her through them without a pause.

"Okay, this is, like, *really* simple, but listen carefully. We'll put you on in the middle of the first, second, and third innings. One question each inning. The questions will appear on the message board behind the center-field fence and will be announced over the p.a. system. They'll all be multiple choice except the tie-breaker. A, B, and C. You'll each have three paddles, one with each letter. You just hold up the paddle with the letter for your answer. And that's all there is to it! Any questions?"

There weren't any questions.

"Okay! I'll come here to get you about ten minutes before the national anthem. It'll be, like, *really* good if you already have your caps and gowns on, okay?"

Okay.

She exited. Three more "blond" dancers came in, at least two of whom had clearly used the magic of chemistry to assist nature in its hair-coloring endeavors. One of them immediately went to the far wall and sat cross-legged beneath a sign sternly warning, "**DON'T EVEN THINK ABOUT SMOKING IN HERE.**" She rested the backs of her forearms on her knees with her hands slightly cupped, closed her eyes, and apparently floated off into her own universe.

"Don't touch those things," the first entrant said to the beer-server, who was fingering what looked like translucent plastic tubes with pistol grips lined up vertically on a shelf next to the microwave over the refrigerator. "Beer and carbon-dioxide don't mix. And where's Dani?"

"I don't think she's gonna make it," the reprimanded dancer said with a winsome pout. "Better call one of the subs, 'cause a five-girl line doing the splits could look kinda lame."

Melissa began opening the large cardboard box that held her cap and gown. As she did so, she prayed silently but fervently for the national anthem.

Around the time the brunette in the blazer was wrapping up her Ask the Professor symposium, Rep was walking past a souvenir shop about two blocks from the main pedestrian gate of the Naval Academy. Among the dozens of bumper stickers and wall plaques displayed in the window, one jumped out at him:

TO ERR IS HUMAN, TO FORGIVE DIVINE
NEITHER IS UNITED STATES MARINE CORPS POLICY

He felt a little belly drop as he read the message, a premonitory tease suggestive of the don't-open-that-door music in a horror movie. But he didn't think anything about it.

Chapter Twenty-four

At six-fifty-eight Rep passed through the Visitors' Center Gate at the United States Naval Academy. He showed his passport to a marine who seemed impossibly young and very alert. The marine checked Rep's name against a list. Then he checked it again. After the second check he waved Rep through the gate. Seven minutes later, Rep was shaking hands with a white-haired man who had a cross on the collar tabs of his khaki uniform shirt.

"Thank you for arranging this," Rep said.

"If Frank Seton asks me to do something, I try to do it," the chaplain said. "He's a by-the-book guy, but whenever he's been here I've been able to count on him. Besides, it was getting to be about time for a chaplain's conference anyway."

"Are meetings like this a regular thing?"

"Somewhere between semi-regular and highly irregular. We can get away with them about twice each term. Stress is part of the training here, but when it looks like some of the plebes are at their limits we call one of these just to give them a night off. This is the only place at the Naval Academy besides the firing range where *no one* can yell at a plebe."

A midshipman, tall and rail thin and with his hair cut so short you couldn't tell whether it was blond or light brown, approached hesitantly.

"Did you want to see me, Father?"

"Yes, Mr. Lindstrom. I'd like you to meet Reppert Pennyworth. He's a lawyer from Milwaukee, working with the attorney who's handling your case. He'd like to have a word with you."

"Uh, sure, I guess."

"You can use my office, if you like."

"Office" was a bit generous. The enclosure the priest pointed to in the far corner of the basement room might have passed for a walk-in closet. Rep and Lindstrom headed for it. They passed knots of plebes who weren't doing anything special—lounging on Naughahyde couches, talking desultorily, flipping through old copies of *Sports Illustrated*—but seemed to bask in idleness itself as an unutterable luxury. Lindstrom looked earnestly at Rep as soon as they slipped inside the office.

"When I called Aunt Lena last Sunday she seemed pretty spaced out. Just, like, flat. No life in her voice at all. How is she doing?"

"Well, it's pretty rough for her right now. You know she's out of jail, so that's good, but she's still facing the possibility of a murder charge as a result of Ole's death. She's afraid they'll just keep dithering. She wants the whole mess behind her in time for her to come out here for the end of plebe year."

Rep hoped that this comment had heartened Linstrom a bit, but it was hard to tell. The change in the mid's expression was microscopic. Rep closed the door and sat on one of the spartan guest chairs. Lindstrom perched tentatively on the other. Rep leaned forward, forearms on his knees, trying to signal that they could talk some more about Lena if Lindstrom wanted to but that Rep was ready to move to the main purpose of his visit. The politely stoic mask meeting Rep's gaze told him that Lindstrom wasn't going to say another unprompted word.

"Did Ole ever talk to you about using you in campaign material?"

"Oh, yeah."

"Tell me about that. What did he have in mind?"

"He didn't really get into specifics too much. He just asked when my summer duty tours would be and when I'd have leave so that he could set up a shoot when I got back to Wisconsin. He told me to be sure to bring a set of whites and a set of service dress blues, so he could see which one worked better. 'Which one the camera liked better' was the way he put it."

"Do you know how Lena felt about that?"

"She didn't like it, I know that. She hated the idea of him using me for window dressing—that was how she said it—but it was more than that. She was afraid he was trying to set me up for a political career of my own after I leave the Navy. Thing is, I plan on taking my commission in the Marines and staying twenty-five years. That'd make me a little old to run for the Sylvanus County board."

"Lifer, huh?"

"Oh, yeah. Of course, that was my plan last December, too, when it looked like I was gonna be six months and out. I'm guessing last December is what you really want to talk about."

"That's right. I know you've been over it a dozen times with three or four different people, but maybe you could just tell me about it."

"Sure. But it's gonna take awhile."

"I have plenty of time."

At about that moment, six-sixteen p.m. in Milwaukee, Melissa gamely followed her fellow professors from the first row of box seats to the roof of the Brewers' dugout. The perky brunette and a guy in a Brewers uniform were already up there, the former offering a megawatt grin that Melissa chose to interpret as encouraging. Most of the fans who'd made it into the park so far were ignoring them, which was fine with Melissa. Even before she got her second foot on the roof, though, hoots and whistles burst from the upper deck of the grandstand where students from the four participating colleges sat in sharply discounted seats.

Seconds later the student cheering morphed from good natured and laid back to sharply competitive. A whisper of apprehension fluttered through Melissa's gut. No longer was this just a mildly embarrassing lark. The collegians assembled in the grandstand, many no doubt amply lubricated with the beverage that gave Miller Park its name, were suddenly taking the thing very seriously. Melissa realized that the UWM contingent, barking defiance at their peers from rival schools, would expect her to hold her own against the other professors. She swallowed hard.

The brunette explained to the crowd how the trivia game would be played. She introduced the Brewer on the dugout roof as "Coach Dale Sveum," who got wild and sustained applause because as interim manager he had taken the Brewers to the playoffs last year. Then, after a dramatic pause and a deep breath, she said, "Now let's play round one of Ask the Professor!"

They all turned to the message board to see the first question, while the p.a. announcer read it aloud:

WHAT IS THE MAXIMUM POSSIBLE NUMBER OF SACRIFICE FLIES THAT ONE TEAM CAN HIT IN A SINGLE INNING?

A. ONE
B. TWO
C. THREE

Thank Heaven, an easy one to start off, Melissa thought. She turned back toward the grandstand while fumbling for her B paddle. A run can't score after the third out in an inning, so the answer had to be two. She confidently raised her paddle, noting with a tincture of disappointment that all of her colleagues had also chosen B.

She heard derisive laughter and dismayed groans. Puzzled, she looked at her paddle. Her heart sank. In her nervousness she had held up the wrong side. Instead of B she had shown a blank to the crowd.

"Three out of four got it right!" the blonde said. "Pretty good!"

Koehler stepped forward and gestured for the microphone. The blonde obligingly tilted it toward him.

"Strictly speaking," he said over the crowd's buzz, "Professor Pennyworth's answer is the correct one. A sacrifice fly can be scored on an error as well as an out. If the left-fielder drops a fly ball on the warning track with less than two out and a runner at third scores, the play is scored as a Sacrifice Fly/Error-Seven, and the hitter is credited with an RBI and not charged with a time at-bat. Technically, then, there is no theoretical limit on the number of sacrifice flies a team can get in one inning, and the correct answer is 'None of the Above,' as Professor Pennyworth said."

Ear-splitting cheers and angry obscenities from the upper grandstand greeted this exposition. They flummoxed the brunette for only a second. She swung the microphone toward Sveum, who looked like he would much rather be trying to decide whether to call for a sacrifice bunt or a hit-and-run in the bottom of the ninth.

"Your call, Coach!"

Sveum jerked his thumb toward Koehler.

"What he said."

"All right!" the brunette said. "Everyone scores a point in round one of Ask the Professor!"

"Thanks," Melissa whispered to Koehler as they completed their descent from the dugout roof.

"What can I say? I'm a showoff. Believe me, the pleasure was all mine."

◇◇◇

"...Next thing I know I'm naked on the lobby floor getting mouth-to-mouth from gunny."

It was seven-thirty-eight (eastern time), and Rep's last twenty-two minutes with Lindstrom had gone pretty much like that. Once he got to the December incident, Lindstrom talked as if he were dictating telegrams. He made a generic comment and then he stopped speaking. If Rep wanted any specific details or concrete facts, he had to pry them out with painstaking questions in a process that reminded him of digging muddy pebbles from between the sole-treads of winter boots in late March.

"Do you remember anything about the girl, except that she had long, black hair?"

"Just that. And that she was hot, I guess."

"How old would you say she was?"

"I don't know for certain. I mean, older than me, for sure. Her hair made it look like she was trying to seem younger than she was, but it didn't. She wasn't real old, like sixty or like that, but she wasn't just out of college, for sure."

"Could the hair have been a wig?"

"Coulda, I guess. Her hair wasn't really what I was looking at." Lindstrom accompanied this comment with a blush instead of a smirk, glancing hurriedly downward in becoming embarrassment.

Pulse racing a bit, Rep took out his Dictaphone.

"Did the girl's voice sound anything like this?"

He thumbed the knurled switch to PLAY. He had recorded Gephardt's clipped, disdainful voice off of his hotel room phone, and it now began to resonate in the tiny office. Lindstrom listened through the end of the message and then emphatically shook his head.

"No way. The girl's voice wasn't anything like as clean as that one."

"What do mean by 'clean'?"

"You know, kind of well-shaped tones, like a newscaster or someone that you might hear on television. The girl who took me had a kind of edge to her voice, kind of raspy, and she didn't have that kind of high class pronunciation. More like party girl, if you know what I mean."

Rep turned off the Dictaphone as he felt his interest in the interview begin to seep away. His theory wasn't doing so well. Whatever Gephardt had done, it didn't look like she was the one who had enticed Lindstrom into a motel room and drugged him. Still, he felt he should follow up on Lindstrom's last comment.

"I'm not sure I do know what you mean," Rep said. "What does party-girl pronunciation sound like?"

"Oh, you know. Like real breathy, and kind of come-on, you know, like 'let's get it *on*' and 'I want it *now*' and 'I want some *ack*-shawn.'"

Rep refocused on Lindstrom and looked intently at him.

"'*Ack*-shawn'? That's the way she pronounced 'action'?"

"Oh yeah."

Oops, Rep thought.

Round Two of Ask the Professor began at six-forty-five (Milwaukee time), after the top of the second inning. Melissa saw a lot more people in the stands now. Fans who had lingered at their tailgate parties in the parking lots through the first inning had now made their way into the stadium and were filling the seats. Melissa and her colleagues turned toward the message board to read the question for this round:

WHAT IS THE *TOTAL* NUMBER OF WAYS THAT
A BATTER CAN REACH FIRST BASE WITHOUT
THE BAT TOUCHING THE BALL?

A. THREE
B. FOUR
C. FIVE

Melissa couldn't believe her luck. The question came like an answered prayer. She had actually read this esoteric bit of baseball arcana in a very obscure mystery from the early 'nineties. She could still remember (approximately) the New York tough-guy argot wrapped around the information: "Five. Like the number of the amendment you plead in front of grand juries." She found her C paddle and this time made sure she had it facing the right way.

As they turned around, she heard Koehler muttering to himself in obvious doubt as he counted on his fingers: "Walk. Hit-by-pitch. Catcher's interference. Passed ball on a third strike."

"There's a fifth," she whispered to him.

"Catcher's balk!" he answered. "You're absolutely right! If the catcher steps on or in front of home plate without possession of the ball during an attempted squeeze or steal of home, the batter is awarded first base."

Koehler held up a C to match hers.

"Thanks!"

"We're even," Melissa said.

The other two professors hastily switched answers as they saw Koehler's.

"The correct answer is C!" the brunette said. "Everyone scores again!"

"Shame on you two," Koehler tsked to other professors as they made their way back to the stands. "You looked at your neighbor's work."

"Guilty as charged," Watkins said. "But I don't think you have standing to complain about it."

"Law professor," Koehler said to Melissa, shaking his head in mock disapproval as he gestured toward the professor from Marquette.

Melissa didn't think to turn her cell phone back on until there were two outs in the bottom of the second. She saw that she had missed a call from Rep and dialed him back.

"My theory about Veronica Gephardt is wrong," he said. "A much better candidate for femme fatale is Laurel Fox."

"Where are you now?"

"About halfway between the academy and the bar and grill Frank suggested, Federal House. I'll get something to eat and then go back to my room and wait for another call."

"Another call? Why would you be getting another call?"

"Someone claiming to be Wolf's uncle left a message for me about how maybe he could get me in touch with Wolf and maybe he couldn't and said he'd get back to me."

"Reppert, dearest love," Melissa said, exasperation dripping from each syllable as the inning ended, "what if this completely unknown person calls back and suggests that you come to an obscure motel in the boonies to get in touch with Ms. Wolf?"

"I would express disappointment at his lack of imagination and politely decline. I might ask him incredulously if he really thought a lame dodge that worked on a callow eighteen-year old would succeed with a worldly and sophisticated trademark and copyright lawyer."

"Suppose our hypothetical caller comes up with a less derivative variation?" she demanded then. "Something that's not quite as obviously a trap but still potentially hazardous?"

"I'll ask myself what you would do and be guided by your example."

"Rep," Melissa said fiercely, thinking of some of the things she had done and feeling his sly comment like a kick in the pants, "so help me, if you take some insane risk in a display of misguided machismo just because you've flown several hundred miles on a wild goose chase and now your blood is up, the next time I'm within three feet of you I'll smack you hard enough to knock your glasses off."

"You won't, you know. I wouldn't hit you back and you know it, and then you'd be ashamed of yourself. No worries, though. I'm not a farm boy and I've seen painted women before."

They exchanged expressions of exasperated love and he ended the call.

Annapolis has its charms if you're walking instead of driving along its cobbled streets, and one of them in April is weather that seems very mild to a Milwaukeean. Rep savored the pleasant evening as he completed his journey to the Federal House Bar & Grille. He didn't particularly notice the grizzled man in the red windbreaker who kept pace with him on the opposite side of each street he entered, and he probably wouldn't have thought anything about him if he had.

The top of the third went quickly, so Melissa and company were back on top of the dugout, fussing again with caps and gowns, before Rep was inside Federal House.

"Round Three is the tie-breaker!" the brunette said. "So it won't be multiple choice!"

"Essay?" Quaid groaned.

"As long as we don't have to show our work," Melissa sighed.

"All right, here's the question! On Easter Sunday, 1987, the Brewers won their twelfth game in a row to go twelve-and-oh on the young season! They won that game on a walk-off home run in the bottom of the twelfth inning! Name the Brewer who hit that dramatic, game-winning homer!"

Melissa glanced down the line and saw three faces as blank as her own must be.

"I think this calls for a collaborative effort," she said.

"I agree," Watkins said. "Let's caucus."

The brunette looked a bit non-plussed as the four contestants huddled. The countdown music from *Jeopardy!* began playing over the public address system.

"Does anyone have any idea?" Koehler asked.

"In 1987 I was a freshman at Saint Teresa's Academy in Kansas City and I was a lot more worried about homework and detentions than baseball," Melissa said. "But Sveum was blushing like a teenager at his first mixer as that question was read."

"Let's go with it."

"Aye."

"It's unanimous."

"Our collective answer," Koehler announced as they broke the huddle, "is Dale Sveum."

The brunette's confirmation was lost in the crowd's roar, for the professors were apparently the only four people at Miller Park that night who hadn't known the answer instantly. After hamming it up a bit with sweeping waves in response to the sarcastic cheers, they hopped down from the dugout for the last time. Instead of pausing immediately in their complementary box seats for the bottom of the third, all four headed back to the prep room under the stands so that they could shed their caps and gowns. With the stadium full and the roof closed, they were sweltering.

"That was quite clever, making that oblique connection," Koehler said to Melissa.

"Thanks."

"In a very roundabout way, it reminds me of Ole back in 1957. Alaska statehood was a fairly hot issue. Democrats weren't crazy about it because they figured it just meant two more Republican senators and three more Republican electoral votes. But Ole was a Kennedy guy. He knew the delegates the state sent to the Democratic National Convention would be Democrats even if the congressman it elected would inevitably be a Republican. He figured he could snag Alaska delegates for Jack Kennedy by getting him behind the statehood bill. He sold the idea to Kennedy and managed to get full credit for him from everyone in Alaska, including the GOP. Even Egan, the point man on statehood."

Nodding distractedly at the anecdote, Melissa took three more strides toward the elevator and then, still twenty feet away, stopped cold. Oblivious to the milling fans gaping at someone in full academic regalia standing stock still in the midst of the bustling concourse, she matched Koehler's offhand comment against the data she'd accumulated about Ole Lindstrom and his murder, starting with Rep's description of the club room in the Lindstrom home. Then she burrowed furiously under her robe to retrieve her phone.

She called Rep first, but he didn't answer. Then she called Kuchinski, laughing in spite of herself as she heard the *Perry Mason Theme* that he used as a ring-tone. It had gotten through *Duh-Duh-Duh-DUH!-duh-duh-duh-duh!* when he answered.

"This will sound off-the-wall, but trust me," she said. "I want you to get in touch with whoever has custody of the evidence in the Lindstrom murder case. Ask them to count the stars on the flag that was wrapped around his body."

◇◇◇

Rep walked serenely into the Federal House Bar & Grille, followed a hostess to a dark wood booth, sat down, and began studying the menu. He intended to take full advantage of the opportunity to dine without female supervision. He was still trying to decide between a bacon cheeseburger and a T-bone when he heard a voice over his left shoulder.

"Hi."

Rep had to twist around to see the speaker, who was not grizzled and was not wearing a red windbreaker.

"Good evening, Mr. Halftoe," Rep said. "Would you care to join me?"

"I would," Halftoe said, stepping forward and slipping onto the bench opposite Rep's. "I'm in the mood for a little firewater, as my people supposedly call it. I understand that you want to talk to Laurel Wolf."

Chapter Twenty-five

"Whoever told you I want to talk to Laurel was right," Rep said. "Can you arrange it?"

"That depends on how you look at it. I don't know where she is, and I don't know anybody who does."

"Good. That means you can't be accused of harboring a fugitive. If I were wearing a wire any cops who were listening would now be yawning and going back to their crosswords."

"I guess I would've made make a good lawyer." Halftoe grinned, showing teeth more even than any adult gets without help from the American Dental Association.

"Stick with being a bagman. It's better for your reputation."

"It's 'bundler,' not 'bagman.' Good line, though. I like it."

"So now we're on the record that you can't take me to her. Tell me what you can do."

"I can get you on the phone with a guy who'll listen to you. If he likes what he hears, and I like what I hear, he'll patch you through to Laurel Wolf."

An auburn-haired waitress approached. Her smile seemed designed to meet the minimum standard defined by a union contract. Her expression said, "Look, but don't touch." Rep estimated the distance between the hem of her red leather miniskirt and the tops of her knees at fifteen inches. Her halter top was also red, also leather, and equally skimpy relative to the flesh it was nominally intended to cover.

"Can I get you fellas anything to drink while you're looking at the menu?"

"Actually, I think we're about ready to order," Rep said. "Bacon cheeseburger medium rare, with fries and extra barbecue sauce."

"You get a second side order."

"Better make it cottage cheese. I'm on a diet."

"What to drink?" asked the waitress, who had apparently heard that one before.

"Miller Genuine Draft."

"Don't have it."

"Coors?"

"Nope."

"Leininkugel? Point Beer?"

"No and no. Best I can do is Budweiser."

"Water, then. No ice. Fewer calories, lower carbs, and it tastes about the same."

She turned toward Halftoe.

"How about you, sir?"

"Cosmopolitan."

"Anything to eat?" she asked, keeping her tone professionally neutral.

"Sure, why not? Plate of hot wings and a Coke chaser."

"I'll bring your food and drinks together."

She sashayed off. Halftoe followed the departure with a connoisseur's eye.

"When she comes back you'd better pinch her fanny or she'll think we're gay," he said.

"I'm afraid she'd beat me up. Besides, I'm not the one who ordered a cosmopolitan."

"I'm going for metrosexual. Chicks in the Midwest really dig it."

"Okay," Rep said. "So. This guy who has to like what he hears. What's his number?"

"Don't you think this venue is a little public for a conversation like that?"

"Public is one of the things I like about it."

"I was thinking we could go back to your hotel room."

"Not gonna happen."

"Pretty please."

"No."

"How badly do you want to talk to Laurel?"

"Badly—but not that badly."

"Don't you trust me?"

"Nope. Besides, my wife said that *she'd* beat me up if I pulled something as reckless as that—and she scares me even more than the waitress does."

They continued the unpromising discussion for about seven minutes, suspending it briefly when the waitress came back, bearing a tray. With brisk efficiency she distributed the orders. Halftoe killed a third of the cosmopolitan in one gulp, then picked up a mini-drumstick and began playing with it without showing much interest in consumption.

"You're making this a lot harder than it should be, but maybe I can find a way to make it work," he said. "First, give me an idea of what you plan to say to Laurel if I manage to get you in touch with her."

"If I did that then you'd have information you want from me and I wouldn't be one inch closer to a chat with her. The American Bar Association would never let me lecture on negotiating tactics again."

Halftoe snapped his gaze away from Rep, emitting a little hiss of frustration as he did so. Then, squaring his torso against the back of the booth, he pulled his mobile phone from his shirt pocket, flipped it open with a disgusted, have-it-your-way petulance, and hit a speed dial button.

"He wants to do it where we are, in the restaurant.... No, it's not crowded yet. It's Friday night and the early crowd has cleared out. Most of the action now is at the bar.... Okay."

Halftoe handed the phone across the table. Rep accepted it and, with a sharply regretful pang, laid most of a bacon cheeseburger back on his plate.

"This is Rep Pennyworth. What's on your mind?"

"Why do you want to talk to Laurel?" a low, male voice asked.

"To tell her some things I think she should know."

"Like how you fingered her to the cops?"

"She already knows that."

"Why are you so concerned about her all of a sudden?"

"It's like jazz. If you have to ask, you wouldn't understand."

"Not good enough. I need more than snappy patter."

Rep frowned. The guy had a point, but explaining would be a challenge. He was concerned about Laurel Wolf for two reasons—one that he couldn't confess, and one that he wasn't sure he could articulate.

"Let me put it this way," he said after a couple of moments. "Someone murdered my client. I don't know who or why, but if Laurel Wolf isn't the who then there's a pretty good chance the why has something to do with people I care about—starting with me."

"What good is talking to Laurel going to do? She's not going to answer any questions."

"It can't hurt and it might help."

Rep listened to static while whoever he was talking to pretended to think things over—or, perhaps, actually did.

"All right," the voice said at last. "I'll try to patch us through."

Rep heard beeps, clicks, two ring-tones, and a female voice with roughly the register and tone of Wolf's.

"This is Laurel."

"I have Pennyworth on the line. He's the lawyer who said he wanted to talk to you."

"It's your party, shyster," the woman's voice said. "You wanna talk, talk."

"Whoever told you to torch the Lindstrom place is trying to frame you for Ole Lindstrom's murder."

"And you think that because—why, exactly?"

"Let's call it a dream I had."

"Is that your idea of joke? Because I'm not in the mood for paleface racist bullshit."

"I'll tell you the dream and then you decide whether it's racist." Rep waited through a couple of seconds of silence. "My dream began with someone in a motel room. I can't tell whether it's a man or a woman. You know how dreams are. It's not one of the franchise chain motels, more of a seedy kind of place where you pay cash and no one checks license plate numbers. Suddenly someone else is in the room. Definitely a woman. She's very excited. She says they have to leave in a hurry. Something has gone wrong. That kind of thing. You with me so far?"

"I'm keeping up, but it sounds more like a second-rate cable cop show than a dream."

"Anyway, they both leave the room and peel out. Then a strange thing happens. All of a sudden I'm checking into the same motel. Not really my kind of place, but I'm wet and cold and little banged up, and it's any port in a storm. What do you think of my dream?"

"I think it's a pretty unlikely coincidence."

"Not really. The seedy hotel is near Loki, but not too near, and it doesn't keep meticulous records. Just the kind of place you'd pick if you wanted a base of operations for an assignation—or an arson. And because it's near but not too near Loki, it's the kind of place I might stumble over when all I care about is running water and clean sheets. It happens that I did stumble over it, or my wife did, and a car peeled out of the parking lot right around the time the VACANCY light came on. Now what do you think?"

"I think you're wasting my time," the female voice said—but it spoke without conviction.

"Maybe. But I started trying to reach you by leaving the same message with three different people. If I'm wrong, all three of them should have treated it as a crank call. The only reason any of them should have paid any attention to it was that their caller i.d.s would have shown that the call came from the very motel I saw in my dream. Maybe that's just another unlikely coincidence—but the coincidences are starting to pile up here. And if it isn't a coincidence, then your life is in danger."

"In danger from who? People who were trying to keep you from going to the police with some white man's fairy tale about recognizing my voice?"

"Yes."

"I thought you said the bad guys were trying to frame me."

"They are, but they don't want the police to get you. You'd be a much more convenient suspect dead than alive."

"Right. Got it. Sure." The voice dripped with sarcasm. "So this is the part where you say I should go to the police myself, right?"

"I have a conflict of interest. The only advice I can ethically give you is to consult an attorney who doesn't. But if that other lawyer tells you to make sure you get the truth down on paper or in a computer disk that can be sent to the cops if you turn up missing, I wouldn't be surprised."

Rep listened to what he told himself was thoughtful silence for six or seven seconds before he heard the voice again.

"Anything else?"

"Just one thing," he said. "When I almost nailed you with the SUV door during your escape from the Lindstrom house, what did you say?"

"That's it," the male voice said brusquely. "End of conversation."

With the abrupt click from the broken connection still sounding in his ear, Rep returned the mobile phone to Halftoe, who smiled mordantly as he took it.

"The guy told you she wasn't going to answer any questions, didn't he?"

"And she didn't. But he did. He told me whoever I was talking to didn't know the answer."

Rep went contentedly back to work on his bacon cheeseburger. Halftoe looked at him with undisguised exasperation for a couple of bites, then polished off four hot wings in one minute flat, finished his cosmopolitan, drank half the Coke, and stood up.

"I'm gonna hit the head. I'll be right back."

"If the waitress comes, do you want me to have her put the rest of the wings in a doggie-bag?" Rep asked Halftoe's back. Except for an I-can't-believe-this head shake, Halftoe ignored him.

By the time Halftoe returned, about five minutes later, the bacon cheeseburger was almost gone and Rep's pile of French fries much diminished. The cottage cheese, however, remained untouched. Relaxed and all smiles now, Halftoe sat down and attacked his buffalo wings with apparently genuine enthusiasm. He was finishing the last of them when the waitress reappeared.

"How about dessert, gentlemen?"

"Not for me," Rep said.

"I'll pass too," Halftoe said as he stripped a sauce-sodden wing clean with his perfectly even teeth. After a couple of desultory napkin swipes on his right hand, he pulled a wad of currency from his right-hand coat pocket and peeled a hundred-dollar bill from it. "Let me get this."

"If you insist," Rep said.

The waitress took the bill without comment and padded away.

"Okay," Halftoe said to Rep then, folding his hands and leaning forward in a suggestive, man-to-man, just-between-us-guys kind of way. "With Ole's unfortunate death, your professional engagement in that matter is over, right?"

"True," Rep admitted. "Death of the client terminates the retainer."

"So you're now available for other work."

"Keeping busy pays the rent."

"You've handled yourself pretty well in this mess. Stayed loyal to your client, kept your eye on the ball. That impresses people."

"Thank you."

"Chenequa Gaming Enterprises, Inc. has lots of trademark and copyright work. They have some good lawyers working for them already, but they like to spread their business around. What's your standard retainer for new corporate clients?"

"It depends," Rep said. "How does twenty-five thousand sound?"

"Sounds doable."

"Tell you what," Rep said, digging out one of his cards and sliding it across the table to Halftoe. "Have someone email me a list of potential adverse parties. I'll have a conflict check run first thing Monday morning, and as soon as we're clear I'll crank out an engagement letter and we can get to work."

Halftoe pocketed the card with one hand and took the wad of cash out with the other.

"Better idea." He peeled off ten bills. "There has to be some work that you won't be conflicted out of. We'll make this a deposit on the retainer. They'll wire the rest as soon as you get the paperwork done. Meanwhile, there's a project you can get to work on tonight. There are some people in D.C. getting ready to chat up the Bureau of Indian Affairs on Monday. We can run in and see them for half-an-hour or so."

Rep was shaking his head when the waitress returned with Halftoe's change. Her eyes widened at the pile of hundreds untouched in the center of the table.

"We have a special tonight," she said. "If that's the tip you get dessert for free."

"This is your tip, munchkin," Wolf said, plucking a ten from the change she had brought. "Remember me in your prayers."

"'Munchkin?' Never mind. You fellas have a good night."

Rep waited until she was ten feet away before he spoke again.

"Let's do it by the book. I'd love to represent Chenequa, but it's never a good idea to cut corners. No need for cash. Their credit is good. I'll jump through the hoops and we can hit the ground running Monday afternoon."

"Fair enough," Halftoe said with an equanimity that surprised Rep. "Monday it is."

They got up and made their way through the dimly-lit and increasingly boisterous establishment toward the door. When they got outside, Halftoe pointed to a sleek, black Chrysler Imperial that had apparently been circulating around the area and was now approaching.

"At least let me give you a ride back to your hotel," he said.

"Thanks, but I always like to get a walk in after dinner."

He started to move away. Halftoe subtly grabbed his right bicep and stopped him cold. At the same moment, Rep noticed the driver of the Chrysler get out. The man was quite large. He wasn't smiling.

"Here it is," Halftoe said quietly. "We need to talk. I have to find out what you know and what you're guessing about and what you're just making up. So you're going to come with me."

Rep's belly dropped. He'd dodged every bullet so far, but he hadn't anticipated being kidnapped in the heart of Annapolis, in front of two or three dozen witnesses.

He tried to jerk his right arm away from Halftoe's grip, while simultaneously swinging his left fist around to hit Halftoe as hard as he could. He aimed for the diaphragm, but he hit Halftoe's chest instead.

"Nice shot, junior," Halftoe said, grinning. "By the way, yell all you want to. People are used to it down here. They'll just think you're drunk and my buddy and I are doing a Good Samaritan thing."

The other guy had reached them now. He got a grip on Rep's left arm.

"Let's go," Halftoe said.

"Let's not," an unhurried drawl interjected.

All three people in the group turned toward the unexpected injunction. It came from a guy with at least a two-day growth of salt-and-pepper beard. He was wearing a shiny red windbreaker.

"Remember me?" he asked Halftoe. "I'm the harmless codger you asked for directions to Federal House about an hour ago. You said you had a mid at the Academy and you wanted to meet him there."

"Sure." Halftoe beamed. "Your directions were right on. Took me straight to the front door."

"Federal House Bar and Grille is off-limits to midshipmen."

This comment left Halftoe speechless for about two seconds.

"So I lied," he shrugged then. "What do you want?"

"I want to take a stroll with this gent. Now, if you don't like that idea, we could play a little game I call 'gunny roulette.'"

"Tell you what, gramps," Halftoe said, pulling a twenty from his pocket with his free hand and holding it out to the interloper. "Go on in there and have a couple on me."

Less than a second later, the iron grip on Rep's right arm relaxed. The next thing he knew, Halftoe was on his knees, doubled over with his arms wrapped around his middle. Rep didn't even glimpse the punch that had felled him. One instant Halftoe was standing there holding out a twenty and the next he was kissing cobblestones, sounding like he wanted to vomit.

"What?" the guy on the other side of Rep yelled. "What'd you do?"

Shoving Rep away like a rag doll, he surged after the guy in the windbreaker as Rep tripped over Halftoe and sprawled on the pavement. The assistant thug looked like he knew what he was doing, getting his hands up briskly and keeping his footwork clean. He shot a quick, sharp jab at the gunny. Partially blocked, the punch hit the gunny on the right side of his head instead of his face, but it still sounded like a baseball bat solidly hitting a ball. Rep scrambled to his feet so that he could pitch in somehow.

He never got the chance. The fight was over before he had both feet back underneath him. The gunny didn't flinch or retreat in reaction to the punch. He just plowed forward without wasted motion. The next thing Rep saw was the head of Halftoe's fellow thug snap backwards as the heel of the gunny's right hand smashed into the base of the thug's nose. Remarkably, the blow didn't knock the thug over—but it didn't have to. Three quick steps staggering backward, a quarter-second or so to think things over, and the thug decided that he had urgent business elsewhere. Within seconds he was around the nearest corner in inglorious retreat.

"Thanks," Rep said, holding out his hand. "Rep Penny-worth."

"Champ Mayer," the guy in the windbreaker said as he shook with Rep. "Commander Seton asked me to keep an eye on you while you were here. Sounded silly at the time, but that's why he's an officer and I was just a jarhead sergeant."

"How would you like a drink or two at the Loew's Hotel?"

"I'd take that very kindly."

"Good." Rep took out his mobile phone as they began to walk away from the scene. "I have to call my wife and let her know that things are a little dicier than we thought they were."

"You go right ahead and make that call, son. Lots better for wives to hear things before they read them in the papers. That's always job-one."

Chapter Twenty-six

"What was that cheer?" Rep asked when he and Melissa finally connected with each other live during the break between the sixth and seventh innings. "Home run?"

"Not exactly. The Diamond Dancers just came out for their next routine. Gold lamé miniskirts and silver-sequined blue tops are a bit gaudy for my tastes, but they seem to be crowd-pleasers."

"*O tempora, o mores,*" Rep sighed. "To old-school types like Ty Cobb, Ted Williams, and me, that kind of thing doesn't exactly scream 'baseball.'"

Melissa made a sympathetic noise, but Rep's standard-issue rant didn't really engage her. In the course of tonight's game she had witnessed baseball blasphemies far graver than the Diamond Dancers.

In the middle of the sixth inning, for example, she had seen a seven-foot bratwurst with spindly arms and legs beat a seven-foot hot dog in a footrace around the grandstand warning track, while three other giant sausages trailed behind. The fans had cheered this event wildly, even though most of the sausages didn't really seem to be trying.

The fifth inning had featured grinning twenty-somethings in Brewers t-shirts spilling onto the field with those three-foot translucent tubes Melissa had seen in the prep room, using them to shoot tightly rolled t-shirts into the upper deck. The carbon-dioxide propellant that the head dancer had referred to did its job. The plastic cannons sent the apparel far over her head in long, gracefully arching parabolas.

In the fourth inning, a randomly chosen fan had tried to guess which of three animated baseball caps on the message board hid an animated baseball. The fans not only cheered but shamelessly yelled the answer at him. Melissa thought that was cheating, but no one seemed to care.

"Tell me you're okay," she said to her husband.

"I've had an interesting night, but I'm safe and sound," Rep said.

"Interesting in what way, beloved?"

"I'll tell you all about it sometime, from a distance exceeding three feet."

"You promised you wouldn't take any risks."

"I didn't, but some risks tried to take me. It all worked out fine, though, with some help from Frank and Gunnery Sergeant Mayer. The bottom line is that this mess is a lot nastier than we thought it was."

"What do you mean?"

Rep explained. Melissa frowned. She had three frowns in her repertoire, one suggesting irritation, one dismay, and one concentration. She had used all three before Rep paused.

"Did you at least get to talk to Laurel Wolf?"

"No, I got to talk to someone pretending to be Laurel Wolf. She was pretty good at it, but she was faking. In fact, I'd give you three-to-one it was the other Laurel—Laurel Fox."

"You'd lose," Melissa said.

"How can you be so sure? There aren't that many women running around in this Chinese fire-drill who could have brought it off."

"Because Laurel Fox is about forty feet from me right now, doing the splits."

"She's a Brewers Diamond Dancer?"

"I think she's filling in for one. For an old-school type, by the way, you seem rather familiar with the group's act."

"I think someone on ESPN must have mentioned it during *Baseball Tonight.*"

"Uh *huh.* Well, get a good night's sleep and hurry home, darling. Walt may have some news for us tomorrow that will bear analysis."

"I can't wait."

Melissa clicked the phone off and pensively watched the Diamond Dancers hustle off the field. *"There aren't that many women in this Chinese fire-drill...."* Rep was right about that. Laurel Fox was one of them, along with Lena and Veronica Gephardt. But Fox was the one who got paid to "lay down tracks," according to Carlsen—and who apparently used a machine to do it. The last of the dancers was twenty feet up the walkway behind her when Melissa impulsively jumped from her seat and scurried after them.

Panting a bit as she went, she followed the athletic young lasses through the concourse. She missed the elevator they took, but found a discreet set of stairs that took her to the prep room level. The door had closed behind the last of them while Melissa was still ten feet away. A black guard in a red t-shirt with EVENT SECURITY silk-screened on it in gold jumped in front of her.

"You can't go in there, miss!"

"God bless you for the 'miss,' but I'm one of the professors from the event earlier in the game. I have to pick up my cap and gown."

The guard's lips split in a broad grin and he pistol-shot her with his right index finger.

"Riiiight. Unlimited sacrifice flies in one inning. I loved that."

He rapped sharply on the door and then opened it a couple of inches.

"Heads up, girls, don't panic. It's the lady prof here for her monkey suit."

Melissa pushed through to find a gaggle of Diamond Dancers sponging off, slipping out of costumes and into robes, talking on mobile phones and, in one case, giggling a bit manically as she used one of the plastic t-shirt cannons to fire her gold lamé miniskirt against purple cinderblock. Melissa saw Fox directly in front of the no-smoking sign, hastily pulling on a pink hoodie. She strode over to the younger woman.

"We need to talk."

"Sorry, boss," Fox muttered without looking at her. "I'm on break 'til the top of the ninth."

"It's important."

"Not as important as getting out of this Campfire Girls meeting for twenty minutes. Move it or lose it, sis."

Fox brushed past Melissa and slipped through the door. Melissa turned quickly to follow her.

"Don't forget your cap and gown!" one of the other Diamond Dancers called, holding out the flat, brown cardboard box with "UWM" scrawled in Magic Marker across its lid.

Melissa paused for just a moment to accept the parcel on her way out the door. As she scurried upstairs and onto the concourse, she realized that the wasted moment might be crucial. The concession stands at Miller Park don't sell alcoholic beverages after the seventh inning. Forty-thousand people were by now within five outs of last call, and a fair percentage of them weren't taking any chances. Melissa found herself submerged helplessly in a churning wave of beer-seeking humanity, with no Laurel Fox in sight.

She came to a complete stop, deployed her sharp right elbow to discourage a brace of serial jostlers, mentally smacked the side of her head, and firmly instructed herself to *think!* She remembered Rep's description of his first encounter with Fox. Unless he was grotesquely exaggerating—and her husband wasn't given to hyperbole—the single most logical place for Fox to go was a designated smoking area. Miller Park has two on the right field side of the stadium, and Melissa headed for the nearer one.

Tracking Fox down, of course, would only be half the battle. If the insight sparked by Rep's offhand comment was going to get her anywhere, she would have to figure out some way to grab a piece of Fox's apparently limited attention span and somehow motivate her to speak. Rep's description of his conversation with a fake Laurel Wolf, combined with his comments about the device looking like an old-fashioned answering machine that Fox had lugged out of Future Cubed, gave her the germ of an idea. To do anything about it, though, she'd need some help. While she picked her way through the surging crowd, she opened her mobile phone and hastily thumb-punched a nine-hundred number into it.

As she had expected, she reached a recorded message. It seemed to shout in her ear because she'd had to crank the phone up to maximum volume in order to hear Rep in the grandstand. The recording wasn't new to her, but it still brought a disgusted moué to her lips and a hint of blush pink to the tops of her ears.

"Have you been naughty? Do you need—"

"This is spoiled sibling's friend," she said sharply, speaking over the insinuating patter and hoping that Rep's mom was just screening calls and would pick up. "He said you could give me some advice—"

"Hello, spoiled sibling's friend," a throaty, no-nonsense voice cut in. "Advice about what?"

"I've heard about machines you can use to modify your voice when you talk over the telephone or make a recording—if you want to use one person to play multiple parts on a radio ad, for example."

"Or if you want one person who can talk like a man or a woman on a nine-hundred telephone call. Machines like that exist, all right."

"Is there one that looks like a mini-control board about a foot square with four black control levers that you can slide up and down?" The urgency in Melissa's tone clicked up a notch as she saw the first sign for the designated smoking area.

"That sounds like the Boss Voice Transformer VT-One model made by Executive Pro Voice Changer. Runs between five-hundred-fifty and six-hundred dollars. I recorded some scene scripts a while back on audio cassettes: two women and two men, and with that thing I could do all four voices myself."

"Is that the one you'd expect someone who was really serious to use?"

"Probably. There's a cheaper unit called the PCV-One that sells for less than two-fifty, but it's really just a toy. To create different voices convincingly, you have to control both pitch and harmonics. Anything much cheaper than the Boss only affects one."

"Thanks. That's a big help."

Melissa paused in front of the entrance to the smoking enclave and braced herself. Not being prissy about cigarettes is one thing, and braving this toxic miasma was something else. The bluish-gray cloud floating over the two-dozen people on the patio promised a concentrated second-hand smoke experience several orders of magnitude worse than anything she'd undergone since high school. After a deep breath she strode onto the patio and worked her way steadily over to Fox, who was on the far side, leaning against a waist-high metal rail and dragging hard on an American Spirit.

"*Don't* tell me you want to bum a smoke," she said when she spotted Melissa. "You could be the snarky little snot from the anti-tobacco commercials, the one who just shakes her head with this pissy, superior smile on her face when someone offers her a cigarette. Don't bother faking it."

"Farthest thing from my mind. I tracked you down to tell you something you want to know, whether you realize it or not."

Fox rolled her eyes and whiffed smoke disgustedly over her shoulder.

"The only reason I don't just blow you off is that I'm trapped here until I finish this and the one that's going to come after it. So go ahead. You talk and I'll smoke."

"I'll keep it short." Melissa flourished her mobile phone to suggest the source of her information. "Someone pretending to be Laurel Wolf talked to my husband by phone tonight. You might say it was a party line."

"I don't get it."

"Other people were listening. I don't know if they got the call traced, but they have figured out that whoever was talking to Rep was in Milwaukee and was using a Boss Voice Transformer VT-One to fake Wolf's voice. I don't think those are very common here."

Fox's disdainful expression evaporated and her face transformed. Her eyes rounded to dinner-plate dimensions, her mouth gaped, and her face turned stop-sign red. She snapped her own phone open and punched a single speed-dial number into it.

The language that began her conversation a few seconds later was bluer than the smoke surrounding them. Her first epithet, delivered in a kind of spitting screech, accused whoever answered of practicing what seventeenth-century English judges primly referred to as "sodomy *per os*," although Fox used the Anglo-Saxon terminology. Furious and fluently obscene observations on the stupidity, incompetence, and dubious ancestry of her interlocutor followed. Before she had finished, a buzz-cut in a chief petty officer's uniform pulled a thick cigar from the corner of his mouth and walked away as his cheeks flushed. Fox paid no attention.

"They've *made* me, you vermin!" she yelped into the phone. "How could you let this happen? You *promised* me."

Well, THIS is suggestive, Melissa thought.

Fox stopped bleating for about thirty seconds. Her body relaxed a bit, and as she straightened up her face resolved into something more recognizably human.

"Just a sec," she said in a much calmer voice as she looked back at Melissa and lowered the mouthpiece below her chin. "This is, ah, kind of, like, confidential, so...."

Fox accompanied this with left-handed shooing motions. Melissa nodded understandingly and retreated toward the smoking area's gate. She watched as Fox continued the phone conversation for another couple of minutes. The younger woman was much calmer now. She brought her cigarette to her lips deliberately rather than desperately, and pulled on it with a thoughtful, contemplative expression. As soon as she ended the call she walked over to Melissa, clearly doing her best to look contrite.

"Sorry about being so bitchy just now," she said in a voice barely above a whisper. "Stress and...you know...stress."

"Sure."

"I appreciate you telling me that stuff. You were right. I needed to know that."

"You're welcome."

A spasm that seemed to mingle pain, frustration, and fear rippled across Fox's face, like an underwater wave in a clear pond. From the stadium behind her Melissa could hear the *Beer Barrel Polka* winding down on the organ. That meant the top of the seventh was over and the crowd was nearing the end of the seventh-inning stretch, watching a pair of young couples stomp through an elementary polka on the top of each dugout. The kitschy scene, which she'd witnessed at every ball game she'd attended in Milwaukee, always struck Melissa as poignantly ordinary, unpretentious, and American. She regretted missing it. But she couldn't leave Fox now, even though she was pretty sure she had the information she wanted.

"Look," Fox said then, "I'm in a bit of a fix here. I'd like to talk to you about it in depth, privately, so we can really get into what's going on."

"Of course. I can stand the smoke if you need another cigarette. I don't think there's any danger of anyone here paying much attention to what we say. Otherwise, I'm sure we can find a quiet place somewhere in the stadium."

"I do want to grab another smoke before I go back to the Babysitters Club, and then I'm going to have to hustle because we have one more routine to do before the top of the ninth. I hate to ask this, but could you maybe wait 'til the game is over so we could hook up and really have a little heart-to-heart?"

Melissa hesitated for a moment. Fox was asking her to make the same kind of reckless, grandstand play that she'd threatened to smack Rep for if he pulled it. But the risk seemed manageable. She was in a baseball stadium with tens of thousands of other people, including an array of what seemed to be thoroughly competent security officers. Besides, whatever felonies and misdemeanors Fox may have abetted, the woman in front of her seemed scared and vulnerable—and, equally important, ready to talk.

"Sure," Melissa said. "I'll meet you outside the prep room as soon as I can get there after the last out."

"Great," Fox said, a fresh cigarette already headed for her lips. "I really appreciate it."

There were already two outs in the bottom of the seventh by the time Melissa got back to her seat. Her colleagues had long since gone home, and the crowd as a whole was steadily thinning. When the inning ended a couple of minutes later the early exodus of fans hoping to beat the traffic and confident of victory accelerated. The kids with the plastic cannons hustled out and shot more t-shirts into the crowd. That was it for in-game distraction. Nine outs later, with only a walk and a double-play for the sake of variety, the game was over.

She made her way back to the prep room. Fox was waiting for her just outside, holding the door slightly ajar to keep it from closing and locking. The other Diamond Dancers had apparently left. Fox gave her a semi-conspiratorial nod and pushed into the room ahead of her. She flopped wearily into a chair near the door while Melissa found a seat on a bench across the room.

"Do you know what 'bundlers' are?"

"In general terms," Melissa said. "They're people who pull together political campaign contributions, supposedly from individuals associated with a business, and put the money together in one big pot. The idea is to make influential donations to politicians on behalf of the business without violating the legal limits on contributions."

"Right. Well, apparently the law can be pretty rough on these guys. If they don't obey a lot of ticky-tacky little rules exactly, they get treated almost like racketeers."

"That's because they are racketeers. It's dirty business even if you play by the rules. If you break them, it's a combination of extortion and bribery."

"Whatever," Fox said. "Anyway, the guys involved in it can get pretty rough—especially if they think someone is scamming them on some of their contributions."

"Rough enough to kill Ole Lindstrom?"

"Rough enough to crease up Laurel Fox is all I care about. Something happened. Some not-my-department kind of thing. I don't know what it was. But if they think I'm mixed up in it, I could be in pretty big trouble."

"Aside from suggesting that you get a lawyer and go to the police, I'm not sure how I can help."

"Tell me what *you* know. 'Cause if your husband is involved enough in this to have someone listening in on his phone calls, then you know a lot more than I do."

"Most of what I know we learned confidentially from other people. I don't feel comfortable disclosing it—especially if it might get them crosswise of thugs like you've been describing."

Melissa's phone chirped. Seeing Kuchinski's number, she mouthed an apology to Fox and answered.

"You were absolutely right," Kuchinski boomed, as Melissa realized too late that, in this quiet room, the voice was easily loud enough for Fox to her. "The flag wrapped around Ole had forty-nine stars."

"Walt, I'll call you back in about ten minutes," she said hastily. "I can't talk right now."

"Got it."

The line went dead. Melissa looked up, preparing to offer Fox a verbal apology. The words choked in her throat like an inconvenient fish bone. Fox was pointing a small, silver-plated and ivory-handled automatic at her chest.

"It'll be more than ten minutes," she said. "Slide your phone over here along the floor."

"Well," Melissa sighed as she moved to comply, "that's what I get for bad manners."

Chapter Twenty-seven

"Okay," Fox said, checking her watch, "here's the way we're going to work it. First of all, I don't want to kill you."

"You mean I've been practicing perfect Acts of Contrition for nothing?"

Melissa's glib pose was spurious, and it seemed so transparent to her that she thought Fox had to see through it. In reality, the muzzle pointed at her chest terrified her. She felt a cold, yawning void in her belly. Her right calf started to shake and it took a conscious effort of will to stop it. Her throat felt blocked, as if she were about to vomit. She knew that if she unclenched her fists her fingers would tremble. She was putting on the act because she figured it was her only shot at survival, but she had to deploy every atom of concentration she could muster to manage even the pathetic semblance of poise she was showing now to Fox.

"Just listen, okay?" Fox demanded crossly.

"I'm listening."

"Security will be spending the next half-hour shooing the fat cats out of the luxury suites. The TGI Friday's restaurant in the left-field stands is open for another two hours, and the guards will concentrate on the main concourses until it closes. They won't get around to a final check on this room until then."

"You obviously know the routine."

"I've filled in as a Diamond Dancer before. I've also 'filled in' inside some of the luxury suites, if you know what I mean."

"Thank you for sharing."

Fox glanced at her watch.

"In thirteen minutes, you and I are going to walk out that door and meet somebody. The three of us will go upstairs and then leave the stadium through the Club/Suites entrance, like stragglers from one of the luxury suites. We'll do all of this very quietly and without drawing attention to ourselves—understand?"

"Don't worry about me," Melissa said. "I'll be a perfect lamb."

"You'd better be. Because the other way to handle it is for me to club you over the head with this gun while my friend holds you, so the two of us can walk you out as if you were drunk or strung out on bad downers or something."

"Could you repeat the part about how I'm not going to get killed? I liked that."

"Only you and I will know my little Glok Twenty-three is there. I'll use it if I have to, but as long as you don't yell for help or make a break for it I won't have to. And there won't be any point in running for it because I know this stadium a lot better than you do and unless you stumble over a guard, which you won't, I'll track you down—and when I find you I'll be very cranky."

"So if I cooperate I get to go on living until we're a mile or two away from the stadium, somewhere in the Menominee River Valley, right?"

"No one wants to kill you."

"Even to stay out of prison?"

"We're not worried about some low-rent campaign finance rap. We want the information you have because there are very nasty people who think my friend and I have scammed them, and we have to show them that we haven't. Murder would just screw things up."

"It already has," Melissa said.

"What, Ole? No way. My money is on Wolf for that one. If it wasn't her it was Lena or Gephardt."

"It was Gary Carlsen. The friend you've been talking about."

"No way. Ole was a meal ticket for Gary. That Gephardt thing would have kept Gary in latte grandes for ten years. It might even have gotten him to the big time."

"There were forty-nine stars on the flag, Laurel. Not fifty."

"So what?"

"The only time the American flag had just forty-nine stars was the seven-and-a-half months from January 3, 1959, when Alaska was admitted to the union as the forty-ninth state, and August 21, 1959, when Hawaii was admitted as the fiftieth."

"If the Brewers ever do a geography trivia promotion, you should come back out for it."

"Fifty years later, there aren't many forty-nine-star flags lying around outside Alaska. But one of them was hanging in Ole Lindstrom's club room. The governor of Alaska had a forty-nine star flag flown over the Capitol on the day Alaska was formally admitted, and sent it to Ole to thank him for getting Kennedy behind the Alaska statehood bill."

"And you're telling me this because...why?"

"Because it proves that Ole was killed in the club room in his home in Loki, not in Milwaukee—killed by someone he knew and trusted enough to get close to him; someone who could have snuck out the safe deposit box key sometime when Ole wasn't looking. The crime scene was relatively clean because the blood and tissue from the death blow spattered on the flag hung on the wall behind his desk. Carlsen wrapped Ole's body in the flag and moved it to Milwaukee to cover up the fact that the murder happened in Loki, and to throw suspicion on Laurel Wolf. Before he moved the body, he took one of the other flags stashed in the club room and used it to replace the forty-nine-star flag on the wall."

"But this supposed killer couldn't expect that to work. Sooner or later, Lena was bound to count the stars on the displayed flag and she'd know that it couldn't have been the one this political hack from Alaska sent to Ole."

"That's why Carlsen talked Laurel Wolf into torching the place. I don't know whether he told her that Ole had evidence tying Native American political movements to illegal campaign finance activity or something else. Whatever it was, though, it worked. She set a fire that destroyed the decoy flag."

"It sounds like he was really scrambling," Fox said sarcastically. "Apparently it wasn't a very well-planned murder."

"It wasn't planned at all. Carlsen suddenly found Ole threatening a neat little campaign finance scam that he'd put together. He had to improvise."

"Ole wasn't any boy scout," Fox said, shrugging. "Everything in campaign finance is dirty one way or another."

"Maybe—but it only turns into a scam when you don't stay bought."

"What's that supposed to mean?"

"Carlsen was trying to sell the tribes the same Persian carpet twice. Chenequa Gaming thought Gephardt was bought and paid for by the donations it made to the Wisconsin Policy Project. They even had a receipt for their purchase, in the form of the formal recognition she provided in the program for her domestic violence symposium. I'm betting that some smooth talk between Carlsen and Randy Halftoe played a role in that."

"No scam so far. That's just salesmanship. Seduction isn't rape."

"The scam came when Carlsen injected Indian gaming as an issue into the Gephardt's nascent campaign for attorney general. That was pure extortion. He was telling the tribes that Gephardt wouldn't stay bought—that they just had to keep paying and paying and paying, until he had all he wanted. He used you to drug Midshipman Lindstrom and steal his military i.d., service dress blues, and safe-deposit box key so that he could get the back-up disk with the critical donor information on it. His plan was to keep taking payoffs in the form of 'contributions' to his political action committees. When he figured he'd milked that for all it was worth, he'd have Gephardt drop the gaming issue and focus on something else. He could have told her the polling was skewing south on it or something. She's a political naïf with suite-smarts instead of street-smarts, so she would have believed him."

"That's nothing to kill anyone over. That's almost legal. That may actually *be* legal."

"His problem wasn't the feds, it was Ole. Ole found out about it. That's what Lena meant when she said that Ole wasn't trying to bleed anybody. He wasn't in it for the money. He just wanted another chance to play at the big table, as Lena put it. He summoned Carlsen to a meeting in Loki and confronted him about it. There was an argument. It turned violent. Carlsen hit Ole on the head with something, and suddenly he had a corpse on his hands."

"If anyone hit Ole on the head, it was Lena," Fox said. "After all, she has a history of doing that."

"The first assault on Ole was also by Carlsen. The safe deposit box required two keys. He had Harald's but he had to sneak Ole's out as well. He'd managed that and then, after he'd gotten the disk, he snuck into the house to put it back before Ole missed it. Ole came home before Carlsen expected him to. He knocked Ole out in order to make his getaway, then drove back up and called nine-one-one just in time to pin the assault and battery on Lena."

"Whatever, I guess," Fox said, rolling her eyes in unfeigned boredom.

"Aren't you getting the picture here, Laurel? You're already on the fringes of one murder and you're about to get up to your eyebrows in another one. There's no way Carlsen can leave me alive. No matter what I tell him he can't prove he wasn't scamming the bundler-thugs because he *was* scamming them."

"I won't let him kill you," Fox said, her gaze suddenly focused and intense. "No one's going to pin a murder rap on my cute little ass."

"Laurel Wolf probably wasn't planning on having one pinned on hers, either, but cops from two counties and the FBI are looking for her. Carlsen's aiders and abettors don't come out well."

Melissa thought she saw a shadow of doubt cloud Fox's face for a moment. She wondered if she was kidding herself.

"That's not going to happen," Fox said, looking again at her watch. "No killing, unless you force the issue. Okay, time for us to go. Just keep your cool, walk right in front of me with a nice, steady pace, and don't try anything."

Fox stood up. With the barrel of her pistol she summoned Melissa over toward the door, standing to one side so that she could position herself just behind her and slightly to her left. Melissa stood up. She felt her gut quiver.

Never mind, she told herself. *You've got one shot. Don't blow it. Focus.*

She took one deliberate step forward and then managed another. Muscle memory took over from there and without excessive quaking she moved toward the door. Melissa was a professor in her mid-thirties who could have lost five pounds without hurting anything, and Fox was an impressively athletic entertainer in her late twenties. Professor versus athlete in a fair fight—Melissa had a pretty good idea of how that one would come out. She had, at most, one chance and she had to make it count.

She reached the door. She sensed Fox slipping behind her. She imagined that she felt the pistol's muzzle against her spine, but the rational synapses still functioning in her brain told her that Fox almost certainly had the weapon concealed. She felt two irritating rivulets of sweat coursing from her shoulder blades toward her waist.

"Now, open the door and walk slowly through the doorway."

Melissa grasped the doorknob and turned it. With surreal clarity she heard the knob's tongue click out of the jamb and recede into the doorknob itself. She started to jerk the door open, but Fox said, "Easy now," as if she were reading Melissa's mind. Melissa took the hint and pulled more tentatively on the knob. She got the door a little more than one body-width wide and stepped through it, with Fox crowding on her heels.

Ten feet away, in the dim recesses of an otherwise empty corridor, Melissa saw Carlsen. He looked seriously wired. He started striding forward.

Melissa stepped across the threshold with her right foot. As she began to move her left, she turned her head slightly so that she could talk over her shoulder to Fox.

"You know that phone of mine you took? I hit REDIAL before I slid it over to you. It's been connected all this time to a lawyer's number, recording everything we said on his answering machine."

"WHAT?"

Fox snapped her head down as she reached for Melissa's mobile phone stashed in the pouch of her hoodie. Planting the ball of her left foot and leaving her left leg extended, Melissa twisted decisively to her left. She grabbed a fistful of hoodie near Fox's shoulder with her right hand and snatch of sweatpants near the dancer's hip with her left. She jerked and shoved. Hard. With a yelp like a cat in heat Fox tripped over Melissa's leg and sprawled on the concrete floor.

Carlsen raced forward, preparing to block any flight by Melissa, but Melissa had no intention of fleeing. She stepped back into the prep room and slammed the door. It took a moment of sweaty fumbling to find the button that locked the door from the inside, but she managed it.

"GODDAMMIT!" she heard instantly from outside the door. "You *lied* to me, you bitch!"

Melissa thought that Fox was in a poor position to be making moral judgments, but she figured she'd save the one-liners for later. There was a black phone on top of the counter above minirefrigerator. She grabbed the receiver and punched zero.

"Hello!" a cheery voice chirped. "Thank you for contacting Stadium Administration at Miller Park! For operating hours during the National League Championship Season, say, 'Hours' or punch One. For—"

Melissa hit nine-one-one.

"Invalid entry," a different voice, not nearly as cheerful, said.

"OPEN THIS DOOR!" a male voice barked from outside. "If I have to blow the lock off, you won't like what happens next!"

Melissa hit one on the phone.

"During the season, regular—"

"Help!" Melissa yelled.

"I'm sorry! I don't recognize that instruction!"

Melissa heard a fingernails-on-chalkboard scratching sound behind her. She spun around. The front edge of a credit card was sticking through, in between the door and the jamb. Detective stories she read referred to this as " 'loiding a lock," and it almost invariably worked in fiction. She wasn't sure that it worked in the real world, but she had a sick feeling that she was about to find out.

Two against one, they have at least one gun, and I don't have any. I don't like the odds.

She flung the receiver in frustration at the wall. Instead of a satisfying plastic-on-cinderblock smash, this gesture produced a hollow *thonk!* The receiver had hit the barrel of one of the t-shirt cannons.

She heard a metallic *snick* followed by a click and swiveled to look back at the door. It didn't open. Instead, the credit card went up and started laboriously back down.

"Almost got it that time," Carlsen said, his voice no longer agitated. "This one should do it. You've got maybe twenty seconds."

That sounded about right to Melissa. She opened the refrigerator. She wasn't sure what was in there, but she knew it had to include cans of Miller Genuine Draft. If nothing else, she could fling those at her assailants and hope for the best. She was getting ready to grab a couple when a sound from her very recent past came back to her.

Thonk!

She looked back toward the rear wall. Three t-shirt cannons stood there. Devices that had hurled tightly rolled t-shirts weighing perhaps half-a-pound eighty or ninety feet.

She grabbed the nearest one and looked feverishly at the breech. A handle, a CO-2 canister, and a trigger. She turned back to the refrigerator and grabbed a can of beer. She was afraid that the can would be too heavy for her weapon, but that looked like the only ammunition she had available. Then something cold and hard hit her wrist and fell to the floor.

It was three Klements Bratwurst, still frozen solid together. Someone had stashed them on top of the beer cans. She grabbed the chilly trio and dropped it down the muzzle of the t-shirt cannon.

Snick!

She pulled the sliding handle back to its lock point.

Click!

"Got it!" This came from outside the door.

The door started to open. Melissa leveled what was now a brat cannon at the moving door. Carlsen suddenly filled the doorway, eyes avidly lit and Fox's pistol gripped in his right hand.

"YES!" he yelled triumphantly.

Melissa pulled the trigger. She heard an emphatic *WHOOMPF.* Carlsen had eight-tenths of a second to look utterly baffled before three frozen Klements Bratwurst hit him flush on the mouth and nose. He flipped backward as if he'd been mule-kicked and his back and head smacked the concrete.

"What did you do?" Fox wailed. "You killed him!"

"Probably not," Melissa said. "That would be a wurst case scenario."

Fox reached for the pistol while Melissa reached for beer. Hearing Frank's taunting reprimand from more than twenty years before—"*Don't throw like a GIRL!*"—she cocked the first frosty can behind her right ear and hurled it directly overhand.

The can hit Fox on her collarbone with enough force to burst a seam (on the can) and send sudsy liquid spewing all over her face. Fox shrieked and reflexively retreated. A respite but no more than that, for Fox was still within twelve inches of the Glok something-or-other that was undoubtedly loaded with ordnance more lethal than sausage.

Melissa picked up a second can and, with more confidence this time, chucked it like she was trying to put an old-school, 'sixties era, National League, dead-red fastball right down the middle. It caught Fox squarely on her adorable surgically-improved nose and her Botox-enhanced lips.

She didn't make a sound. She just keeled over rather dreamily and collapsed, lying motionless while spilling beer soaked her golden hair.

Melissa hustled to retrieve the pistol, then retreated with it back into the room. She wasn't altogether sure what to do next. Fox and Carlsen were *dehors le combat* for the moment, but their bodies were blocking the door and it would be awkward if either of them came to while she was trying to pick her way past them. On the other hand, she had no confidence in her ability to use the handgun she'd just grabbed. She had only fired one pistol shot in her life, and it had missed the target by eight feet.

The sound of rapidly running footsteps in the hallway resolved her dilemma. A few seconds later, two security guards came racing up, filling the doorway with their bulk. One of them was the guy who had let Melissa back into the prep room.

"What's going on here, professor?"

Melissa gave him the short version.

"You mean these two were trying to kidnap you and you shot the male perp with frozen bratwurst?"

"Yes."

The guard looked down at Carlsen, cackling with glee.

"Welcome to Milwaukee, flatlander!" (Chicagoans— "flatlanders" in Milwaukeean—didn't deserve this association with Carlsen, a pure-bred dairy-stater. All Milwaukee cops, however, presume that bad guys come from Chicago.)

The other security guard examined Fox's broken face and, almost tenderly, picked up the can of Miller Genuine Draft still leaking malty liquid onto the floor near her head. His eyes looked forlorn as dew-like, anguished tears pearled the tops of his cheeks.

"What a waste of premium lager," he moaned.

Chapter Twenty-eight

Friday, May 22, 2009

On September 12, 1857, United States Navy Captain William Lewis Herndon went down with the ship he commanded, the *SS Central America*, when it foundered in a storm off North Carolina. After making every effort to save the doomed vessel, he firmly ordered that women and children be saved first in the available lifeboats, and then in disregard of his own safety stayed at his post when the lifeboats returned to pick up what remaining passengers they could. In recognition of his heroism, a gray obelisk about twenty feet high, called the Herndon Monument, stands on the grounds of the Naval Academy.

On May 22, 2009, Rep, Melissa, and Lena Lindstrom moved away from Tecumseh Court in front of Bancroft Hall at the Academy, where they had watched morning formation, and found a shady spot about thirty yards from the Herndon Monument. Several hundred other civilians milled about in the same general area. Attached firmly by sealing tape to the top of the monument was a plebe's cap—circular, with an upturned brim around its entire circumference, derisively referred to as a "Dixie Cup." A thick coat of viscous grease covered the monument from top to pediment.

"Nine-fifty-nine," Lena said. "Harald said he'd be the one in a white t-shirt and blue shorts, with short hair."

At precisely ten a.m., a signal cannon boomed over the Severn River, less than a quarter- mile away. A collective shout nearly as deafening as the gun's report erupted from T-Court, and the pathway from there to the Herndon Monument filled with plebes racing for the greasy obelisk. There were more than a thousand of them. They all wore blue shorts and white t-shirts and they all had short hair.

Mass confusion seemed to reign for the first few minutes. Then a group of plebes ringed the monument, arms locked and facing outward. Other plebes stripped off their t-shirts and, boosted by classmates, climbed on the shoulders of the group around the base. They began wiping grease off the monument, throwing sodden t-shirts back to the crowd and catching fresh t-shirts thrown to them by those still at ground level.

As they cleared more and more grease from the monument, a second ring formed on the shoulders of the grimacing lower group. This one was less organized and much shakier than the first. A couple of lithe plebes took a stab at clambering up the second tier, and for a tantalizing moment it looked like the whole thing might be over in twenty minutes. But that didn't happen. A grasping hand would get within five or six feet of the Dixie Cup, but then the improvised human pyramid would crumble under the strain and give way.

This continued for well over an hour. Surge, hope, failure, and re-formation in a continuing and ever more tantalizing cycle as new bodies replaced the exhausted ones on the first and second tiers, and voices barked frustrated instructions: "All right, let's get organized. A line of people between one-hundred-seventy and one-hundred-ninety pounds here! Now!" The signal gun boomed at the hour, in case anyone was napping. The cycle continued.

The climax seemed to come without warning. The same things happened, but this time the base held and the fresh plebe climbed a little higher. He came within fingers' reach of the Dixie Cup. He loosened most of the tape holding it to the top before he fell back, cascading down the mountain of bodies. Almost immediately a second plebe made his way nearly to the summit of the now greaseless monument. This one pulled the Dixie Cup off. He raised it triumphantly above his right shoulder, shouting something Rep couldn't make out. Then he replaced the Dixie Cup with a visored officer's cap. A hoarse chant went up from the group.

"PLEBES NO MORE! PLEBES NO MORE! PLEBES NO MORE!"

The chant eventually died down as a group escorted the plebe who had gotten the caps changed over to the chapel steps, where the superintendent was waiting for him.

"What's his prize?" Rep asked.

"An honorary pair of admiral's shoulder boards," Melissa said. "Tradition has it that the plebe who grabs the cap will be the first in his class to make admiral."

"How many times has that happened?"

"It has never happened. But tradition is impervious to fact."

A bare-chested plebe with dirty sweat crusted on his torso came pelting up to them. He hugged Lena.

"Well, Harald, it's over, I guess," she said.

"I guess it is."

"It's good to see you."

"You too."

These long-winded Scandinavians, Rep thought, shaking his head, through about ten seconds of ensuing silence.

"Well," Harald said, "I've gotta shower and change, and then we can get to lunch."

"You can shower and change a little later," Lena said firmly. "There are some things I need to tell you right now."

Rep and Melissa moved discreetly away. Fifty feet or so on the other side of the walkway, they found relative privacy.

"What do you suppose they're talking about?" Melissa asked. "Laurel Fox and Gary Carlsen competing to see who can sing loudest?"

"I think it probably has something to do with Ole Lindstrom being killed because he tried to prevent the corruption of a corrupt system from corrupting him. He spent his entire life practicing politics as an honorable profession. He died for honor."

"Well, that's something that bears telling, I guess—as Lena might put it. By the way, speaking of Ole and his death, how did Walt know to contact stadium security and have them start looking for me? I was lying to Fox about pushing re-dial. That was just a bluff."

"Walt told the guards he thought he heard someone say something threatening in the background, and he heard fear in your voice."

"But he couldn't have. Laurel hadn't said anything, and I hadn't even seen the gun yet. I was worried that she'd overheard his comment because I had the phone turned up so loud, but I wasn't terrified yet."

"Yeah, he was just kidding the guards about all that. Like the cops in the O.J. Simpson case saying they thought they saw blood through the window. What really bothered him was that he couldn't imagine your not wanting to talk right away about the forty-nine-star business. Plus, he knew you were at the stadium but he couldn't hear any stadium noise in the background. He couldn't tell the guards he was playing a hunch, so he made some stuff up."

"Well I'm glad he did. The rescue squad came at a very opportune moment."

"Although they didn't actually rescue you," Rep noted. "You'd already won the battle by turning it into a food fight."

"Thank you for pointing that out, dear. Ironically, when I was fifteen I got a Saturday detention for doing basically the same thing."

"Irony is where you find it," Rep said. "By the way, speaking of detentions, Professor Pennyworth, is there anything you'd like to say?"

"Oh, yes. That." Melissa lowered her eyes demurely and bowed her head in a suggestion of contrition.

"Yes. That."

She raised her head and squared her shoulders.

"After threatening to hit you hard enough to knock your glasses off if you recklessly rushed headlong into mortal peril, I proceeded to do exactly that myself. I shouldn't have threatened to hit you. It was quite wrong of me."

"Indeed."

"Headstrong."

"True."

"Misguided."

"Correct."

"Inexcusable."

"Right again."

"I humbly apologize."

"I accept your apology—with all my heart."

Melissa sighed. Through hooded eyes she glanced hopefully at her husband's features, looking for an upturn in the corners of his lips. She didn't see it. Her beloved spouse had the moral high ground and seemed determined not to surrender it. She spoke again, with just a whisper of apprehension.

"One must be careful about what one says."

She re-squared her shoulders, closed her eyes, and held out her right hand, palm down. Rep waited for three seconds. Then he gripped her fingers tenderly and gently raised her hand.

"What you did was reckless, willful, misguided, headstrong, inexcusable—and magnificent." He kissed the back of her hand. "I hope you're still threatening to hit me once in awhile fifty years from now."

"That's the most romantic allusion to spousal battery that I've ever heard," she murmured as she fell into his embrace.

"You didn't really think I was going to slap your wrist, did you?" he asked.

"Of course not, dear," she said. But she kept her right hand tucked safely behind her back, just in case.

Afterword

The Stafford Flour advertisement discovered in the course of the story by Gary Carlsen actually appeared in print in the United States during the 1930s. A complete depiction of the advertisement can be found in All-American Ads – '30s, Jim Heiman (ed.), (Taschen GmbH 2003).

To receive a free catalog of Poisoned Pen Press titles, please contact us in one of the following ways:

Phone: 1-800-421-3976
Facsimile: 1-480-949-1707
Email: info@poisonedpenpress.com
Website: www.poisonedpenpress.com

Poisoned Pen Press
6962 E. First Ave. Ste. 103
Scottsdale, AZ 85251